the BOY

the BOY

by

Betty Jane Hegerat

OOLICHAN BOOKS
FERNIE, BRITISH COLUMBIA, CANADA
2011

Library and Archives Canada Cataloguing in Publication

Hegerat, Betty Jane, 1948-

    The boy / Betty Jane Hegerat.

ISBN 978-0-88982-275-7

    1. Cook, Robert Raymond, 1937-1960--Fiction. 2. Hegerat, Betty Jane, 1948-.

I. Title.

PS8615.E325B69 2011   C813'.6   C2011-901006-2

We gratefully acknowledge the financial support of the Canada Council for the Arts, the British Columbia Arts Council through the BC Ministry of Tourism, Culture, and the Arts, and the Government of Canada through the Canada Book Fund, for our publishing activities.

Published by
Oolichan Books
P.O. Box 2278
Fernie, British Columbia
Canada V0B 1M0

www.oolichan.com

Cover design by David Drummond - daviddrummond.blogspot.com. Cover photo by David P. MacNaughton, courtesy of the Legal Archives Society of Alberta.

Printed in Canada on 100% post consumer recycled FSC®-certified paper.

MIX
Paper from
responsible sources
FSC
www.fsc.org FSC® C013916

this book is dedicated to the memory of the Cook family
Ray, Daisy, Gerry, Patty, Chrissy, Kathy, and Linda
and Bobby, the boy who was lost along the way

It begins with fiction. An image of a boy with scabby knees, a thatch of dull blonde hair, eyes like hummingbirds. A boy circling a house. Window to window, dirt-rimed fingers on the sills. A boy on tiptoes, peeking, ducking, smirking before he slinks away. It begins with a woman inside the house, dizzy with this window, that window, and *where is the little bugger now?*

The Boy

June, 1994

Louise hates these end-of-school celebrations. What she really wants, is to go home and have a glass of wine in solitude, but always there is the round of drinks with her fellow teachers, the very people she's looked forward to escaping for two months.

As the evening wears on and the pub gets noisier, she waits impatiently for the woman who's giving her a ride to tire of the forced hilarity. There is a man at the next table who seems as much an outlier to his party as she is to hers. He looks familiar, but she can't imagine where she could have met him. Chronic tan, crew-cut hair, that way of looping his arm over the back of the chair, so that he looks mildly amused but not really part of the company. He reminds her of the farmers in her extended family. The waiter, she's noticed, has refilled the man's glass of Coke as many times as he's filled hers. A teetotaller? Or the driver for tonight? He looks up and catches her staring. Winks, then tilts his head and seems to puzzle a minute. Finally, he nods, puts his finger to his lips and stands up. Without a moment's thought, Louise stands too, and follows him to the end of the bar. No one at either table seems to have noticed their leaving.

"Louise, right?" The green eyes are so familiar. "Ninety-two Corolla, four door deluxe, sun roof, Desert Sand. How's the car running?"

"Amazing," she says. Now she remembers that he'd seemed out of place at the car dealership as well. Too polite and soft-spoken to be a salesman. He sold her the car two years ago, and he remembers her name? The colour of the paint? "You have some memory." Trying hard to recall his name.

"Jake Peters." He sticks out his hand, and when she extends hers, instead of shaking it, he holds it in his warm grip. "The memory is the secret to my success as a salesman." A grimace. "I've been trying for ten years to find a better way to use this gift, but I guess I'm stuck in the rut."

Ah, the career rut. Even with summer stretching ahead of her, Louise is anticipating the blue funk that will wash over the whole month of August as she thinks about going back to the classroom. "I know all about it," she says. "I never thought I'd spend a lifetime teaching, but I seem headed in that direction."

"What did you imagine yourself doing instead?" he asks, and steers her by the elbow to a place at the bar.

She imagines herself married, raising a family. Now there's a good line for picking up a guy in a bar. "Anything but," Louise says. She looks back at the teachers. Surely someone will have noticed. Is there anyone less likely in the room to be hit on by this totally presentable man than Louise Kernan? She glances at his hands where he's conveniently rested them on the bar. Gold band on his ring finger, right hand. She felt it there when he held her hand. Nothing on the left.

"Not married," he says. She has no finesse at this game. "I lost my wife two years ago."

A widower? The word sounds archaic, but so does "lost" in reference to a spouse. Unless he means he's lost her in some other way. "I'm sorry," Louise says. "That must have been terribly hard."

The bartender is waiting for them to order. "I don't think I can handle any more Coke," Jake says. "How about you?"

Louise shakes her head. "I was ready to leave before the ice cubes in the first glassful melted."

Jake slaps his palms down on the counter. "I'll take you home, but how about we find a good cup of coffee somewhere first?" The bartender shrugs and moves on.

Coffee? No more caffeine. Louise wants to sleep away the first day of summer holidays. She wonders how Jake feels about herbal tea. "Your friends aren't counting on you to drive?"

"Heck no. I almost never come out with them. We're celebrating a promotion and I think everyone came because they're glad to be getting rid of the guy. How they get home is their problem."

Louise stops at the teachers' table to collect her jacket, says she's run into an old friend, and the party doesn't seem to miss a beat as she walks away.

At Tim Horton's, over Jake's chicken sandwich and three refills of coffee, he talks and Louise sips weak tea and listens. Married fourteen years ago, one son, who'll be twelve years old in another month. His wife diagnosed with pancreatic cancer and dead six months later. Jake lifts the bread on the sandwich and gives the chicken a liberal salting. The last two years have been tough, but he's beginning to feel the ground under his feet again. No, Louise decides, Jake Peters is not like the men in her family— except for the salting. Not one of them would have opened up to a stranger in this way. Jake is treating her like someone he's known for years. Like a cousin, or an old school friend. The way, Louise thinks with resignation, men always treat her.

"I guess," she says, "your wife was still alive then, when I bought my car." God, that sounded so cold. And irrelevant. What did the buying of a car have to do with the dying of a wife?

"I think," Jake says, "the day you came in was my first day back at work. Maybe that's why I remember you so well. I went home that afternoon right after we closed the deal. I decided one gentle customer, you, was all I could handle in one day." She feels heat in her cheeks, the blotchy embarrassment that she can never control and which is not even remotely as charming as a schoolgirl's pink blush of modesty. "Your son?" she asks, to shift the attention. "Tell me about him."

"Danny's a good kid at heart, and smart too, just not real motivated when it comes to school work, and maybe a bit rambunctious, you know what boys are like?"

The child, Daniel, is a problem at school. This Louise knows from that one sentence. The kind of child teachers roll their eyes over in the staffroom at the beginning of the year. *Who's the poor schmuck who's ended up with the Peters kid?* Still, she reminds herself, he's lost his mother, and shouldn't she give him compassionate benefit of the doubt? His teachers must have cut him some slack for at least the year after.

"We're a lot closer since his mom died," Jake says. "I guess that's about the only good thing that's happened. Brenda always dealt with the school and the neighbours when Danny got into mischief, and I have to admit I was glad to work long hours and hope for the best. Now, I spend all my spare time with him." He glances at his watch. "I'd better get home. My next door neighbour said she'd look in on Dan tonight, but he won't go to bed until I get back."

When Louise looks into the tired smile of the man across the table, she sees a petulant boy superimposed. A kid daring her to make more of this encounter than a lonely man confiding to a familiar face. A one-off occasion, as most of Louise's encounters with decent men tend to be.

They pull into the parking lot at Louise's townhouse. "Aw man, I've been talking your ear off. I don't know what uncorked me tonight. Can I make it up to you by being a good listener next time?"

Next time? For once Louise is grateful for the poorly-lit parking lot. He can't see that her face has burst into flame. "I'd put you to sleep with my life story," she says. "There's not much to tell."

"Okay," he says, "then we'll go dancing instead of just drinking coffee." He brushes a wisp of hair off her cheek and tucks it behind her ear. Louise wonders if he can feel the heat from her skin. "You have the most beautiful hair," he says. "That's how I recognized you tonight."

Schoolteacher hair, her friends all tease her. Cut it! Go short and perky. Instead, she clings to the French braid that takes fifteen minutes every morning, the end result a plait as thick as her forearm, and still a rich brown, although she will soon have to cease plucking the white strands. Louise is not perky and a short hairdo on top of her chunky body would look ridiculous.

"I'm a terrible dancer," she says, wishing the hand was still there, but it has dropped again as gracefully as it rose to her hair. "But I love movies." She's astonished by her eagerness, and embarrassed too.

"Perfect," he says, "so long as it's not *Dumb and Dumber*, or *Ace Ventura*, or *Mighty Ducks*, or anything else in that vein."

So they make a date to see *Four Weddings and a Funeral*, Louise's suggestion, and it isn't until she closes her front door and takes a long deep breath that she realizes the very title is another gaff on her part.

Roads Back

July, 2004

I re-read the first scenes of the story, then powered-off the computer, hoping to silence Louise. My husband and I were going out for dinner with friends, and I welcomed the escape. I'd been dogged by the voices of characters before in the early stages of writing stories and had always loved the process because I'd learned that if I listened the story would find its own way onto the page. Louise was a challenge; demanding but elusive, compelling but disquieting. Instead of telling me the story herself, she seemed to expect me to tell her what was going to happen next. How could I know that? And yet, behind the image of Louise in my mind, there was sometimes a dark shadow, something she couldn't see, and I didn't want to illuminate. Power off.

So far, I knew Louise had married late and had inherited a stepson—a half-grown unruly boy named Danny. I knew that I would uproot Louise from Edmonton and transplant her to a small Alberta town. Churning underneath that small cache of information, though, was darkness I felt too cowardly to explore. So I'd been trying to confine this new story to a short piece of fiction, find an ending and let it go. I was excited about a first novel which was set to be published in the fall, 2006, and had just finished final edits. I was trying to find a home for a collection of short stories, and I did not want to get mired down in another book length project. But Louise was not going away, nor was she giving me the help I needed. I'd begun to wonder if there was another voice I was ignoring. Someone else in the story? The child?

As long as I'd been writing fiction, I'd been trying to dump the baggage I carried from my social work career. As well as the obvious professional commitment to confidentiality, I have a deep sense of privacy, and while I've been a necessary intruder in many lives, I do not feel I have the right to steal specific story material from them. The universality of the human condition is one thing, but individual stories are another. After I had children of my own, a question that haunted me in child welfare work, and especially in adoptions, was "How does someone learn to love someone else's child?" With babies it was easy, but I'd known many older children who weren't especially loveable, nor even likeable. Was that where I was going with Louise?

Ask your characters what they want, I tell my creative writing classes.

*Do I want to love Danny? Of course. Is it going
to happen? You like fairy tale endings?*

That was all Louise would give me. So far all I had was tension between stepmother and stepson, old news.

On this particular day in July, the story had run into a brick wall. Or so it seemed to me, but when I saved the meager writing of that day, I could almost hear Louise sniff. If I hadn't muted her, I'm sure she would have told me that I was laying the bricks myself.

My husband, Robert, and I had a dinner date with long-time friends, Dave and Dorna Young. We'd already cancelled the trip to the Longview Steakhouse twice that spring because of snow. Longview is only an hour away from

Calgary, but when a blizzard swoops across the Rockies, Highway 22X is as bleak as tundra. That afternoon, when thunderclouds had begun to pile up in the north, underbellies white with hail, I'd felt sure the dinner was off again. By five o'clock the only souvenirs of the storm were the shredded hostas in my garden and a few drifts of slush on the shady side of the house. The sky had been washed clean; azure silk stretched cloudless over the foothills.

For the first half of the drive from Calgary to Longview we talked about children. The Young's two children, our three; we'd been friends for more than thirty years, there was a lot to talk about. Long ago we'd fretted over toilet training, tantrums, kindergarten crises, bad teachers, bullying. Then we'd run the gauntlet of junior high and high school and the lure of drugs and booze, and will they survive? Our youngest was sixteen, Dave and Dorna's son nineteen. The older three—their daughter twenty-two, our middle son twenty-three, our daughter twenty-six—were just finishing university, still in need of propping up.

When? Robert asked. When will we get to relax? I recalled a ninety-year-old woman I'd met when I worked in a geriatric program shortly after I finished my social work degree. I'd asked about her family, and she in turn asked if I had children. Not yet, I said, but hoped to have a baby soon. Oh, the joys and the sorrows of it all, she said. My youngest of the five is sixty-five and not a day goes by that I don't worry about each one of them.

But that, I said, in reply to the groans in the car, doesn't mean we can't relax tonight.

When we stopped for gas in Turner Valley, the other three got out to stretch their legs. While I waited, Louise nudged her way into my thoughts.

Is this where I'm going? This town?

I stared across the street at a clapboard house. The windows were boarded from the inside, pieces of two-by-four nailed across the front door to keep out anyone not daunted by the sagging front porch whose first two steps had cratered. In spite of neglect, perhaps because of it, an old rugosa rose, probably a Hansa, was lush with new growth beside the step. In another two weeks, a mass of mauve-pink blooms would cover the window of what I guessed must be the master bedroom, if such a humble house had a master.

I indulged in a fantasy of buying an old house in this town, restoring it with floral wallpaper, fifty's arborite and lino in the kitchen—a weekend retreat. A fine place for writers, because if I squinted I saw ghosts—a woman on the porch, children tumbling across the patch of packed dirt at the side of a house. A man, hands on his hips, watching from a shadowy garage set diagonally on the end of the property. The overhead garage door hanging askew, probably permanently rusted into the open position. The leaves of many autumns past having drifted in to settle against layers of cardboard and rags.

Is it my house you're imagining? Don't move me into that sad place.

I rolled down my window. The air was tinged with the scent of petunias spilling out of a barrel in front of the gas pumps. A nice touch, but after the first whiff, the smell of gas prevailed.

And in the garage across the street? I mentally scuffled through the debris on the floor, imagined the smell of decay, of rotting leaves. And grease.

I closed my eyes and I was eleven years old, reading a copy of the *Edmonton Journal* my mother had hidden under a stack of *Star Weekly Weekend* magazines because she did not want me to know the gruesome details of a nearby crime. Reading about bodies hidden under layers of greasy rags and cardboard. Heart-thumpingly vivid.

When the other three came back to the car, I pointed down the street. Would a garage in a small town have a grease pit? But even as I asked the question, the empty house became just another old building, benign in the gold light of a spring evening. Why my interest in grease pits? Surely an old rose bush was more in my realm.

Did any of them remember the Cook murders, back when we were all just kids? Stettler, Alberta. Robert Raymond Cook. The whole family bludgeoned to death, bodies hidden in a grease pit in the garage.

Bludgeoned. A word that was new to my vocabulary when I was eleven years old. I remembered sitting on the back step, my mouth full of that blunt, ugly, word. But it was pictures more than words that began roiling up out of my memory now. I conjured a small clapboard bungalow, a flashy convertible, a madman rampaging through the central Alberta countryside. The eldest son of the murdered family.

The son? The son murdered the family?

I couldn't remember how the story ended. There was an escape, a recapture, and then? All this had happened more than forty years ago. Surely sometime in my adulthood there'd been a mention of Robert Raymond Cook, but if so, it had passed me by without this tweak—no, this clutching of the throat—of my memory.

Dave remembered the murder story, he said, but only vaguely. Dorna and Robert shook their heads.

For the last ten minutes of the drive I concentrated on the scenery, miles of mint green ranchland rolling toward bruise-coloured mountains. When we parked on Main Street, Longview, I vowed to douse the morbid memories and enjoy the evening. This quiet little town with its one long commercial street and scattering of possibly two dozen houses was postcard serene, and from our table next to the window we looked out at the hills, the tall grass bending always to the east.

The sons of the Moroccan family who owned the busy restaurant with its French bistro menu, country kitchen ambiance, were working that night. One in the kitchen, one waiting on tables. Before Longview, they'd owned a successful restaurant in Calgary, but had moved to this small town, this space just up the street from Ian Tyson's Navajo Rug coffee house, for the quieter life.

Could I see my children working alongside us in a family business? Working alongside each other for more than an hour without bickering and plotting their escape? Different cultures, different sense of family obligation, we agreed quietly over our dinner but not without a slightly wistful note in all our voices. And as for the safety and serenity of the small town? The members of the Cook family were bludgeoned to death in small town Alberta. Stettler.

I do remember that murder, Dave said. Hard to imagine what could provoke a son to murder his family. Hard to imagine.

Before I had children, I'd never imagined sons at all. My fantasies were of a gaggle of auburn-haired daughters, cheerful cherubs who became tall, quick-witted girls who grew into headstrong capable women. Our daughter was born ten weeks early and grew into a petite, blonde, sweet-natured girl, then hit the crucible of junior high. I'd forgotten, repressed probably, the nastiness of grade eight girls. None of this is the stuff of fantasy. These are things from which we cannot shield our children, but our daughter survived. I made a mental note to ask her sometime, what she remembered of junior high. When our second child was born, I'd looked at the robust boy in my arms and wondered what I needed to know to raise a son. He and our third, another son, plunged me into the world of boys. My two sons and their many friends grew from puppy-dog toddlers to noisy exuberant boys and were now on the cusp of becoming men. There were times when the sheer force of their energy overwhelmed my house. There were times when I saw flashes of anger that seemed to come from a place I did not want my child to inhabit.

Ha. When you haven't had the pleasure of the first twelve years with the boy, there's a real reason to feel overwhelmed. And more.

I filed away the garage, the grease pit, bludgeoned bodies, until we were home again and I sat down, compulsively as ever, to check my email before bed. Then I "googled" the murderer, Robert Raymond Cook.

Good. Let's get down to it.

Exactly. I'm going to find out what happened and be done with it.

I don't think so.

Seven members of the Cook family were murdered in June, 1959. Robert Raymond Cook was tried twice, convicted, lost an appeal to the Supreme Court of Canada, lost a last ditch bid for a commuted sentence and was hanged at Fort Saskatchewan Provincial Gaol on November 14, 1960. He claimed the infamy, I discovered, of being the last man hanged in Alberta. Little wonder, I thought, that I'd filed the Cook case away so quickly in my young mind. Justice had been swift, the case probably old news within a year.

Aside from this thumbnail sketch on the "Great Alberta Law Cases" page of the *Alberta Online Encyclopedia*, there were few links. Three books on the subject. I jotted down the titles. Maybe the next time I was at the library…Maybe.

Leave it, I told myself. This was a gruesome story. Better to spend my time on Louise's story. The Cooks—all eight of them—had been dead for almost fifty years. There were enough new murder stories to trouble anyone's dreams.

In the morning, I blamed the several cups of coffee at the Steakhouse for my insomnia, but it was the memory of the Cook murders that had kept me awake. How much of it real, how much imagined? How much did it matter?

Oh, it matters. I have a feeling this is going to be important. To me.

Louise was right. When I sat at the computer that morning, I finally acknowledged that her story wasn't just about family dynamics, a rebellious teenaged stepson, a crisis, a resolution. There was a reason for my recall of the Cook story. Write boldly! Hadn't I given that advice to other writers? If the writing frightens you, you're finally getting somewhere?

I found myself contemplating a trip to Stettler, although that was surely not where Louise's story was set. Nor should it be necessary for me to travel around rural Alberta to get the feel of small town life. I'd lived it.

The Boy

July 1994

Since the night they met in the bar, Louise and Jake had been to four movies, drunk countless cups of coffee together, and driven out into the country to Jake's hometown of Valmer for a quick look-see, as he put it, at a couple of houses he was interested in.

On their third date, Jake told Louise that Daniel had been caught shoplifting a *Playboy* magazine the day before. Before she could respond, Jake launched into a monologue on how the city was a bad influence on Daniel, and if he and Brenda had stayed in the small town where they both grew up, the boy would have been fine. Everyone knew him there and came to Jake and Brenda if there was a problem instead of running to the principal or the police. If that sort of thing had happened in Valmer, Jake said, the store owner would have sent Danny away with a stern warning, then phoned Brenda to tell her about the mischief so they could deal with it at home. But in Edmonton, the manager of the drugstore called the police, claiming this was the third time he'd been suspicious of Daniel's activities, and although it was the first time he'd caught him in the act, he'd bet money there had been previous thefts. No charges were laid, but they would be the next time.

Even though Louise still hasn't met the boy, she knows from teaching at least a half dozen other "Dannys" that it's only a matter of time until he's in trouble again. She has enough problem children to deal with at school. Should she let another one of these little con artists into her personal life because he's convinced his father that the world is to blame for his mischief? But there is the gentleness with which Jake treats her, the pleasure of being out in public with what her mother would call "a fine figure of a man," and the fact that for the first time in her adult life, Louise is tempted to believe that she's pretty. Jake told her so.

Still, a whole month into their relationship, Louise is making excuses for postponing her meeting with Danny. Jake's hours at the car showroom run to evenings and weekends, and Louise takes advantage of her summer vacation to spend three mornings a week visiting her mom at the nursing home and two mornings dropping in on her dad at the house.

Jake was impressed when she told him about her dutiful daughter routine. "Not many people are that committed to their folks. They're lucky to have you!"

Well, no. She's always felt she was the lucky one. An only child, a surprise in her mother's mid-forties after years of assuming they'd never have a child, her parents doted on her. She grew up in a household so calm that it's taken her years to stop flinching every time she hears voices raised in disagreement. Even loud friendly dissent makes her uncomfortable. Her parents enrolled her in piano, ballet, art lessons, figure skating, anything in which she expressed even a ripple of interest, and there was never a hint of disappointment shown when she gave up and moved on to something else. Louise responded to that gentle nurturing in the same way she now basks in Jake's attention—gratefully, and with a fierce desire to be worthy of his interest.

Jake's interest in her, though, except for a few gentle caresses of her hair or her cheek, a hand cupped around her elbow when she gets in and out of the car, chaste, tight-lipped, good night kisses, seems so brotherly that Louise is expecting to be dumped. One of her best friends at school, a gay teacher who started the same year as Louise, has told her many times that she needs to learn how to flirt. That she gives off no erotic signals at all. Has he considered, she's asked him, that her lack of enthusiasm might be the *result* of being repeatedly rejected rather than the *cause*?

"Oh honey," he said, "you just keep on trying; don't turn into everybody's big sister."

Then Jake phones and says he really wants her to meet Daniel. That if they are going to get serious—oh yes, she wants to shout, please let's get serious—she should be willing to fit into his life; and his son is a big part of that life.

"Okay," she says. "Why don't the two of you come to my house for dinner?"

"No, let's make it my place. Danny's better at home. He can say hi, visit for a few minutes and take off to his room if he wants to. I'll cook."

She agrees, but after she hangs up the phone she's tempted to call back. Tell Jake she has a strong sense that she's making a mistake, and she's going to save them both whatever it is she fears. But she also fears hurting this kind man who's told her she's the first woman he's called more than once since he started going out again. And she's decided that if he's going to dump her, or she has to dump him, she's going to bed with him at least once before that happens. She's thirty-six years old and has yet to have a relationship that's gone beyond a few dates and some sweaty tussling that is not what she's ever imagined as love-making.

Danny looks like his dad, short for his age, probably able to pass for ten rather than twelve, but Louise doesn't see anything like the naïve immaturity Jake has described. There is a slyness to those green eyes, the way they dart away as soon as Louise makes contact with them, then flick back to check if she's given up or is still watching him. He has the same square jaw as his dad, same heavy blond hair that refuses to lie flat in spite of the goop he uses to slick it down. Jake's solution is a brush cut, but Dan looks as though he hasn't been in a barber's chair since his mother died.

Louise has brought a gift. A skater's magazine, because Jake told her a skateboard is at the top of Danny's wish list for his birthday. He will be twelve in another week. He takes the package enthusiastically enough, but frowns when he pulls the magazine out of the paper. His nose needs wiping. Something Louise can't abide in her grade threes, never mind a boy this size. Jake has told her Danny has allergies.

"I have this one. Why did you buy me a skateboarding magazine?" He throws the book on the coffee table.

What did he think it was? *Playboy?*

"Daniel." Jake's voice is quiet, but loaded with warning.

"Thanks," Danny mutters.

"You're welcome. Your dad told me you were interested in skateboarding. Give it to one of your friends," Louise says. She pulls her wallet out of her bag.

"Louise, no." Jake puts a hand on her arm. "You don't have to do that."

"I want to," she says, pulling out a ten dollar bill. "Here. Buy something else." Cheap for a birthday present? She doesn't know the kid. This is meant to be a peace offering of sorts. She and Jake and Daniel all stand looking at the bill in her outstretched hand. Finally Danny shrugs and takes it from her.

"Thanks," he says again, this time without the scowl. He looks at her quizzically for a minute. "Hey, I thought my dad liked pretty girls."

Louise wants the beige carpet under her feet to open and swallow her. Or better yet, to swallow the boy.

"Daniel!" Jake clamps a hand on his son's shoulder. "Don't pay any attention to him," he says, turning toward Louise. "It's a joke. A very stale joke he made up a while back and as of tonight, it's retired." He goes nose-to-nose with Danny. "For good. Get it?"

"Got it," Danny says, wrenching himself away from his dad. Then he turns and stomps out of the room.

Danny doesn't come back until Jake calls him for dinner, and he eats his plate of spaghetti in silence. Someone has obviously taken time to teach him to keep his elbows off the table, to manage pasta without wearing it on his chin. No slurping, or burping and when he's done, he carries his plate to the sink, rinses it, stacks it in the dishwasher.

He comes back to the table and stands beside Jake's chair. "So can I?"

"Okay. But only half an hour. That joke cost you." Jake stands up. "Excuse me a minute, Louise. I'm going to get the Nintendo out of lock-up. We decided when it came into the house that it was going to be a privilege, not a right."

We? Louise knows Daniel wasn't party to this decision. She feels as though his mother, Jake's dead wife has joined them. Louise is in another woman's house.

Danny lags behind. As he passes Louise, the words slip out of the corner of his mouth. "All the other ones thought the joke was funny."

"I'll just bet they did," she says quietly. "Enjoy your game, Daniel."

He slouches out of the room. Not surprising that Jake Peters has never had more than two dates with anyone before her. Oh no, she is not giving up. She has a reputation for never having been bested by a student, and damned if she's going to let this miserable little tick burrow into her skin so easily.

When Jake comes back, she clears the table while he makes coffee. "He has good table manners, your son," she says. Like the parent teacher interviews at school when the only positive thing she can say about a struggling child is that he's polite.

"When he wants to," Jake says. He takes the stack of plates from her hands and puts his arms around her. "He behaved like a little jerk. But you know what?" She tilts her head to look up at him. "I think he likes you."

"Oh really, Jake."

"No, honestly. He says he's sorry he made that stupid wisecrack."

"I'll bet he is," she says, "because this time it fit."

"Oh come now. You're fishing for a compliment, because you can't possibly be that insecure." He pulls her so tight she can feel his heart thumping against her breasts. Such a good strong heart. She's glad he can't see her face, the blush over how pathetic she must have sounded. "Have your coffee," he says. "I'm going next door to ask my neighbour to keep an eye out for Dan for a couple of hours. We are going back to your place."

As they're leaving, a woman who looks older, more frail than many of the people who are resident at the nursing home where Louise's mother lives, is making her cautious way up the front walk.

"Alice!" Jake takes her arm. "You don't have to sit over

here. Just so long as he knows you have an eye on the house he'll behave."

Now that she's standing straight, shoulders back in almost military posture, the woman looks a little less like she's the one in need of care. She pushes her glasses up onto her nose, tilts her head and stares at Louise, blinking like an owl. "Well you don't look scary at all," she says. "Daniel told me he was awfully nervous about his dad bringing home a teacher." She shrugs free of Jake's hold, and pats him on the arm. "I know I don't have to sit here, but I happen to like the boy's company. He's a sweetie, isn't he?" She looks so stern that Louise can only nod in agreement. "Actually, I came over so he can tell me what he thinks of you."

Louise forces a smile. Wouldn't she love to stay around and eavesdrop on that one? No, not in the least.

"Looks like Danny has a friend in Alice," she says when they're in the car and driving toward her apartment, the direction she's been hoping the evening would take. She wonders if Jake told Alice where they were going. Or Danny. No, she does not want to be in any imagining of Danny's.

"Ah, she's a snoopy old bat," he says, "but she has a kind heart and I don't know what I'd have done without her help with Brenda in the end."

"She was Brenda's friend too?"

"I wouldn't say that. Brenda found Alice a bit much, kind of rude, but Alice and Danny have been pals since we moved in when he was a little guy. Just so you know, she's been telling me for months that I need to find someone."

They're stopped at a red light, and when he drums his fingers on the steering wheel, Louise reminds herself that he's probably been more nervous about tonight than either she or Danny.

She lays her hand over his to still the jumpy fingers. "Don't worry, Jake. I'm sure Danny and I will get used to each other." But there is no way, she thinks, even though she has decided that she is going to marry Jake, that she will ever really be Daniel's mother.

As for a move from the city being the answer to Danny's problems, Louise hopes she won't have to see Jake's romantic notion kicked down the main street of some Alberta town.

Valmer? Does it by any chance bear a striking resemblance to that town with the broken-down garage?

No. Wrong landscape. I'm thinking more central Alberta.

Stettler region?

Close.

Roads Back

I didn't go to Stettler immediately after dredging up the information about the Cook murders. I was tempted, but without a clear mission, without the remotest idea of what I intended to do with any of this horrific story, there seemed little point. Instead, I found myself returning in memory to the towns where I'd grown up. The summer of 1959, the summer of Robert Raymond Cook, returned with the memory of a girl who'd been one of my best friends in the year after we moved to Camrose from the much smaller town of New Sarepta thirty miles away. I had no recollection of how long that friendship lasted. No memory of Rose beyond elementary school, but I was as sure as I could be that it was Rose who told me about the Cook murders. I could hear her slight lisp, see wide brown eyes, high cheek bones, long brown hair.

Rose lived three blocks away. It impressed me so, at ten, to be living in a place that was measured in blocks, to have an address instead of a post office box. New Sarepta had no more than half a dozen streets when we lived there; a creamery, post office, service station, general store, church, school, and hotel. And a coffee shop, owned and operated by my parents. We had living quarters in the back, and my mom cooked and served meals, while my dad drove away early every morning to check well sites for Edmonton Pipeline. Oil pump jacks in farm fields were as much a part of the landscape as barns and fields of barley. The year before I was born, oil well Leduc Number #1, just twenty miles away from New Sarepta, "blew" and there were good paying jobs to be had for every able-bodied man around. And for men from away as well. Our small town had an unusual number of strangers passing through, and many of them passed through our door.

I was so shy about this business of feeding strangers that went on in our home, that I lurked at the side of the house rather than out front or inside where men's dark green work shirts hunched like turtles over coffee mugs thick as bathroom sink porcelain. Their big bums spread on the red shiny stools where, after the coffee shop closed, a child could twirl until she was falling-down-dizzy.

Saturday night after closing, Mom would be on hands and knees doing a "proper" scrubbing, the pail of water emptied again and again. I can still evoke the smell of Johnson's paste wax that clumped in our throats late into the evening, hear the rustle of sheets of newspaper spread over the thick wax until it dried. On Sunday night, my sister and I in thick grey socks skated under the blue fluorescent light until every dull patch was swirled to a high shine.

When I slipped through the front door into the shop with its long stretch of counter, I would see my mother's permed head in the pass-through to the kitchen, apron straps crisscrossing the back of her dress, one elbow crooked over the pan of onions. When the special of the day was hot hamburger sandwiches, our house, clear to the bedrooms at the back, reeked of onions and grease.

We only moved thirty miles when we left New Sarepta and the coffee shop, but at ten, it was a world away to me, and a welcome one. No more strange men in our house, no more muddy streets.

Camrose had paved streets with numbers, parks, a movie theatre, library, and a social structure. Here my mother seemed to tag each of my friends with the occupation of the father. The banker's daughter, the funeral director's son, the school principal's kids, the optometrist's boy. But those like us, the working class, went untagged. When we moved to Camrose my mother worked as a seamstress at a dress shop, my dad still driving out to the oilfields. I never knew the occupation of Rose's dad. She was the girl from the family of ten kids. That description eclipsed all else, even though large families were common then. The small, crowded house was the reason my mother gave for refusing permission for me to sleep over at Rose's. She saw no reason for children to spend the night anywhere but in their own beds. My mother couldn't imagine how all those children fit into a small bungalow, and she certainly wasn't inflicting another on Rose's beleaguered mother.

It wasn't a slumber party Rose had on her mind when she pounded into our yard that day, Monday, June 30 when the news of the Cook murders broke. It was likely the last day of school. No early exits in those days. I imagine that Rose and I had hauled our bags of end-of-the-year grade five books and papers to our respective houses, that she reappeared just before suppertime, which at our house was the early hour of five o'clock, as soon as my dad walked through the door.

Memory tells me I was outside, sitting on the back step, pouting. Because my mother had refused another sleepover? Because I was prone to pouting and it was the surest way to irk my mother? In my memory, too, there is the smell of meat frying, my mother busy in the kitchen but keeping an eye on me through the open window, ready to come out and tell me that if I was sulking and bored already, she'd find some work to keep me busy. Boredom irked her even more than pouting.

Then Rose, wide-eyed, breathless, hair dangling around

her ears from the ponytail that never lasted the day, racing along the cotoneaster hedge that separated our yard from the alley. Bringing the news. Dead bodies in a hole in the floor in a garage. Bodies of little children. This is the news I remember.

Rose would have heard it from one of her brothers. But her brothers were forever trying to scare her with creepy stories about graveyards and people buried alive and rats climbing into babies' cribs and gnawing off their fingers and toes. We didn't even have rats in Alberta and yet she believed them. So why would I believe a story about a pit full of bodies?

Because it was on the radio, she said, and Rose's oldest brother knew the person who they said had done the awful killing. Robert Raymond Cook. I can hear Rose pronouncing his name like she was broadcasting the news herself. All summer long we would hear him formally named.

No, I insisted, this couldn't be true. Especially when she told me that he was the son, the brother of the dead children. I didn't have brothers, just one older sister, but I did have a sense of what brothers would or wouldn't do. Tease, torment, bully, but not murder. It must have been a stranger. If Stettler was anything like the small town we'd left behind, then a stranger was the answer.

My mother verified Rose's story when she came outside to find out what we were quarrelling about. She had heard the news from Stettler, and if she had heard, it had to be true. It was not the sort of information she deemed suitable for eleven-year-old girls, though, and she sent Rose home. The radio that usually played during supper so my dad could hear the weather report was turned off. The *Edmonton Journal* disappeared the next evening as quickly as the paperboy dropped it on the front step. But Rose was my pipeline, and eventually we got the story in its ghastly entirety. The children had been "bludgeoned" to death. I got out the *Miriam Webster* for that one, and for "stench" which I heard my dad quietly ponder to my mother. My dad didn't share my mom's strict prohibitions on what we were allowed to hear. If my mom was out, or distracted, he would let us sneak into the living room and watch *Alfred Hitchcock Presents.* My mother was sure Hitchcock would plant the seeds of nightmare. *Lassie, Ozzie and Harriet,* those were shows suitable for children. If I could find my dad out in the garage, or in the basement, away from her keen ears, he would give me at least a censored version of the Cook story. Rose could be counted on to fill in the gore.

So, there were seven bodies, five children, the eldest a year younger than me. The son was a jailbird, just out of "the clink" my dad would have said, a few days before the killings. And if I asked how Robert Raymond Cook was captured, Rose might have described a car chase, with her brother in the lead, heading Cook off at the junction service station. My dad would probably have told me that they didn't have to catch Cook. He was parked outside the coffee shop in downtown Stettler, showing off his new car.

It turned out Rose's brother didn't really know Robert Raymond Cook, except that he'd been at a party Cook crashed a year or two before. But what seemed to be accepted by everyone as truth from the moment the news hit the front page, was that Robert Raymond Cook "did it."

Cook was sent to Ponoka, to the provincial mental hospital, for psychiatric examination before his trial. That was the second chapter in the story I had stored in my memory. For anybody growing up in Alberta, Ponoka was synonymous with craziness. It still is. Yesterday, from the window of this room, I heard my neighbour saying goodbye to a visitor. "I should be in Ponoka by now!" the woman said. Laughed and drove away, leaving me to wonder what was driving her mad.

If Cook was sent to Ponoka then, in my eleven-year-old mind, he was as crazy as could be. And guilty. Much of my memory of that summer is set on the three block stretch between my house and Rose's. We must have trudged back and forth, whispering about murder, about brothers and boys. Though the Cook murders had dislodged it from our minds temporarily, another murder earlier in June had been centre stage. A girl in Ontario, exactly our age, out riding her bike, had never come home. Her body had been found in a field two days later, strangled, sexually assaulted. I didn't need *Miriam Webster* for those words. At eleven, Rose and I were better informed about sex than we were about violence. A fourteen-year-old boy, Stephen Truscott, had already been charged with the murder of Lynne Harper when the Cook family was murdered.

It was officially summer, two lazy months during which Rose and I would have ventured out on the gravel roads around town, Cheez Whiz sandwiches wrapped in waxed paper and milk bottles full of Kool-Aid in the baskets on the front of our bikes. So long as we were back by suppertime, no one would have worried. But on July 10, Robert Raymond Cook broke out of Ponoka, and our wandering came to a quick halt. My mother didn't need to place restrictions. Rose and I imagined a murderer, one with particular interest in children, hiding behind every tree, and even if we'd been allowed, we weren't likely to wander farther than the play-ground within shouting distance of my house.

Even though he was captured three days later, the final chapter in my memory of Robert Raymond Cook, it seemed as though our summer-time freedom was irrevocably lost.

So this is your story now?

No. That's as far as we need to go with my story.

Well you're ignoring mine. And what about the Cooks?

What about them? They've been dead for forty-six years.

What happened to them?

I am not writing a story about bludgeoning and hanging.

Not that part. What happened before. Why did he kill them?

Why does it matter?

That's the question, isn't it? I knew you weren't finished with them yet.

Roads Back

I found three books on the Cook case. *The Robert Cook Murder Case,* published by Gopher Books, Saskatoon, Saskatchewan, was part of a series on infamous prairie murder cases by Frank W. Anderson. I ordered the book from a bookstore in Saskatoon, and tracked the other two books to the Calgary Public library which had one copy of each at the main branch.

They Were Hanged, by Alan Hustak, is an account of the last man executed in every province in Canada before the death penalty was eliminated in 1976. Photos of doomed men, one woman, introduce each chapter. Too much for me, I flipped to the picture of Robert Cook, the same image that must have accompanied the long ago newspaper articles because it was a match for the one that had been gaining focus in my mind since the drive to Longview. The Hustak account is short and sympathetic to Cook, I found to my surprise. Full of questions about the circumstantial nature of the evidence and political motives for denying the request for a commuted sentence. But at the end of it, another reader had penned, "They should have hanged Bob Cook '7' times." And he signed his note, "JD."

The photo on the cover of *The Work of Justice, The Trials of Robert Raymond Cook* by J. Pecover was also familiar; a photo of a young man in suit jacket and tie, hair combed straight back, looking as though he could have been on his way to a school dance, or a first job interview. The book is four hundred and forty-nine pages, with two epigraphs:

"Who shall put his finger on the work of justice and say, 'It is there.' Justice is like the kingdom of God; it is not without us as a fact; it is within us as a great yearning."
— George Elliott

"The whole case agianst me consists of suspision and if theres any justice in this world something will be done. However I am beginning to have serious doubts as to weither or not there is any such thing as justice."
— "Letter from the death cell" Robert Raymond Cook

There is a foreword by Sheila Watson, author of *The Double Hook,* a novel which, I remembered with a jolt, opens with a man killing his mother. Even in the ten minutes I spent at a table in the library, skim reading, I found myself reaching for my pencil and the pad of post-it notes I carried in my bag. I put the pencil away. I would find my own copy for marking and defacing. Mr. Pecover, I decided, had a lot to tell me. The back cover said only: "Jack Pecover is a retired lawyer and an alumni member of the Canadian Rodeo Cowboys Association." What I knew from the heft of this book was that Jack Pecover had spent a long time and a huge amount of energy examining the trials of Robert Raymond Cook.

An online search for the book led me to a used bookseller in Calgary. He would be at the Sunday morning flea market at the Hillhurst Sunnyside Community Centre, he told me in reply to my email.

There was one lone customer at the bookseller's stall

when I arrived on Sunday morning, a woman working her way through stacks of romance novels. In spite of the suffocating heat in the building, the man behind the table was wearing a heavy cardigan sweater. He seemed to be waiting for me; before I could speak, he dipped into a stash under the table and handed me the book.

I flipped to the publication date: 1996. This copy looked new, although the pages gave off the unmistakable musty smell of old book. I wondered who'd owned this, why they dumped it. I asked the seller if he'd had the book for long.

He shrugged, said it wasn't exactly a hot number, but he'd sold a few copies in the past couple of years.

Then, I asked him if he remembered the murder case, a question I'd been posing to many people. He looked the right vintage. But he was from Quebec, he told me, where they have their own long list of bloody backwoods crime. Twenty bucks, he said, obviously not interested in chatting.

The romance woman, balancing her pile of books under her chin, wanted his attention. I pulled a twenty dollar bill out of my wallet and he snipped it up with two fingers and a wink.

All afternoon, I sat in the garden swing and read. By the time I reluctantly put the book aside, new images of Robert Raymond Cook had lifted off the pages; a boy barely able to peer over the steering wheel of a stolen car; the police chief in the village of Hanna, Alberta, in hot pursuit, muttering, that's young Cook for sure. A boy who loved animals, and who was forever bringing home stray dogs. A boy who was markedly fond of younger children. A young man who carried photos of his five siblings and showed them proudly.

While I read, my sixteen year-old son and two of his friends were pounding out music in the basement. In a few minutes, they'd stomp up to the kitchen to chomp through a mountain of food before they moved to the basketball hoop. Goofy teenagers, with nothing more pressing on their minds than how to spend the rest of a sultry afternoon.

By the time Robert Raymond Cook was sixteen years old, he had graduated from reform school to big-time jail. His mother died when he was nine years old. In the solitary company of his mechanic father, he'd learned to drive by the time he was ten, and developed a passion for other people's cars. From his first incarceration for car theft when he was fourteen years old, until his execution at twenty-three, he spent all but 243 days of 3247 days in prison. I imagined him, a young teenager, playing basketball in the exercise yard of the Lethbridge provincial jail.

I made the mistake of returning to the book later that night. At three in the morning, I was wide-eyed, grisly bits of information running in my head like squirrels in cages.

The next day, I buried *The Work of Justice* under a pile of other books I'd set aside for summer reading. Anne Marie McDonald's, *The Way the Crow Flies*, was at the top of the pile. I knew the book was about a murder, but it was fiction.

McDonald's fiction threw me right back into 1959. Although *The Way the Crow Flies* is fiction, a novel, it seemed to me clearly informed by the Lynne Harper/Steven Truscott murder case. Once again, I was eleven years old, imagining a girl just my age riding into a summer afternoon on her bike, and never coming home again. I went back to the internet for information about Steven Truscott.

Fourteen year old Truscott was scheduled to be hanged for the murder of Lynne Harper two days before Robert Raymond Cook was sentenced to death. Truscott's sentence was commuted. A similar plea for clemency was made on

Cook's behalf, and according to J. Pecover, author of my flea-market-found book, the odds seemed good. John Diefenbaker, who was Prime Minister at the time, was outspoken in his hatred of the death penalty. Unfortunately for Cook, there was an election looming and Diefenbaker was advised that he would lose the west if he showed clemency in a crime so heinous as the Cook murders.

I finished *The Way the Crow Flies,* satisfied in the end that it is a fictitious rendering. I knew all I needed to know about the Cook murders, and it was time to go back to Louise's story. Fiction. I knew how to spin a story. Surely I could leave the Cook family to their rest.

Why are you so sure they're at rest? If it were me…

It is not you, Louise. Danny is not a murderer.

How do we know this?

You know it because I'm telling you it's so.

And if I don't believe you? Maybe you're wrong.

I'd like to remind you that I'm in charge here.

Ah, but you keep changing the story. Maybe Ray and Daisy Cook thought they knew Robert. Do you think they called him Robert? Why did the reporters always use his full name? So there would be no mistaking another Cook for the murderer?

I suppose. Maybe Ray and Daisy called him Bob. Or Bobby.

Bobby? A Bobby does not bludgeon little children.

Okay, so he was not Bobby. He was Robert Raymond Cook and he killed his family.

An entire family. Including his stepmother, half brothers, half sisters.

So?

So what about me?

You are not Daisy. You don't have any other children.

Well unless the story stops here, that's a distinct possibility, isn't it?

The Boy

December 1994

Christmas, and this year Louise has a new family to circle around the tree. She and Jake were married on December 7 in a civil ceremony, Jake's cousin and one of Louise's teaching friends as witnesses. Jake thought it best to leave Danny out of the ceremony, but include him later for the small dinner party at the Italian restaurant where Jake had proposed to Louise. An old-fashioned, candlelit presentation of a diamond.

"Would you rather," Jake asked, "have picked it out yourself? Phyllis said I should have let you do that, but I wanted to surprise you."

"No," she said, quickly. "It's lovely, Jake." She felt a stab of jealousy. He'd shown the engagement ring to his cousin first? Had he asked her advice about whether or not he should marry Louise? How would Jake's family—all of them, he'd told her had adored Brenda—look on a new wife? Louise turned herself inside out with questions.

The day they chose the wedding bands, she questioned the wisdom of excluding Danny from the wedding.

"Let it go, Louise," Jake said, with the same authority Louise had heard in his voice when he spoke to Daniel. Louise stared down at the diamond on her left hand, then at the man in the driver's seat next to her. When she'd told her dad about the engagement, he'd hesitated before congratulating her. Was she absolutely sure, he'd asked, and she'd taken a deep breath and spilled out all of her doubts. But then, he'd patted her hand and told her Jake was a good man, and although the boy was a bit of a concern, when was life ever perfect?

This was not going to be a perfect union, and that was all the more reason to make herself very clear. "I will not let anything go without a reasonable discussion, Jake. If I'm going to be part of this family, we make decisions together, including decisions about Daniel."

"All right." Jake didn't take his eyes off the road. "We'll be a democracy. I have no trouble with that. But Dan gets a say as well, and he's cast the deciding vote on this one. I didn't want to hurt your feelings, but he's already refused to have any part of the wedding. We'll be lucky to get him to the party afterward."

Jake sent Daniel to school the morning of the wedding. Better than leaving him at home, moping, he said, and they'd pick him up after school, go somewhere for a celebratory Slurpee before they took him home and cleaned him up for the reception. At the school, they waited until every last straggling child had exited the building, and then Jake went inside to look for his son. Daniel had gone home at lunch time, the secretary told him, and the neighbour who was the emergency contact on the school records had called to say he wasn't feeling well and wouldn't be back for the afternoon.

While Jake went next door to Alice's to collect Danny, Louise waited in the house. They were a long time returning. At the front door, Dan brushed past her without a word, straight to his bedroom. Jake coaxed him out later, even though this time Louise cast her vote in favour of leaving him at home to sulk.

At the restaurant, Danny sat with arms folded, head down through the toasts. But when Louise glanced at him later, he was enthusiastically tucking into a plate of pasta. He looked up, twirled a strand of spaghetti around his fork, and sucked it slowly into his mouth, never taking his eyes from hers.

Now it is Christmas and the three of them are on their way to Louise's dad's house with a miniature decorated tree, presents, and a fully-cooked Christmas dinner in several boxes. Jake has roasted the turkey and prepared the mashed potatoes and gravy. He is, Louise discovered, a decent cook when it comes to traditional country cuisine. Every Sunday, he takes over the kitchen and serves up a meat and potatoes meal. Exactly as his mother taught him, he says, but a skill he didn't practice at all during his first marriage because Brenda was a better cook. Brenda was a sensational cook. Brenda was also a seamstress, Louise has been told, and sewed all her own clothes, the curtains, the cushion covers, and some sweatpants for Danny that he still wears even though they are so small now they fit like tights.

This Christmas morning, though, Danny emerged from his room dressed in jeans and the Edmonton Oilers hockey jersey Jake bought for him. They opened their gifts last night and after the hockey shirt, Daniel didn't seem to care about anything else, not even the Nintendo game and the skater shoes the price of which made Louise gasp. The whole pile of gifts frankly appalled her. She'd asked Daniel for a wish list. He rattled off electronic games, phones, items that were beyond her concept of gifts, and into the realm of adult toys that one should earn rather than expect to be given. Finally, she picked two movies on his list that sounded reasonable. She was, Jake told her gently, pretty hard-nosed on this stuff and it wasn't as though they couldn't afford it. Was she going to be this tight with their kids?

"Yes," she said. "I've waited a long time for kids, I've had the chance to watch a lot of parents, and I'm warning you, Jake, that I'm going to be tough."

He raised his eyebrows. "About everything? We haven't seen a tough side of you, I don't think. Are you just breaking in here slowly? Dan and I should be very careful?"

She laughed finally. "Hey, I'm tough, but I'm fair. If I do my job right, you shouldn't even notice."

In fact, in these first weeks things had gone far more smoothly than she expected. But she knew all about honeymoon periods with kids, and when she opened Daniel's present she had confirmation that what was happening at home was probably no indicator at all of what he was doing outside.

The perfume was one she didn't know, but she could tell this wasn't the variety found on the open shelves at the drugstore. Daniel watched her face while she opened the package and she likely didn't disappoint him, because she was genuinely touched that he would choose something feminine and personal. She'd expected a box of candy, or a coffee mug. A teacher gift.

Later, she asked Jake how much money he'd given Daniel for his Christmas shopping.

"Why do you want to know?"

"Because that Lancôme perfume he bought for me has to have cost at least forty, maybe even fifty dollars. It must have broken the budget."

"Nah, he said it was under twenty, Louise. No offense,

but I can't see him spending fifty dollars on a present for anyone, especially something like perfume."

Danny's present to Jake was a can of cashews. Tradition, he said. When Danny was about six, his mom had told him that cashews were the perfect gift for his dad, and ever since that had been the stock gift. It was a joke between them by now, Jake said, and he and Danny would eat the nuts together while they watched the next Oilers game on television.

"How much did you give him?" she asked again.

"Sixty bucks," he said. "Ten dollars each for the five people he was buying for and an extra ten if he went a bit over. As we agreed, small gifts, it's the thought that counts."

Daniel bought gifts for Louise, Jake, Jake's mother, Alice next door, and Louise's dad. Nothing for his friends? Louise quietly asked Jake when she saw the list.

"No," he said abruptly. "He doesn't have anyone that close."

Last night, Danny took a box of Turtles over to Alice. They were, he claimed, her favourite candy. Considering that Alice wore top dentures that slipped onto her lower lip when she allowed herself a stern smile, Louise doubted that, but chocolates seemed a suitable gift for a neighbour. For his grandmother, who Louise still hadn't met, Dan bought a package of notepaper which was wrapped and sent away a week before Christmas. Grandma Peters had sent a cheque made out to Jake that was to go directly into an educational fund, and a pair of cowboy patterned pyjamas, size sixteen. Danny had put them on last night and clowned around, flapping the long sleeves, yodeling. Funny at first, but finally Jake asked him to cut it, and to make sure he wrote a thank you note on Boxing Day. Another family tradition courtesy of Brenda, all presents were acknowledged with handwritten notes on Boxing Day.

And is she, Louise can't help wondering, expected to keep up all the traditions? Is that the stepmother's job? It would be different if Jake was divorced, and there was a real mother across town, upholding tradition. Louise, awake early this morning with an unsettled stomach, stood at the window waiting for dawn, and thought she could see Brenda's footsteps in the deep snow around the house.

Louise's dad is in good spirits when they arrive. As Louise could have predicted, he likes Jake, and he and Danny have discovered a mutual love of hockey. The boy, he told Louise a few days ago, will be fine. Nothing there that a little kindness can't cure. Danny's gift to his new step-grandfather is a hockey puck emblazoned with the Oilers logo. Danny, to his credit, convincingly fakes some enthusiasm for the gift-wrapped collection of old Tom Swift books.

"Really, Dad," Louise says, when Dan has gone into the kitchen to help Jake unload the food. "You couldn't get me interested in those dated old stories. What makes you think a kid in the electronic age will find them remotely interesting?"

He looks hurt. Louise knows that if her mother were here, she would stand beside him, and gently chide Louise. A gift is a gift, she would say. And the look on her face would say, I thought we taught you this.

"Do you think he'd rather have cash?"

Yes, she's positive of that, but she shakes her head. "I'm sorry. It was a generous gesture." Maybe she can explain to Danny how much her dad loved those books and how he kept them for his own children, but ungrateful little girl that she was, she didn't appreciate them. A boy, she will tell him, would probably not have disappointed him. "Much better than cash. What are you going to do with your hockey puck?"

He picks the puck up from the coffee table and tosses it in the air, catches it with a grin. "I'm enjoying that a young fellow thought an old guy like me would like this. And I thought he seemed pretty pleased with the books. He's a good boy at heart, Louise."

She's told her dad briefly of Danny's problems at school, his lack of friends. Nothing about the shoplifting. Theft and lying were two things her parents would never abide. They would be sympathetic to a child with problems, but if the law were ever involved there would serious questions about character and responsibility, the good-heartedness notwithstanding.

Louise has told her mother, as clearly and gently as possible, about her marriage, about this boy who will be her stepson, but there is no way of knowing if she understood. Jake has visited at the nursing home with her a half dozen times, but they agreed after the one time Danny came along, that there was no point in taking him again. Louise's mom is beyond having a relationship with her new grandson. The place stunk, Danny said as soon as they entered the building and he thought it was hilarious that a bingo game was going on in the lounge. Bingo for zombies. When they found Louise's mom in the rows of wheelchairs and pushed her down to the lounge so they could have privacy for the visit, Danny sat silently through the laboured conversation, staring at his feet.

Louise looks around this room with the tiny artificial tree twinkling on the piano next to her mom and dad's wedding picture. There is scant resemblance between the radiant young woman in the photo and the mother she visits at the nursing home. She sits down and runs her fingers over the furry keys. Her dad has given the cleaning woman two weeks off with pay for Christmas, but Louise doubts the living room has been dusted since Hallowe'en.

"All right then. The gravy's bubbling, and the potatoes and the turkey will be fine for another fifteen minutes in the oven. Do you want me to do the salad?" Behind her, Jake puts his hands on her shoulders. "Serenade us and we'll do your bidding."

Louise twirls round on the piano stool and lifts her face for a kiss. Even though Danny has his back to them, eyes glued to the television, Jake still glances his son's way before he brushes Louise's lips. "Too rusty to do any serenading," she says. "Why don't you pour wine for you and Dad, and I'll get out the serving bowls and set the table."

"Get Danny to do the table," he says. "He knows how."

Dan surprises Louise by coming willingly to do the job when Jake asks. With a great flourish, he spreads the linen cloth on the dining room table and clumps down the rose-patterned china. Louise keeps her back to him, bites her tongue to keep from telling him to be careful, be careful, be careful, as the silverware clatters against the rims of the old plates. She busies herself spooning cranberry sauce into the rose-coloured glass bowl that to her knowledge has never been used for any other purpose, trying not to glance across the kitchen, through the archway that leads to the dining room. The kitchen is muggy with steaming food. She swallows hard, her stomach churning suddenly instead of hungry for the feast. When she finally turns around, Danny is standing with arms folded, everything in its proper place.

"See," he says. "I'm not as stupid as you think."

He had a haircut last week, and his face looks exposed,

vulnerable without the thick swath across his forehead. He stares at her, rare eye contact, and she shakes her head, walks across the room to him, but touches the tablecloth with her fingertips rather than touching him. She and Daniel have not exchanged a single physical touch. They walk carefully around one another, never even brushing sleeves. One night she sat down beside him on the sofa while he was watching television, and he picked up a pillow and stood it on end between them.

"Danny, no. I don't think you're stupid. Not at all."

The kitchen door opens then, and Jake and her dad come into the room. "Lovely!" Jake said. "Looks like a celebration. Does the bird need to sit a while before I carve, or can we get right to it?"

Danny flops down onto one of the dining room chairs and puts his elbows on the table, his chin in his hands. "Let's just eat. I'm hungry."

On Boxing Day Jake and Daniel are up early to check out the big sale at Future Shop. Not a chance, Louise says, when Jake asks if she wants to come along. Push through crowds for more things she doesn't need or want? She tries not to sound self-righteous or critical. She adds the extra excuse that she's a bit queasy this morning. Too much turkey.

She's relieved when they're out the door and she has the house to herself. She feels like a visitor here. She's put most of her furniture into storage, not wanting to crowd this space, waiting for Jake to let go of the idea of small town life so that she can convince him that the best plan is to buy another house in the city, one that they will all choose, where they can start fresh. A house without Brenda's curtains,

Brenda's cushions, Brenda's books and records, Brenda's sewing machine. These are the things that should be stored.

An hour later, Jake and Daniel are back, empty-handed, Jake white-faced, Daniel rushing past her to his room. While he was looking at the VCRs, thinking they could use a new one, Jake tells her, Danny went off on his own. He told Jake he'd meet him at the car, because he wanted to go to Sport Chek as well. No more than ten minutes later, a security guard tapped Jake on the shoulder. His son had just tried to slip out the door with a CD in each pocket of his jacket.

Daniel has been let off with a warning once again. Jake paces up and down the kitchen, punching his fist into the palm of the other hand. "You know what's even worse than his stealing those CDs?" From her chair at the table where she's been sipping gingerale, eating dry soda crackers, Louise just nods. She knows he isn't looking for a dialogue, and now is not the time to tell him that she suspects that what she has is not the flu after all. Half of her class was away with flu the last few days of school, but this morning, she is sure that hers is not a viral problem. "He lied. He told me he didn't know how they got there. Said some kids he knows from school who are always picking on him were in the store and he thinks they slipped the CDs into his pockets."

Louise stands finally, and steps into Jake's path in the middle of the kitchen. She holds out her arms. "Is that possible?"

He leans on her, shakes his head, his chin bristling against her hair. "I don't know. Do other kids hate him? Is he being bullied? Brenda used to say he was a victim, that he let himself get set up over and over again. But I've never really seen it."

"Jake, we need to get help for Danny. I know a good psychologist."

"Would we all have to go? I hate that kind of stuff, Louise."

Me, too, she thinks, but I've never had to consider seriously the possibility before. "I think we can start with just Danny."

"Okay," he says, "but this clinches it. I want to move back to the country. We know people there, Danny will have friends, and it's close enough for the two of us to commute to work together for the rest of the year."

"And who will look after Danny while we're commuting and working in the city?"

"No problem," he says vaguely. "I have a couple of cousins right in town with kids that age. I'm sure we can find someone for before and after school. And it'll only be until June."

They've decided that Louise will take a year off teaching, help her dad sell the house and move into a seniors' complex next door to the nursing home, and with luck, she'd be pregnant before it was time to decide whether or not to go back to work in the fall. As much as she wants another house, she's not sure about small town life. She's been charmed by the friendliness of the people she's met on the couple of visits to Jake's family in Valmer. But she's a city girl, and the thought of having to plan her life around trips to Edmonton is not appealing. She's been hoping Jake isn't really serious. What about the library, the German deli, the Greek bakery, the restaurants when nothing in the fridge looks appealing at 6:00? What about the friends who phone for a spur of the moment coffee or lunch?

"What about Danny?" Jake asks. "Isn't he worth at least giving it a try?"

Ah, yes, what *about* Danny? They'd planned to watch a movie together tonight, the three of them. Eat turkey sandwiches in front of the television. Maybe establish a new Boxing Day tradition, Louise had dared to dream. She's pretty sure Daniel is not writing thank you notes in his room.

On a Saturday afternoon in late January, Louise rings the doorbell at her dad's house, a courtesy she's always followed, but finally uses her key when there is no sound of movement from within. Through kitchen, dining room, living room, she calls until she opens the bedroom door and finds him sprawled between bed and floor, one hand clawed for the quilt, the other clutching the telephone hand piece. There is no life in this pose, nor any doubt when she sees blood-swollen ankles protruding from striped pyjama bottoms. Still, Louise kneels beside her father, trying to warm his cold cheeks between her palms.

The exact time of his death, the medical examiner tells her, isn't an easy thing to determine. This is not television or the movies. Some time between late evening and early morning Friday, most likely. What does it matter? Louise keeps trying to convince herself there was nothing she could have done to prevent this.

She realizes that she has been preparing for the death of her mother, assuming that she would struggle with a guilty mix of relief and sorrow, but she and her dad would cope, comfort one another. Now, numb and disoriented, she plods through the funeral arrangements and the small private service—just a handful of relatives and close friends—without shedding a tear.

The morning after the funeral, she wakes with a strange sense of urgency, swings her feet to the floor, but when she tries to stand, her legs collapse under her. Three times she tries, three times she falls back onto the pillows. Finally, she curls up in a tight ball and weeps. When she's finally spent herself and is silent except for the rhythmic trembling exhalations of her breath, the bedroom door creaks open and she hears Danny's hesitating footsteps approach the bed, then stop a few feet away. Jake left for work an hour ago, with a kiss and a promise to be home early.

"Louise?" Danny's voice cracks on her name.

"It's okay," she whispers, throat raw from the sobbing. "I just feel sad because my dad died. I needed to cry, but I'll be okay now."

She pulls herself up on the pillows and looks at the boy. He seems so small at times, times like this, and at other times when he enters a room he seems to grow to fill the entire space, sucking up the air. She brushes the hair from her face and tries to smile. Her "flu" has been properly diagnosed. She's pregnant, but she and Jake have agreed that it's best to wait a bit before telling Danny.

"Should I make you tea?" he asks. "I always made tea for my mom when she cried."

"That would be very nice, Danny." She glances at the clock. "We'll have a cup of tea, and then I'll drive you to school."

"Don't you have to go to school?"

"No, I have a few days off because of my dad."

"What are you going to do?"

"I have to go visit my mom." There was no question of Louise's mom attending the funeral. The big question is how to tell her that her beloved husband of almost fifty years has gone on without her. Louise has been looking forward to bringing her mother the news about the baby, sure that when she takes the wrinkled hand and places it on her belly, a light will go on. She planned to take her dad to the nursing home that day and tell the two of them together. As always, she waited too long. Surely it would have made a difference. Maybe a few extra heartbeats would have strengthened that muscle.

"Why tell her about your dad at all?" Jake asked. "What's the point in trying to crack through that shell in order to make her sad?"

Louise would like to agree with Jake. It would be so much simpler that way. But when she sat down at the piano yesterday after all the funeral guests had finally eaten their egg salad sandwiches, drunk their one glass of wine, sipped a cup of coffee with a few nibbles from the avalanche of sweets that poured in from neighbours, she held the wedding photo in her hand and looked into her mother's face. She would want to know. If she'd been given the dignity of voting on these matters before dementia moved in, she would have voted to know.

Self-conscious suddenly to be lying here, the rumpled nightgown twisted around her thighs, she pulls the quilt over her legs.

"Can I come with you?" he says.

"Where? To see my mom?"

He nods. Louise looks away to the frost-encrusted bedroom window, and imagines sitting beside her mother's wheelchair, holding the claw-like hand. How does Danny fit into that picture? If she takes him along, she'll have an excuse to tell, and then leave quickly. I have to get Danny to school now, she'll say to her mom, kiss her forehead and walk away. She will, of course, alert someone on the staff that she's broken this news, but she's sure they will only glance at the woman slumped in the chair, nod, and then she and Dan will stride through the snow to the car.

"We'll see," she tells him. "Yes, tea would be nice."

He turns and walks out of the bedroom. The hockey jersey, she realizes, has been on his body every day for a whole week. Even yesterday, when Jake was trying to coax Danny into changing into a button shirt and khakis, Louise held up her hand.

"It doesn't matter a bit," she said. "We don't need to wear black. Let him wear the shirt." But today? Today he is going to school and someone will surely notice that the boy smells bad.

She dresses, and braids her hair. In the kitchen the pot of tea is on the table with two mugs, a jar of honey, a piece of toast on a plate. The phone rings before she can thank Danny. Jake, checking to ask if she's okay.

"Danny's making breakfast," she says. "I'm going to see Mom this morning, and he wants to come along. Okay with you if he misses an hour of school? I'll write the note."

There's a pause. "Why would you want to take Danny? Surely it would be better to be alone with your mom."

"Oh, I don't know," she says. "I think the company might make it easier."

"Louise, remember who we're talking about here. I'm glad Danny came through with the cornflakes, or whatever, but he's not predictable. What if he says something off- the-wall and upsets you?"

Across the kitchen, her stepson is hunched over a bowl of Honeynut Cheerios. He looks up at her, blank, milk dribbling down his chin.

"Maybe you're right," she says.

"I don't imagine he's going to be too disappointed, considering his reaction the other time we took him along."

Louise doesn't get a chance to concoct a complicated

excuse as to why Daniel shouldn't come with her. She's barely past, "Your dad doesn't think…" when he stands up and grabs his jacket from the back of the chair.

"No, wait," she says, "I'll give you a ride."

"Drink your tea. See you later." He slams the door behind him.

Off to a good start, aren't we, Danny and I? Is that the way it went with Robert Cook and his stepmother?

There's not much in the books about Daisy. She married Ray Cook, became Robert's stepmother, had five children, wrote letters to Robert when he was in jail, sent yellow socks and a red tie for his release in June 1959, and died of a gunshot wound to her head. In her bed, apparently, and then her body was thrown into the hole in the garage floor with those of her husband and children. Enough?

No. That's not about Daisy. That's about Robert Cook.

How is it about Robert?

He killed her.

The more I read, the more I wonder if he did.

We don't care about that. We care about Daisy.

Roads Back

She was a red-headed school teacher. I skimmed the chapters in *The Work of Justice* that chronicle the crime, the arrest, the manhunt and the trials, to find the section on Daisy in the chapter Jack Pecover titles, "The Seven." About Daisy, there's a scant two pages, quotes from girlhood friends, a description of the frugal but tidy house the investigating police officers described. Discounting, of course, the mayhem of the night of June 25, 1959. One paragraph about the five children. But Pecover's book is about the crime, and the process that sent Robert Raymond Cook to the gallows.

Who, I wondered, was there left to tell me about Daisy, about those five children who, had they lived, would now be middle-aged? From Jack Pecover's sketch, the quotes from Daisy's friends, there emerges the portrait of a vivacious woman, no great beauty, but full of fun, quick-witted, and irreverent. One of two daughters, Daisy grew up on a farm, went to school in Hanna, took piano lessons every Saturday, and after a year of Normal School, the old teacher training program, came back to teach in her hometown. Strict, and dedicated to her students. Remembered by some—undoubtedly little Bobby Cook among them—as the "crabby" Miss Gasper, fondly remembered by far more. A talented pianist, who as a teenager, snuck into the Catholic church in Hanna with a friend one afternoon, and played "Elmer's Tune" on the church organ while the other girl tap-danced. A teenager who, because of a promise to her mother that she would stay out of the Hannah beer parlour, hitchhiked to

Drumheller with her friend to get drunk for the first time on brandy. Daisy became a stepmother when she married the widower, Raymond Cook, in 1949, three years after his wife's death. She'd been Robert's teacher, knew the twelve-year-old boy she was inheriting, a boy who had already been in trouble with the law. She was twenty-seven years old. Ray Cook was forty-two.

Daisy, the red-haired schoolteacher, stepmother of Robert Raymond Cook. A woman with a wicked sense of humour. When her second son was born in 1951, Daisy sent a note to a friend: "Roses are red, violets are pink. Our little Kathy was born with a dink. So we named him Pat."

Gerry in 1950, Patrick (Patty), in 1951, Christopher (Chrissy) in 1952, and in 1954 Daisy gave birth to her Kathy. Then Linda in 1956.

Daisy, mother of five children born in six years. A woman with a circle of friends who grieved the violent loss of their fun-loving friend. All of them, I knew, would be old women by now, but the memories Jack Pecover recorded in the 1980s were so poignant that I wanted to find someone, any one of them, and hear about Daisy from a human voice.

I searched directories, made phone calls, sent letters, and did not find a trace of any of the four women quoted in the Pecover book. Then, I stumbled on an obituary in the *Calgary Herald*. Clara Bihuniak, age 83, had passed away peacefully in Edmonton. I had been searching for Clara Behuniak, a woman Daisy's age, someone in her early eighties. Too much coincidence, I thought, a name easily misspelled. I sent a letter to one of the sons of Clara Bihuniak listed in the obit. Four days later, a man called. Yes, his mother was Daisy Cook's friend he said, but he was not the person with whom I needed to talk. Call his aunt, Marion Anderson, his mother's sister, he said. She lived in Calgary.

I knew it wouldn't be that difficult!

When I told Marion Anderson why I was calling, about my interest in the Cook family, she sighed. She was seven years younger than her sister, Clara. She didn't really remember much about the Cook family, or about those times, and she was busy, her family having a yard sale at her house that weekend. She remembered going to a wiener roast to celebrate the end of school when Daisy was teaching, hearing Daisy play the piano. She remembered how committed Daisy was to her students. After Daisy was married and living in Stettler, Marion Anderson had stopped in to visit. Daisy had two little girls, Mrs. Anderson remembered. She seemed surprised when I mentioned the other three children, the three boys. Could I meet with her, I asked, and she hesitated. Call me next week, she said.

I hung up the phone thinking I might have mined as much information in that call as was possible. The people who had the closest connections to the Cook family seemed the most reluctant to talk about the past, while anyone who'd been a by-stander seemed to have no hesitation at all in speculating and sharing their memories. My brother-in-law, who was sixteen at the time, remembered being stopped at a roadblock when Cook was on the loose from Ponoka. He said just being stopped made him feel that he must be guilty of *something*. And he was. At sixteen, he didn't have the category of licence to be driving the farm truck. No one took note. Another relative in Camrose, Pat, knew several people who'd partied with Cook during the brief times he was out of jail and around the area. She was mesmerized by the murder case, she said. On November 14, 1960, she stayed awake listening to her transistor radio until the news sometime after midnight reported that Cook had been hanged. She still wondered if the right man was executed. During the years I was to spend writing this story, Pat would often ask what new pieces I had found to fit into the puzzle.

By now I had newspaper clippings, notes from casual conversations with people who had lived in the area in 1959, recorded interviews—some enlightening, many just recounting the same archived information I'd already found—and no idea how I was going to use any of the pieces. Or why I wanted to. I tried once again to separate Louise's story from the Cook murder story, tried to use what I was gleaning about Daisy Cook to add some veracity to Louise's fears, and yet I couldn't find any real evidence that Daisy was frightened, or in fact—if those who so fervently maintained that Bobby Cook was innocent—that she had reason to be. For now, Daisy and Louise were entwined.

Some kind of sisterhood of stepmothers? If you're thinking Daisy and I are members of the same chapter, I'm cancelling my membership!

You don't get to vote. You're fictional, remember?

Are you sure? Doesn't Daisy feel like fiction too? All of this gets a little blurry sometimes, doesn't it?

A week later I called Mrs. Anderson again, without much optimism that she would have more to add. And that was how it began. She had not, she said, been able to dredge up much memory at all of Daisy, but to my surprise she said that she had been phoning other long-ago residents of Hanna to ask them what they remembered. The same details came up over and over again: Daisy's red hair, her gift for the piano, and the shock to the community when the news of the murders broke. Mrs. Anderson recalled her sisters going to dances with Daisy, knew that they were very fond of their fun-loving friend. Marion Anderson had left Hanna by 1959. She heard the news of the Cook murders on television and phoned her sisters who were both living in Calgary at the time. They were stunned, unable to believe such a thing could befall their friend. But, she said, life goes on, and it was long ago. I suggested meeting with her, but she declined, saying she didn't think it would be worth my time, but she'd be happy to chat now if I had questions.

I asked if she remembered Robert Cook, and she did indeed, but only as a small boy. She and a friend often babysat Robert and his cousin, Garry Bell, when the two boys were about four or five years old. Marion remembered that she and her friend played with paper dolls—they were that young—while they sat awake. They were not allowed to sleep when they babysat, even though the boys were already in bed when they arrived. The parents often went to dances. Bobby and his cousin were pests when they were awake, knocking on the door at Marion's house, pleading with the girls to play with them. She remembered the boys in the kitchen, watching her mother bake cookies. Bobby was a cute boy, she said, and she was surprised later to hear that he'd become a bit of a bully in Stettler, that he picked on other kids. She didn't remember how Daisy dealt with her stepson. Marion had left home by the time Daisy married Ray Cook.

I read Clara Bihuniak's comments to Marion from the Pecover book and she said this sounded exactly as she remembered her sister talking about Daisy. And the comments of Mrs. Joe Reilly, who it turned out was Marion Anderson's other sister, rang true. She was curious about my interest. So was I, I was tempted to say. So was I. A friend had just told me she had no intention of ever buying this book if I was lucky enough to get it published. My interest repulsed her.

I told Marion Anderson that my quest was really on behalf of a character in a story I was writing. I remembered the murders from my own eleven-year-old perspective, but another story, a piece of fiction, seemed to be demanding that I try to find the family in this crime.

Don't blame it on me.

The Boy

July, 1995

In the first months of her pregnancy, Louise didn't have the energy to resist when Jake set out to find them the perfect house in Valmer. Right to the end of the school year, she was wracked with morning, afternoon, and best-part-of-the-evening nausea. When they moved at the end of June, she let Jake do the packing, most of her belongings still in their boxes anyway.

Although Jake insisted the move was for Danny, the boy was even less enthusiastic than Louise. He refused to help with any of the unpacking, wandering outside instead, sitting on the back step, staring at the wooden sidewalk that led to the garage. Or riding his bike up and down the street for an hour at a time, bouncing a basketball off the side of the house until the sound drove Louise mad. Or sometimes just disappearing, but leaving her with the feeling that he was hiding somewhere. Watching her.

The house, she has to admit, is charming. It was built as the parsonage for the Anglican church, but when there was no longer a priest the members of the dwindling congregation had gone to other towns to worship. For the past five years, the elderly widow of the last Anglican priest to serve the parish had lived rent-free in the house. When she was shipped off to a nursing home in Edmonton, Jake, as hometown boy, was given first bid on the house.

Nothing, Louise is sure, has been changed since the house was built, and if she were feeling better, she would be as excited as Jake over the possibilities for upgrading. Meanwhile, even though the place is old, dated, it's in pristine condition. Louise imagines a long line of pious women polishing the banister with Pledge, waxing the black and white tile floor in the kitchen with Johnson's paste wax each week.

When the nausea finally abates, Louise's legs and feet start to swell to elephantine proportions by the end of each day and it's clear there is going to be no radiance to her condition. None whatsoever.

On a sultry day in August, she enlists Danny to drag the boxes labeled "DEN" out of the garage and pile them on the screened front verandah. Here, she decides, she will sit in a wicker chair in the lovely cross-draft and sort through her papers. She's sure that after these months of storage, there is much that she will be happy to discard.

Among the cartons, though, are several labeled in Jake's bold printing and one that says "DEN (Brenda)." She hesitates. Danny disappeared as soon as he finished hauling the boxes. When she looked out the window a few minutes ago, she thought she saw the bike, a swaying dot, at the end of the street. But she can't shake the feeling that she's not alone in spite of the silence.

Letter knife in hand, Louise slits the tape and carefully peels back the flaps on Brenda's archives. At the top of the box there's a file folder of recipes clipped from magazines. Of course. Brenda the amazing cook was always trying something new, Jake's sister told Louise. So the second folder of quilting patterns is no surprise either. Then two photo albums, kittens cavorting on the cover of one, a pony-tailed teenager with a transistor radio pressed to her ear on the other. Pages and pages of friends, birthday parties, school field trips. Louise squints at them, trying to find a likeness to the petite blonde woman in the photos she's seen of Jake's first wife, but it must have been Brenda herself who was the snapper of pictures.

Louise glances at the empty street periodically, stands up twice to walk down into the front garden and look around the side of the house, but there's no sign of Danny. Almost to the bottom of the box, and about to re-pack the mementoes as carefully as she found them, she pulls out a yellowed scrapbook. The first five pages bristle with newspaper clippings, the rest of the book is empty. A series of articles from the *Edmonton Sun*, starting February 26, 1984, ending March 5, 1984. A chronicle of a crime. "The Bobby Cook Story: Part One. Did we hang the wrong man?"

She stares at the photo of a young, bare-chested man against a brick wall. Unshaven, muscular, arms held away from his body, he looks slightly brutish. "Bobby Cook: Was he innocent?" the caption asks.

> "It was a quiet Sunday in June, 1959 when Mounties discovered seven mutilated, blood-spattered, decomposing bodies in a grease pit in the Cook home at Stettler. The victims were identified as Bobby's father, Ray Cook, 53, his step-mother, Daisy, 37, and Bobby's five step-brothers and sisters, aged between three and nine."

Louise lets the scrapbook slide from her lap. What kind of morbid interest possessed Brenda to keep these clippings? People she knew? But 1959? The articles were written twenty-five years after the crime, and must have been in Brenda's keeping, then in Jake's for the next ten years. She picks the book up again, and flips through the pages. The last article: "The Bobby Cook Story 25 Years Later. Some Doubts Remain." A photo of a gravestone. Seven names. Ever Remembered, Ever Loved.

She will ask Jake about this. Forget taping the box shut and pretending she didn't snoop. An innocent enough mistake to open a box accidentally—she'll admit that she was driven by curiosity, apologize for trespassing, ask him what this is about.

The breeze is picking up now, gusts rattling the leaves of the honeysuckle against the screen. The old Fahrenheit thermometer tacked to the doorframe reads eighty-five degrees. Jake tried to teach her the formula for converting back to Celsius, but the pregnancy has reduced her brain to a bowl of mush. "Forget it," she finally says. "It's just bloody hot."

Coal-coloured clouds are piling up in the west, and there is the scent of ozone on the wind. She pushes the boxes against the wall. She needs to put her feet up again—should have done so an hour ago. These past two days, even elevating hasn't reduced the swelling in her ankles. It feels like there are donut-shaped cushions straining under the tight skin.

Louise wanders in to the deep shade of the living room. She settles into Jake's recliner, facing the window. It's been several hours since she felt the baby move. The gigantic maternity t-shirt is limp from the heat. She slides her hands underneath and rests them on her belly, fingertips gently tapping. Usually, this caress wakes the babe, but this time there is no answering flutter.

When she closes her eyes, she senses a flicker of movement on the other side of the room. Opens them, and the curtains are swaying. On the second window, just a foot away, the old lace panels hang slack.

Breathe, she whispers to herself. Get up slowly. But even so, the room spins around her, and she bends over, grabs the edge of the table, takes a deep breath. Another breath, and the whirling stops.

Another three weeks in this swollen state. She's scheduled for induced labour if the baby hasn't arrived by then. Or a C-section at any time, if her blood pressure spikes again. She plods to the other side of the room. When she leans across the sewing machine to press her face to the screen, to look out at the side yard, she drags pieces of flannel onto the floor. Kicks them across the room, and sinks onto the chair, staring out into the back yard. Nothing out there but the vegetable patch in need of water, and the garage wall.

Then she notices the protruding handlebar. He's come back. She wasn't supposed to let him ride his bike, not after he went missing last night, Jake almost crazy with worry when he finally found him after midnight, pedaling down a dark road two miles away, but coming home, he said.

"Danny!"

No sound but the raspy song of grasshoppers. The field behind the house is alive with them. When they walk there in the evening, Louise leaning on Jake, the grasshoppers dance off their legs.

"Daniel Peters!"

Why does she bother? This boy never comes when she calls. He makes a point of waiting, and then appearing from some other direction as though he's come of his own accord.

She should go back to the sewing machine, finish hemming the receiving blankets. She should do the lunch dishes, scrub the frying pan scorched from the grilled cheese sandwich she forgot when Jake's cousin phoned. She wishes she hadn't told Phyllis about the toxemia. Now she phones twice a day to tell Louise to put her feet up. She should tidy the living room, mix the hamburger for supper. She should pee. These days the urge is constant, she never knows if she really needs to go.

The bathroom makes her cringe. She keeps asking Jake to give Danny some instruction so it doesn't look as though he is standing in the doorway and pissing in the general direction of the toilet. She takes a cloth and a can of Comet out of the cupboard and begins to do a clean-up. When she straightens after putting the supplies away, the baby gives a sharp nudge just under her ribcage, and she draws a deep breath. She has her baggy cotton slacks around her knees, is lowering herself cautiously to the toilet, when there is a scrape of sound outside the window, like something, someone pulling themselves up the wall. She is looking at that square of screen when the top of Danny's head appears, and for maybe ten seconds the two of them stare. Then she grabs a towel and heaves it at the window, hears him scramble away.

The roaring in her ears is so loud she doesn't hear the phone until she's back in the living room. She races to the kitchen, snatches the receiver off the hook and as soon as she hears Jake's voice, she screams at him. "You come home right now!"

When she looks out the window, the bike is gone, and God help her, just as she did last night when he disappeared, she hopes that Danny will never come back.

Whoa! It's no wonder the baby's so still. He's afraid too! And what are those newspaper clippings doing in my story?

I'm still amazed that I placed them there.

You mean you don't want to write the Cook story? I've been waiting for weeks for you to either get over it or admit that there might be a book of non-fiction in your future after all.

Really? I thought you were nagging me to finish your story.

Of course. But now you're crossing wires. Are you dragging Daisy into my story, or me into Daisy's?

Neither. Shall we rewrite this last chapter?

No, don't do that. Daisy deserves the attention. I'm willing to give her some space.

Roads Back

Every time I stepped back to 1959, I wanted to open the door of that clapboard bungalow in Stettler, walk into the kitchen and imagine the evening of Thursday, June 25, when Bobby Cook came home from prison. I wanted to imagine Daisy, and what she was thinking, and what was said. I began to write those imaginings, and then I was torn with the sense that I was trespassing, arrogantly assuming the right to impose thoughts and words on someone who had lived a real life. I struggled with my fiction-writing sensibilities. It came like breathing to me to create scenes, and assign motive. To change outcomes. But this story had its own ending, and the only details allowed were the facts.

The most salient facts were missing. No one knew what happened in the house on late Thursday night, June 25, 1959. Or Friday. Or Saturday. But the Sunday discovery of the blood-soaked bed and spattered walls, the pit full of bodies, gave rise to lurid imagining. In fact, I had to put my books aside by late afternoon or I was kept awake by images of little children in pyjamas cowering in the corner of a shabby living room.

The best way to dislodge the grisly bits of information in my head, I decided, was to follow the story to its end, and let everyone rest in peace. I knew from experience that if I stayed too long with a story idea in my head, worked it around without putting all the words on the page, there was the danger that it would be finished before it was written. I found myself secretly hoping that this *would* be the case with the Cook story. And Louise was annoying me enough that I would have been happy to throw her story unfinished into the drawer as well.

What I discovered very early in my pursuit of the Cook family was that there were more questions than answers. Opinion was sharply divided as to Robert Raymond Cook's guilt. There were conflicting stories dredged up out of failing memories, but a deep-seated interest wherever I went. What became abundantly clear was that Robert Raymond Cook was part of the history of central Alberta. Equally clear, that few people remembered the individual members of the family. Even people who lived in the town of Stettler at the time recalled only that there were "several" children, and that they were pitifully small.

So I set out to find these people, restore them from their infamy as the "murdered Cook family" to seven ordinary human beings. And what of their relationship with their son, stepson, half-brother?

That's what I want to know.

Roads Back

Who were these people? I knew where they'd ended. The Pecover book had a photo of a snow-banked headstone in the Hanna cemetery as a frontispiece. So far my search had taken me to Stettler, Red Deer, and Lacombe, but there'd been no particular reason to visit Robert Raymond Cook's home town. It had been over a year since I picked up the Pecover book at the Hillhurst flea market. A long fall and winter of reading, some formal interviewing, a lot of informal talk—so many people who remembered this crime. But I had not felt inclined to trudge through a desolate winter landscape looking for graves.

Then came a day of prairie summer at her best; milky-blue sky a mile high, the scraping song of grasshoppers, dusty smell of gravel roads and new-mown clover, and barely enough breeze to dry the trickle of sweat down my neck. We'd been to Saskatoon for a weekend jaunt with the same friends with whom we'd dined at Longview. They knew I'd been digging around in the Cook case ever since. They were not surprised when I suggested a stop in Hanna.

Which cemetery, the kid at the service station asked when we stopped for directions. The Catholic one or the regular one? I made a blind guess. Regular. About ten miles north, he told me, pointing down the main road that ran through town. His guess was less reliable than mine. It was barely a mile to the wooden archway at the entrance to the cemetery. Like so many country graveyards, this one was set on a hill, bordered along the road by low-growing shrubs, and along the other perimeters by the barbed wire fences of the farmland out of which it was carved.

We fanned out, each to a quadrant. I started at the highest point, thinking there might be a pattern and I'd be able to work my way to 1959 by following the dates of death on the stones. I should have known better from previous cemetery wanderings. There was always a mix of old and new, plots purchased long before the owners had taken up residence. After ten minutes of wandering, contemplated by a herd of cattle—black Aberdeen Angus and white-faced Herefords— now lining the fence on the town side of the graveyard, I made my way into a section that felt less tended, less visited. Here there were more single graves, many occupied in the early forties by young men shipped home from the war. Finally, with a sense that I was closing in, I pushed through a tangle of lilac and caragana bushes into another section. I found myself wanting urgently to be the one who found the Cooks.

I almost tripped over Josephine Cook's grave. Mother of Robert Raymond Cook. The slab of concrete that delineated the casket underneath was chipped and flecked with rust. Creeping charlie and chickweed had choked out the grass in this shady corridor. The headstone was small, unpretentious. Josephine Cook 1915-1946. Perhaps Ray Cook gave thought to being buried next to Josephine some day, owned the adjoining plot which seemed to be vacant. But who would have envisioned the size of the grave necessary to bury his entire family?

A quick scan of the surrounding area and my eyes were drawn to a slight rise perhaps twenty yards away. A head-stone larger than any around it, two big slabs of concrete. I couldn't help wondering morbidly how many coffins were used, how the bodies were divided.

Seven names, one date of death. In touching contrast to the repeated formality of "Robert Raymond Cook" in my reading, the names of his family were carved here in their diminutives: Ray, Daisy, Gerry, Patty, Chrissy, Kathy, and Linda. Ever Remembered, Ever Loved. Someone had left a nosegay of wild purple asters against the stone. The blossoms were wilted, but given the heat of the day, relatively fresh. The fate of this family was so much part of the lore of the area, anyone wandering through the cemetery might have paused to leave the flowers. Then too, there was extended family—Ray's, Daisy's, someone among them who'd chosen the words for the epitaph. Someone who remembered all seven. Who?

With his father's remarriage and the quick arrival of five more children—all of them born between 1950 and 1956—Robert Cook gained a new family, but he spent little of the next ten years in their midst. His life played out with dizzying speed: jail at fourteen, sole survivor of his family at twenty-two, dead at twenty-three. Sixteen months from his arrest for the murders to his execution. Sixteen months without family. According to Dave MacNaughton, Cook's lawyer, after the murders not a single member of the extended family made contact with the boy who had been known as Bobby. No one came forward to choose a final resting place for the infamous grandson, nephew, cousin. Robert Raymond Cook left instructions for the donation of his eyes. One wonders if the doctors who performed the transplant knew what those eyes had seen. Cook's body became the property of the Department of Anatomy at the University of Alberta Faculty of Medicine. There it ended. No grave.

You went to the graveyard to convince yourself that this story was dead and you could let it go?

No. We just happened to be in the vicinity, driving back to Calgary after a weekend in Saskatoon. I thought I might regret the missed opportunity later.

What was missing? You saw the picture of the graves. What more could there be?

Nothing, really. But I wanted to be reminded that there were bodies, real people buried there.

And? Are you any closer to letting them rest in peace?

Well, I may be getting closer, but I think you're becoming as curious as I am about Daisy and young Robert. Or you will be once you get back to those clippings Brenda saved.

Ah, yes, Brenda. And now we meet Josephine? Is that where we're going with this graveyard chapter, back to the dead mothers?

It seems like the logical direction.

Roads Back

Josephine Grover was eighteen years old when she married Raymond Albert Cook in Hanna, Alberta, in 1936. An elderly uncle, when I asked him to reminisce about that period of time on the prairies stroked his chin and frowned. These were the dirty thirties: drought, crop failure, low prices for grain even in the years when there was enough moisture to bring it to harvest, hungry men at the back door wanting to exchange small labour in exchange for a bowl of soup. Legions of men, including my own father, "rode the rails" looking for work. My dad went east to a logging camp, and came back so lean and dirty his mother didn't recognize him when he walked onto the farmyard.

Still, in the reminiscing there was a note of pride. People stuck together in hard times, my uncle told me. When everyone was poor there was a spirit, such a closeness in the community that there were good times to soothe folks through the bad. Among those good times, I imagined, were the dances Josephine and Ray Cook might have attended on the nights Marion Anderson and her friend were hired to watch over young Bobby. Or perhaps, like my parents, they played cards at someone else's house, whist or cribbage around the kitchen table, the air choked with cigarette smoke, a bottle of rye whisky on the counter, the "lunch" of ham sandwiches and perked coffee at the end of the evening.

Robert Raymond Cook was an only child, although according to Jack Pecover's account of the family history, Ray and Josephine considered adopting a second when

Josephine was told that another pregnancy would be life-threatening because of her rheumatic heart. Country dances and family plans notwithstanding, life in the Cook family was troubled. There was a separation, then a reconciliation shortly before Josephine died. Josephine was counseled by a friend to divorce Ray Cook because of his "philandering" but decided to stay in the marriage "to make Ray suffer." Psychiatrists who examined Robert Raymond Cook after the murders likely pondered the significance of domestic strife, the early loss of his mother, the intrusion of a step-mother in turning Bobby Cook into a pint-sized car thief and then a mass murderer. Those were certainly the musings and speculations of the general public.

When his mother died during routine surgery to correct a twisted bowel, Bobby was just nine years old. Too young, his father decided, to attend the funeral. Ironically, thirteen years later, Robert Raymond Cook made a Herculean effort to attend his father's funeral. The service for the murdered family was in Hanna on July 2, 1959. On that same day, Dave MacNaughton, Robert's lawyer, received a letter from Ponoka.

> The doctor here tells me they're not going to allow me to go to the funeral. I've just got to be there, please for Christ sakes arrange it. I've got about $90 they can have for the expenses. If you could only understand how much it means to me. There the only people in the world I have that care if I live or die. So please try and fix it so I can go. ... I truly hope you belive me, for nobody else thinks I am innocent. You probly dont know what it feels like to be completely alone, since there gone.

By the time Robert Raymond Cook wriggled his way through an impossibly small window at the Ponoka Mental Hospital and escaped into the wooded countryside, the seven members of his family had been in their graves for more than a week. When he was captured, Cook said he broke out to attend the funeral, but later he amended his story to say he was on his way to visit the graves. That tendency to amend, to tailor his story to what he believed his audience wanted to hear became a fatal flaw worthy of a Greek tragedy.

In interviews in prison and in the psychiatric examination at Ponoka, Robert Cook gave varied dates for the death of his mother, reported his own age at the time as eight, eleven, twelve, and on one occasion said he was "orphaned" when he was thirteen and "more or less on his own ever since." The night before he died, he spoke about his mother to one of the two pastors who had been his spiritual advisors. He said that Josephine wrapped Christmas presents for him before she died, that he remembered the sadness of opening them on Christmas morning without her. Josephine died in September, during fairly routine surgery, likely expecting to spend Christmas with her son. So organized a young house-wife that she'd done her shopping three months early?

Distorted though his memories of his family may have been, one thing that was certain was that Robert Cook lost everyone of significance in his life. Dave MacNaughton was with Cook when he was told in police cells in Stettler that his father was dead. Although MacNaughton didn't recall the exact words, he remembered that they were hard. Your father is dead, and you're under arrest for murder. No more than that. MacNaughton had no doubts about the honesty of Cook's response: "He wasn't acting when he broke down and said, 'Not dad, not my brothers and sisters.' He couldn't speak after that."

Cook's response was recorded by the police as: "Not my father, not my father." Nowhere in any of the recorded interviews or court transcripts is there a comment from him about Daisy's death.

I was relying heavily on Jack Pecover's book, feeling ever more strongly that I should contact this man and find out what had obsessed him about Robert Raymond Cook's trials, "the work of justice." Although he stated his purpose "simply to present the complexities of the case, allowing readers an outsider's view of how and why a man was sent to death by his community" (pg. xxiv) the text is heavily-laden with anger and frustration, and the author's conviction that justice was not served. I would, I decided, follow my own path to the Cook family. Mine was a different purpose, my question "Why?" rather than "Who?" I would hold off contact with the man who wrote this scathing account as long as possible.

Pecover's book describes Ray and Bobby Cook as being as close as any father and son could hope to be, pals, linked by a passion for cars and pulled even tighter with the loss of Josephine. Ray Cook taught his son to drive at the tender age of seven. After Josephine's death, on evenings and weekends, Ray took Bobby along to the garage where he worked. For three years father and son were tight-knit. Then came Daisy.

Miss Gasper had been one of Bobby Cook's teachers. Though touched by the loss of his mother, she likely knew that the stepson she was acquiring would be a challenge. Bobby had already been in trouble for "joy-riding." He was remembered by a Hanna police officer, Gordon Russell, for his ability to unlock and hot-wire a car with breath-taking speed. At the time, Bobby was so young he was barely visible over the wheel. Cars, trucks, tractors, it seemed any vehicle was a temptation to go for a spin around town.

Daisy May Gasper and Ray Cook were married in July, 1949. Bobby didn't attend their wedding. But he did force his way to the centre of their attention shortly after when he notched up his "borrowing" of cars and for the first time took one of his joyrides beyond the town limits.

That theft is mentioned in a RCMP summary prepared after the murders and dated January 4, 1960:

> At the age of 12 years he took a car belonging to Mr. E. Hart of Botha, Alta. Was eventually stopped by Police. He had been operating the car at a high rate of speed and apparently was not particularly concerned with his behaviour."
> (*The Work of Justice* pg. 33)

Robert Cook may have been unconcerned, but the newly wed Daisy must have held her head in her hands. She was twenty-eight years old, had one year of teacher training and a brief career as the local school marm. Now she was the mother of a twelve- year-old car thief. She was also pregnant. Her first child, Gerald, was born seven months later, in February 1950.

The following summer, July, 1950, Ray and Daisy Cook moved their growing family to Stettler, to a small apartment above McTaggart Motors, the garage where Ray Cook had found employment. Perhaps they hoped a change of scenery would have a positive affect on their eldest son. Shortly after the move, Bobby stole another car. The account of that adventure as told to Jack Pecover by Gordon Russell is livelier than the RCMP report of the earlier crime:

One night he stole a car from Stettler. I was at Castor at the time, my dad was there, the town cop was there and a Mountie. We got a call to put up a road block; a stolen car was coming down the highway from Stettler. Dad went out to stop him and he swerved at Dad and took off. The Mountie said, 'Christ! There's nobody in that car!' We chased him into a coulee near Castor. Dad went up to the car and said, "All right, get out!" but he had abandoned the car and gone up into some trees. He disappeared completely. We hunted for him until about 5 am but couldn't find him. We were standing by the hotel and somebody hollered, "There he is!" He was stealing another car off a used-car lot across the street. We grabbed him." (*The Work of Justice* pg. 34)

The town of Hanna knew Bobby Cook as one of their own, a lad who lost his mother and was seen driving a tractor trailer with his dad beside him when he was barely old enough to look over the steering wheel. A boy prone to mischief with cars in his pre-adolescence. Stettler met him as a juvenile delinquent.

The two towns to which Robert Raymond Cook laid claim as home in his short life straddle the parkland region of Alberta to the north and the grassland region to the south. Around Stettler there is a mosaic of aspen woodlands, fescue grasslands, shrublands and wetlands. As it rolls gently south to Hanna, the landscape becomes grassland, part of the Great Plains that stretch from the Gulf of Mexico, through the United States and up into the Canadian prairies. Hanna is in the Alberta Badlands, where the rivers have carved deep into the bedrock and formed spectacular coulees and ravines. All that open space, so many cars left unattended.

In 1950, Stettler had a population of 2442, Hanna had 2027 citizens. Similar size, both service centres for the surrounding farming districts, only about 80 miles, an hour and a half's drive, apart. Hanna was Bobby Cook's home and it seems unlikely that he was consulted about the move to Stettler.

Unlikely, as well, that he was thrilled with the arrival of a baby brother so soon after Daisy usurped his father's affection. I had a hard time conjuring an image of Ray Cook. In my mind he was a generic small town mechanic, a quiet, hard-working father who left the management of home and family to his young and very capable wife. That part was clear, but it was the younger Ray Cook, husband of Josephine, alleged philander, widowed father of Bobby who both interested and eluded me. In Jack Pecover's interviews, my own interview with Bobby Cook's lawyer, and some casual conversations with people I met who had lived in Stettler during that time, there were hints that Bobby Cook had inherited his attitude toward the law and his slippery fingers from his father. When I pressed for more specific details, though, there seemed always to be a reluctance to speak ill of a man who'd died so tragically.

What was clear throughout, though, was that father and son had a bond, and Daisy and her children drove a wedge into that relationship. In quick succession, Bobby "borrowed" Ray's car for a trip to Hanna to visit his relatives, took a school bus in Hanna for a spin, and stole a car from his dad's employer, McTaggart Motors, in Stettler. He was sentenced to eighteen months in the provincial jail at Lethbridge, almost 250 miles, a four hour drive, from home, likely the farthest he'd ever been from his dad. He was fourteen years old.

The Boy

August, 1996

Jonathon was born the day after Louise found the file of newspaper clippings about the mass murder of the Cook family. There were cans of paint, a roll of carpet, gauzy white fabric for curtains for the nursery, but so far Louise had little interest in turning the spare bedroom into a nursery. Jon slept in a wicker bassinette that was never out of her sight during the day, and snugged up against the bed at night. This was not necessary, Jake told her the second night. Danny slept in his crib in a room down the hall from the day they brought him home from the hospital. Brenda was determined not to spoil her new son, and within a few days he was sleeping through the night.

Jake stopped abruptly, as though he was reading Louise's thoughts on the spoiling of Daniel. She shrugged. It was just easier to feed Jon in the wee hours when he was close, she told Jake. She didn't admit that she couldn't bear the thought of the baby being farther away than arms' reach while she slept. If he were in another room, she would lie awake listening for the tiniest of whimpers, the sound of footsteps in the hall.

In the small hours of this morning when she was nursing the baby, the bedroom door creaked open and Daniel stood silhouetted against the dim light from the hall.

"What is it?" Louise asked softly.

"I thought I heard him crying," the boy said.

"Well he was, but only for a minute and now he's fine."

He nodded, and padded back to his room.

This morning, when Dan came sleep-rumpled to the kitchen, she asked if the baby's crying in the night always woke him.

"I never hear him."

"You mean last night was the first time?"

"What are you talking about? I slept all night." He filled his bowl to almost overflowing with Rice Krispies and then ground them down with the palm of his hand before he added milk.

Jake appeared then, and tousled Daniel's hair as he walked past on the way to the coffee pot. "Me too, pal. Seeing as we're sleeping through all the little guy's squawking in the night, what do you say we let Mom have a nap this afternoon and take Jon for a stroll around town?"

Louise had suggested to Jake that Daniel would likely never think of her as "Mom," but Jake kept on trying. Now that the baby was here, and she felt like a Mom, she'd stopped flinching at the word, but Daniel still scowled. "In the buggy? I'm not pushing any baby carriage around town!" Parked on the verandah was the monstrous English-style pram that Brenda's parents bought when Daniel was born. They retired to Victoria shortly after Brenda died, and so far as Louise knew, there'd been no contact with them since they sent their regrets to the wedding invitation.

"I'll do the driving," Jake said. "He'll be good for an hour while you snooze, won't he, Lou? We'll go down to the coffee shop and let Dan show off his new brother."

"Oh, I don't think …" She was stopped by the cautionary expression on Jake's face. Do not refuse this, it said. Instinctively, she looked toward the living room where Jon was asleep in the bassinette.

Get a grip, she told herself. Jake was the father, and he was as reliable as she was, maybe even more so because he was reasonable, not boiling over with hormones. He was proud of the little guy, and he wanted to show him off.

"Have a good nap," Jake tells her cheerfully after lunch.

Not likely, Louise thinks as she stands at the window watching them leave, Jake stoically pushing the pram, Danny racing ahead on his bike. Instead of sleeping, she pulls the box marked "Brenda" into the living room. From a chair in front of the window she'll be able to watch for their return. The day is overcast, a nasty wind whipping the yellow leaves off the Manitoba maples that form a canopy over the wooden sidewalk. Louise imagines the bumpety ride, Jake taking care to ease the buggy over gaps in the wood, through drifts of leaves. He was positively puffed up when they got the pram out of the garage and dusted it off.

"This thing," he had said, "has a chassis that'll give as good a ride as the Queen's coach. I gave Brenda a real hard time about looking like an English nanny."

Daniel had been poking around in some of the other furniture still packed into the back corner of the garage. He looked up at the mention of his mom's name, stared at the pram. "Was that mine?"

"You bet. You rode in style, my boy. And so will your little brother. I wish we still had some of the other baby stuff around. Nothing but the best was your mom's motto." He fell quickly silent then, no doubt remembering the argument he and Louise had when she was barely pregnant and Jake came home with a fancy crib. He was just walking through Sears, he said, on the way to the hardware department when he saw a whole gaggle of pregnant women heading up the escalator, following the signs for Baby Week. He decided to tag along to the sale. Heck of a deal on the crib, top of the line, so he couldn't pass it up. Louise had already arranged the loan of baby equipment from one of the teachers she worked with. She hated spending money on items that were only going to be used for a few months, hated any kind of extravagant consumption. Hated too, the tension that created with Jake. He wasn't a spendthrift, just impulsive and generous.

The crib, she knows, is out here somewhere, still in the box, and one of these days she will ask him to bring it in and set it up.

She unfolds the flaps on the box with Brenda's name on it, then sits back in the chair a moment to ponder the woman who delighted in buying the very finest for her baby boy. Why keep only the pram? Where have the rest of the baby items gone? At some point hope of another baby ceased and they were too sad a reminder? Brenda has been much on Louise's mind these past two months. In the middle of the night, when she rocks with Jon at her breast, she feels overwhelmed by the baby's helplessness, his dependency on her. How long, she wonders, does a mother anguish over what will become of her child if she isn't there to watch over him? How Brenda must have anguished.

The file of newspaper clippings is at the top of the box. She pulls it out and begins to read.

"Hey, you're supposed to be sleeping. Were we gone too long?"

Louise gathers the papers on her lap into a jumble. Jake is in the doorway with the baby in his arms. She blinks. Glances at her watch. She's been reading for more than an hour, hasn't looked to the window at all.

"What's got you so engrossed there?" He shifts Jon to his shoulder and gently pats the baby's back. When she takes a deep breath and spreads her hands over the newspaper clippings, he crosses the room to sit down on the footstool beside her chair. Jon is awake, gnawing on his fist, beginning to fuss.

"Why did Brenda keep a file on this horrible murder case?"

He tips his head to look at the print. "Cook? Brenda knew the guy. Where did you find this stuff?"

Louise drops the papers into the box, and holds out her arms for Jonathan. Instinctively, she looks toward the door before she pulls up her sweater and settles the baby at her breast. "Where's Danny?"

"Aw," Jake waves his hand dismissively, his eyes on the newspaper clippings, "he got bored as soon as he sucked down his milkshake. He said he was going for a bike ride." He picks up the top sheet of paper, tapping his finger on the photo of Robert Raymond Cook, bare-chested in what looks like a cell. "Brenda knew somebody who knew some-body who went joy-riding with this guy after he killed his folks—everybody knows somebody who knew him, same as with every other ugly story. Imagine the nerve, cleaning himself up, sporting around the country in a snazzy new convertible he bought with his dad's money."

"The man who wrote that article thinks he was innocent."

"Oh yeah, lots of people on that side of the fence but just as many on the other." He stands up, rolls his shoulders, and gives his head a shake. "Gruesome stuff. I'll get rid of this whole box. I doubt there's anything in there we need."

"No, leave it. There are some cookbooks. Leave it, and I'll sort through later." She tries to appear distracted, as though it's no big deal. "Busy day down at the coffee shop?"

"The after-church crowd," he says. "A bunch of grey-haired women fighting to hold the little guy. I drank my coffee and ate my flapper pie, and they still wouldn't give him back."

"No wonder Dan cut out." The boy was well-trained when it came to meeting adults, but Louise has noticed that he never suffers more than five minutes before he comes up with an excuse to leave the room.

"Everybody asked about you." Jake bends down and strokes the baby's cheek with his thumb. "I told them things are getting a little more organized around here and you probably wouldn't mind an invitation to coffee. Maybe you could do the inviting?"

Likely Brenda was planning dinner parties for twelve and volunteering at the hospital three weeks after Daniel was born. "Phyllis is going to stop by this week when she's in town," Louise says. "Frankly, that's about all the socializing I feel up to just now. Maybe in a week or so we can invite the Schultzes over for coffee some evening." The old couple who live next door welcomed them with a basket of cookies the day they moved in, chatted over the fence, offered advice on the garden.

Jake frowns. "They're a bit miffed with me," he says. "Henry and I had words last week."

Even before he explains, Louise knows this is about Daniel. She heard Henry shouting at Daniel one afternoon. "About...?"

"Aw, he says somebody's been in his garage, messing around with his tools. He's missing a few things. Cripes, Lou, he's eighty-five years old. He's probably given the stuff to his kids and forgotten all about it. The place has a padlock and chain across the door that would give Houdini a run for his money."

And a small cardboard-covered window on the alley side, Louise thinks, that wouldn't be difficult for a small body to wriggle through. "You weren't rude to him, were you?" Normally easy-going Jake can be sharp and dismissive. Surely not to an old man, though.

"I told him I'd speak to Dan, but turns out he already did. I wasn't rude, but I probably let him know I thought he was out of line. He should have come to me first."

"And did you speak to Danny?"

He nods. "He said he hasn't been anywhere near that garage, and why would he want to go in anyway because it's full of old junk. Pretty much what I was thinking."

She closes her eyes. She can hear Danny's voice saying those words, see the slight squint of his eyes, his teeth catching his lower lip. She would have snapped back at the boy, asked him how he knew about the junk if he hadn't been in the garage.

"You believed him?"

"Of course I believed him. Judas Priest, Louise! He's my son. I should take the word of a senile old man over that of my own son?"

She looks away so that he won't see the nod in her eyes. Yes, Jake, when the son is a liar, we start from a different place.

"I didn't mention it before," Jake says, "because you have enough on your mind here. It'll blow over."

Blow over, and maybe Jake's questioning will have been enough to deter Danny. Meanwhile she'll speak to Mrs. Schultz. Go over tomorrow with a thank you card for the booties and hat the old woman crocheted for Jon.

Jake walks to the window. "I wonder where that kid got to. I'm going to go for a drive and see if I can find him."

When the baby is asleep in his basket again, Louise returns to the clippings. She's skimmed the newest pieces, an *Edmonton Sun* series written for the twenty-fifth anniversary of the murders. How bizarre, she thinks, to be holding an anniversary for a gruesome murder. The man who wrote the piece didn't hedge. He thought the wrong man had been hanged. Louise thinks suddenly of her dad, how she wishes she could ask him if he remembers this crime, and what he thought. She's sure that if a court of law said it was so, then for her dad it would have been so. Black and white, or at least as dark a shade of grey as it took to make a judgment. She is also sure he would have said, "Hindsight's 20/20, Louise. Everybody's a Monday morning quarterback." She wonders about her mom, whether the name might flick a switch and illuminate one of those patches of long ago memory that occasionally surprise Louise when she visits.

The older pieces are worn at the folds, as soft as flannel to the touch and most of them marred by the dark stain on the envelope in which she found them. A cup of coffee? Young Brenda's bottle of coca-cola splashed across the collection? From what she knows of Brenda, Louise imagines her frowning, blotting the envelope, looking for a new one to replace it with. She riffles through again, looking for the headline that clutched her by the throat just as Jake came through the door. "Place Usurped by Hated Stepmother. Spoiled Son Turns to Crime." Robert Cook was hanged for murdering his father, stepmother, and their five children. Jake is right. Even though the headline is ridiculously sensationalist, worthy of a grocery store check-out tabloid, this is gruesome. She should throw it all away. She piles the papers onto the back of a shelf at the top of the bedroom closet.

Jake's visit with the Sunday morning coffee crowd prompts a phone call from Phyllis on Monday morning. She's planning a baby shower. What day would be best? Jake works evenings all week, they have only one car, Phyllis lives about five miles out of town, and it's a problem to leave Daniel home alone in the evening. But Phyllis is dauntless. One of the women from town will be happy to give Louise a ride, and Dan of course is welcome to come along. He flatly refuses. Boring, he says. Phyllis is from the traditional Mennonite side of Jake's family. No television or computers in their house. The kids, Dan says, are "dorky" and the farm is a drag and Paul, Phyllis's husband, is mean. He made Dan help with chores when he spent a weekend at the farm right after Jon was born.

After Dan's griping, Jake agrees that the boy is old enough to stay home alone. He'll try to get away from work early.

By the time the innocent little party games have been played, the gifts opened, the spread of sandwiches, pickles, dainty sweets set out with coffee which Louise is sure will keep both her and the baby awake well into the early morning, her face aches from smiling. Fortunately, the woman she's ridden with is anxious to leave. She stands at the window fretting. "It's raining dogs and cats," she says, "and I left clothes out on the line."

"You're brave." One of the other women pauses from collecting cups and carrying them to the sink. "I don't hang anything out anymore unless I'm right there with the broom handy." She turns to Phyllis. "We've got a laundry snitcher in town. All sorts of unmentionables disappearing into thin air. Gives me the willies."

"Kids," Phyllis says. "I'll bet you anything it's just kids." She laughs. "Quit buying fancy underwear and they'll leave you alone. How about you, Louise? You had anything go missing?"

Louise shakes her head. Why admit that it hadn't occurred to her to hang clothes out to dry? Or that it's unlikely anyone would have a prurient interest in her nursing bras or elastic-sprung cotton briefs. Although looking around the room, she doubts that any of these women are hiding Victoria's Secrets.

After the haul of baby gifts has been loaded into the car, they are barely into the car when the woman begins ranting again about clothesline raids. Louise tries to come up with rational possibilities that don't involve perverted motives. She tries too, to avoid sounding like she's fabricating a defense, but unease is growing in the soft pit of her belly, something dark filling the space so recently occupied by her son.

The house is dark. No Danny. No Jake. Gifts safely deposited in the front hallway, her chauffeur's headlights disappearing down the street, Louise stands alone in the silent house with the baby in her arms. On her way to the kitchen she flicks on every light switch she passes. There's a note from Jake on the table. They've gone into the city to a movie. Back around midnight. It's just ten thirty.

Louise changes the baby, nurses him again, reflects on his angelic behaviour at the shower, then settles him into the bassinette beside the bed and crosses the hall to Dan's room. She opens the door slowly, surprised as always by the bareness of the space. The weekend they moved into the house, Jake took Danny shopping for something to brighten the walls but the hockey posters are still in their tubes on his desk. The bookcase is empty, boxes stacked unopened in his closet. The bed is made, albeit a bit haphazardly with the quilt simply pulled up over the pillows, one corner dragging on the floor. Feeling guilty, intrusive, but determined to prove herself wrong, she methodically opens and closes drawers, pages her way through the shirts and sweaters hanging in his closet. She folds a pile of clean clothes that she handed Dan from the dryer earlier and leaves them in a tidy pile on the end of the bed, a sign that she's been in his room. He deserves to know this. Tomorrow she'll ask him if he noticed, if he minds. An opening to the discussion on privacy and mutual respect she's been avoiding. Louise knows that Daniel snoops in their bedroom when he's alone in the house. This is a discussion she won't delegate to Jake. She wants a contract from Daniel. But she's suspicious of her own motives; is she setting him up with a promise she knows he'll breach?

Before she leaves the room she straightens the quilt on the sad-looking bed. When she fluffs the pillows, her hand grazes a bit of cool fabric protruding from beneath. The nightgown under the pillow is satin, a watery lilac shade. Not sexy lingerie, but the expensive indulgence more likely of a woman in her forties than a young girl. The sort of gown that a husband might wrap for Christmas. That any wife in this town would be pleased to own.

She buries the gown under the pillow, and tugs the quilt awry before she leaves the room.

When Jake tiptoes into the bedroom just after midnight, Louise feigns sleep. This can wait until morning.

In fact, she waits until after breakfast, when Danny has ridden off on his bike and Jake has finished his third cup of coffee.

"I need to show you something," she says. "But first I need to tell you about this problem around town. Someone's stealing underwear off clotheslines."

He blinks at her, a smile tugging at his tired face. And then he throws his head back and laughs out loud. "That's not news. Louise, every town with clotheslines has a resident pervert who collects panties. So don't hang yours out to dry. You'd think everyone would have figured that out by now." When he picks up the folded newspaper, she taps him on the shoulder.

"Come with me," she says. Without another word, she leads the way into Dan's room, relieved that the evidence is still there but also sick inside when she lifts the pillow. Jake looks down at the garment, draws two long breaths before he gathers the wrinkled silk with his fingers.

"It's his mother's," he says. "This was Brenda's." He is good enough to keep his eyes on the nightgown while she composes herself.

"Oh," she says, "oh, I'm sorry, Jake."

She waits for him to reach for her. He doesn't. Brenda may as well be standing between them.

"How would you know, Lou? I wonder when he salvaged it. A couple of Brenda's friends came over and cleaned out the closet for me because I didn't have the guts to do it myself." He crumples the nightgown in his fist and returns it as they found it before he steers her out of the room.

"I shouldn't have snooped," she says, "but when I heard about that clothesline thing at the shower I had this horrible feeling. I had to know."

"Forget it. I've snooped through his stuff too. It's the only way I know to make sure he's staying out of trouble. But for God's sake, Lou, stopping thinking the worst. The kid is miserable. I took him back into town for a movie last night because he said this place is driving him crazy. Nothing to do, no friends."

Would there be a point to reminding him that Danny didn't have any friends to speak of before they moved?

"He's at a tough age for a big move like this," Jakes says.

Originally her argument, but Jake seems to have forgotten that. She shrugs, not willing to sympathize. They moved. It's too late.

"Maybe I'll take him out for a drive to Phyllis and Paul's this afternoon if they're home. Doesn't hurt to remind him he's got a family that cares about him."

Danny will refuse, but it hurts Louise that Jake thinks he needs to go to Phyllis to find family. And it troubles her even more that while there is an explanation for the nightgown—an explanation so sad she felt limp with despair for the boy when she looked at the pillow after Jake gently returned it to its place—she cannot let go of the possibility that Dan is the clothesline thief. All those hours riding his bike, cruising town. Alone.

Should I have made a big deal of this? Sneaking around clotheslines stealing underwear is a few rungs down, and not even on the same ladder as crashing through road blocks in a stolen car.

Who says for sure he stole the lingerie? Or that he's going to stick with small stuff.

Not me. I'm only the stepmother, remember. What do I know of what goes on in the mind of a teenage boy?

Plenty.

Roads Back

September, 2006

Stefan, my eighteen-year-old son, wandered into my office to ask me a question, and idly picked up a book from my desk. *Sole Survivor, Children Who Murder Their Families.*

Was this a good book? he asked. No, I said, it was an ugly book. Then why was I reading it? When I shrugged, he floated calmly on to ask when I would be finished with this project because there was seriously nothing to eat in the house. He turned the book over in his hands and skimmed the synopses of the case studies on the back. Could he borrow it?

When I was done with it, I told him. But I knew I would never put it in his hands. The thought of my own boy reading about other boys, other girls, killing their parents was more than I could handle.

I was mired down in the huge question of how such monstrous affairs unfold. What are the warning signs? Or is there no prevention, just the heavy hand of fate. Was it a trajectory that led to Robert Raymond Cook's homicidal rampage, or one unfortunate incident that pushed him over the edge?

I was back to obsessing over what went on in the little house on 52nd Street in Stettler. Who would remember? There were the Hoskinses, who, according to Pecover's book, had visited with Ray and Daisy before Robert came home on that night in June. Family friends, they'd planned a picnic together for the Sunday, and waited, puzzled, when the Cooks didn't appear or answer their phone.

I checked directories, and sent letters to two people named Hoskins in Stettler. Four days later a man called. Right family, he said, but wrong man. It was his dad I should speak to. His mom and dad lived in Red Deer now, not Stettler. His grandparents, Jim and Leona Hoskins, were the folks who were friends with Ray and Daisy Cook. His dad, Clark Hoskins, knew the murdered kids. And by chance, his dad was home for the next two weeks. Then he'd be heading back to Yemen. He worked in and out of the Middle East in the oil patch.

A long way from Stettler to Yemen. Alberta's small towns are shrinking, young people moving away, to the cities, to surprising corners of the world. And yet here was Clark Hoskins' son on the phone from Stettler. And the Cook children? They went only as far as the cemetery in Hanna. Maybe Clark Hoskins could give me a sense of where they might have gone.

Okay, now we're getting somewhere. Go to Red Deer and ask Clark Hoskins who they were, those five little kids and their parents. And Daisy! Ask him about Daisy, and don't take "ordinary people" for an answer.

They couldn't have been ordinary people. Not with that other son locked away, but always expected to return.

The killer. Too bad no one saw that coming. Or maybe they did.

Or maybe he wasn't the killer.

Are you expecting Hoskins to give you some clue about that?

When I phoned, he said I'd better know up front that he believes in capital punishment. And that Bobby Cook got what he deserved.

Apart from that newspaper series that so coincidentally showed up in Brenda's papers, everything points that way. How about we just accept that, and you get on with the story.

Ah, but that's problem—now that your story and Daisy's are getting tangled, it matters a whole lot more.

Roads Back

The soft-spoken man sitting across from me was nine years old the summer of the Cook murders. It was such a long time ago, he said. Mostly he didn't think about it much anymore. But every now and again, he'd feel compelled to pick up the book and look at the pictures. He jabbed a finger at the cover of *The Work of Justice, The Trials of Robert Raymond Cook*. His copy looked as worn as my own which was also on the table, a-bristle with post-it notes. His dad, he told me, had talked with Jack Pecover, but had refused interviews with other people who were interested in the case. He'd hated the thought of someone making money from the story.

I'd looked at those pictures many times in the past year, trying to imagine beyond them. As a young boy, Clark Hoskins had spent hours in the small house with the vine-covered verandah, may have ridden in the Chevrolet half-ton truck with the green body and white roof parked parallel to the house, in front of the garage. He likely sat at the grey arborite table in the kitchen, shared a lunch of chicken noodle soup or bologna sandwiches. Curly-haired Gerry Cook, squinting into the sun in the photograph of the five Cook children, was Clark Hoskins' childhood friend.

On the drive from Calgary, I'd been wrestling once again with my motivation for bothering this man, with my obsession with the Cook family and their demise. Every time I took off on a new tangent, I went through the same self-searching. What did I want from this? I was hoping that if I wrote about the crime, I might make sense of a young man raging through a home on a summer night and leaving his father, stepmother, and five young children dead and battered beyond recognition. Sitting there with Clark Hoskins, it seemed an affront to decency to suggest that there was any sense to such an act.

Clark, though, had seemed interested and hospitable since he greeted me at the door. He'd put the coffee on and it burbled away behind us in the sparkling kitchen. I couldn't help thinking of the contrast between this home and the humble house in the photos.

Outside, the fog that had almost kept me home earlier in the morning had begun to lift, and there was a promise of sunshine for the drive back. I'd considered going on to Stettler after talking to Clark. I'd been gathering names, scribbling them in my notebook. An astonishing number of people I knew seemed to have connections in Stettler; an elderly aunt or the father of an old friend who had lived there for years and remembered that summer of 1959 very well, I was assured. But I'd already discovered that the memories of the Cook murders had suffered the same fate as any other story. Each version offered a bit of embellishment, a new twist on Cook's motive, or another theory as to who the real killer might have been. For now, I was confused enough with the conflicting opinions of the "experts" and it was probably best to leave any more wandering of the streets of Stettler until I had a real purpose. The little house at 5018 - 52nd St. was gone, an apartment building in its place. Present day Stettler had little to tell me about the Cook family, unless I could find the people who knew them.

We chatted, Clark and I, about weather, about the scorching heat to which he'd be returning in another week, and the dismal fall we were having here in Alberta, how the climate seemed to be changing. Or maybe, I thought, our memories of the weather were just as susceptible to embellishment as all the other recollections. I'd remembered the summer of 1959 as oppressively hot. When I'd checked the national weather archives, their information said that on those days between the murders and discovery of the bodies, the daytime temperature averaged seventeen degrees with rain showers. In fact, the whole summer had been cool and wet.

For Clark, I was sure, it was a summer hung with cloud. He asked me who else I'd found, and how useful they'd been. He said he doubted much had been left unsaid. Nothing new to uncover. I told him it wasn't the details of the murder case or Cook's trials and execution I was examining, but what went before. It was the family I was interested in, someone who could give me insight into who Ray and Daisy were. I'd told him I was working on a book, one that might weave a fictional strand into the true story. I expected Louise to pipe up inside my head, but she was silent.

So far as anyone who knew the family—he shook his head. He thought his folks had known a few of the Cook's "people," but Ray and Daisy as far as he could recollect, had pretty much kept to their own. Someone in Ray's family had looked after the funeral arrangements. He had no idea who they were.

His own family, he said, probably knew them best. Daisy and Ray Cook were the closest friends his mom and dad had at the time. The families went on picnics together. Gerry Cook had been Clark's best friend. Clark had spent most of his "younger years" at the Cook's house. Spent nights there. Staying with Gerry. He paused between sentences. In that house, he said, and paused again. A lot of time had gone by since those days.

When the phone rang and Clark excused himself to take the call, I picked up my copy of *The Work of Justice*. I wondered if Clark's book opened by habit, as mine did, to the photos. If he'd visited, slept over with Gerry Cook, he may have spent a night on the "Winnipeg couch" in one of the pictures. I remembered these utilitarian pieces of furniture in many homes when I was growing up. Sturdily built of iron and coil springs, they were armless and backless and opened out to form a double bed. The striped mattress on the Winnipeg couch in the photo was blood-stained—blood-soaked, according to the book. The bedroom walls were splashed with blood. The three boys, Gerry, Chrissy and Patty had slept in this bedroom at the back of the house. It held a single bed, the double couch and two dressers. One of the other photos was a group shot of the five children taken one week before the murder. The youngest, Linda, was three years old. She was dressed in a striped t-shirt and overalls, and looking off to the side. I imagined her mother, smiling, telling her to stay put. Just for a minute. Five-year-old Kathy was beside her wearing a sleeveless shirt and a cherub grin. The three boys, Gerry, Chrissy and Patty, nine, eight, and seven years old, all had thick mops of hair neatly trimmed up the sides and wore identical short-sleeved button-up shirts. In another earlier photo on the same page, there were only the three boys; Chrissy just a baby, and Gerry and Patty, all of them wearing the fingerprint of their mother in the one neat curl on the tops of their heads.

I closed the book, and looked out the window into the thinning fog.

When Clark sat down again, he told me that his brother, Dillon, would be a good person for me to speak with. Dillon was older and knew Robert Cook well. The only other person in the Hoskins family who could have told me more was their dad who'd passed away three years ago.

Jim and Leona Hoskins were the last people to see the Cooks alive. When they stopped by for coffee that Thursday night, when they planned the picnic for Sunday, Ray had offered to help Jim move some furniture on Saturday. When Ray didn't appear, Jim went down to the Cook home and found the blinds drawn. There was no answer when he knocked on the door. The next morning, Bobby Cook called from the local jail asking Jim to post bail for him because there'd been some trouble over a car. Now Jim's puzzlement over the family's absence turned to real concern. He refused to help with bail.

It was Dillon who brought back the news that something bad, something very bad had happened at the Cook residence. He'd gone down to the house out of curiosity, and came home crying, this young man of twenty. There were yellow ribbons all around the place, he said, policemen everywhere. They'd shown him a bloody suit jacket. The one in which he'd seen Bobby Cook walk into town just a few days before. Oh yeah, Clark said, I can remember fully the day Dillon went down there and came back crying.

By evening, the Hoskinses knew the fate of their friends. Jim Hoskins was asked to go to the morgue and identify the bodies that night. And that, Clark said, was one of the things that truly did his dad in. One minute there's a friend you talked to on Thursday night and the next minute ... he couldn't recognize any of them to identify them.

Clark looked down at the book, and so did I. A grainy photo of Robert Raymond Cook who seemed to be apprehensively watching something in the foreground. A flip of the cover would open my book to a black and white of the infamous grease pit in the garage, taken shortly after the layers of cardboard had been peeled away. There was a tangle of greasy rags, clothing, two visible faces, and protruding sets of hands. I avoided that photo.

Clark cleared his throat, and folded his hands on the table in front of him. You were asking me what kind of people they were, he said.

As I'd expected, he described ordinary folk. Ray, always working, always fixing, doing something around the place. A good provider for what he had. And Daisy. An ordinary good mother, who loved the children, no doubt about that. Welcomed other kids, made her house a comfortable place to be, but homework before playtime, always a teacher as well as a mom.

And the other son? Bobby, Clark had called him just a few minutes before, and I'd found myself trying to match that name to the newspaper photos and articles which referred to him always as Robert Raymond Cook. In the collection of photos in *The Work of Justice*, there is one of a much younger Cook; a group shot of children, ranging in age from about five to nine years, I'd guess, labeled "Hanna birthday party." Robert Raymond Cook, Bobby, is in the back row, oddly the only child formally dressed in a suit, white shirt and tie and looks a junior version of his neatly-suited self on the cover of J. Pecover's book.

Bobby, Clark said, had seemed like an "okay kid." He'd come along to a relative's farm with the Hoskins family once when he was fresh from jail, and Clark's mother had said that he was destined for trouble. Each time his son came home again, Ray Cook tried to get him a job, give him a new start, and each time he was back in jail again within weeks, it seemed.

Ray Cook had dreamed of owning a service station, and Robert Cook insisted the family was supposed to have left for British Columbia by bus on Friday morning to scout out a location where he and his dad could be partners in a business. He said he'd given Ray $4100 toward the purchase and Ray had left him the car to exchange for a new vehicle for himself.

They may have talked about a partnership, Clark said, and Bobby and Ray may have been serious, but the plan was certainly not in the works that weekend. Ray and Daisy would not have gone off without telling anyone their intent. Of that Jim and Leona Hoskins were sure. They were good neighbours, good friends, people with whom they spent hours playing cards, drinking coffee, sitting around the kitchen. They didn't live "high class." They had "the essentials" and that was it.

I imagined two women, two mothers with young families—Daisy with her five, Leona Hoskins with six children—sitting at the kitchen table in the modest Cook home, a pot of coffee on the stove. Daisy Cook was thirty-seven years old when she died. I wondered if she'd talked with Leona about the delinquent stepson. If anyone in the family talked about Bobby.

He embarrassed them, Clark said. In a small town, everyone knew what everyone else was up to. About 99% of the time Bobby wasn't around, because he was in jail.

He tapped the cover of the book. And then Bobby came back, he said, wearing that blue suit. The Hoskins lived out on the highway back then, and Dillon saw Bobby walking into town that day around noon.

Clark said he was very sure that Bobby knew what he was going to do when he came home that day. That he'd had lots of time in jail to figure it out. He was going to fix them. He was going to get that car, and he was going to have some fun for a weekend.

One of the puzzling aspects of the story is that the family was killed sometime Thursday night or early Friday morning, and though Robert Cook had left Stettler that same night—the last time he saw them alive, he maintained until he died—he returned to Stettler after two days of joy-riding in the new car he bought in Edmonton with money he insisted he'd dug up from long ago heists. Then he cruised Main Street, and went back to the house.

Clark told me that while this seemed like bizarre behaviour for a guilty man, to him it was consistent with the rest of the luck Cook made for himself.

How, I wondered would someone plan the murder of seven people. One murderer and seven victims?

Yes, Clark agreed, the way he killed the kids did make you wonder if he had help. Five kids. Gerry was Clark's age, just about to turn ten. And Chrissy not very much younger. And Patty. The girls were so small, but the boys? Active, energetic kids always running, building tree forts. Today, he said, kids are trained to phone 911, or to run for help. These were not stupid kids. That's always been on his mind. How could someone beat five children to death with the butt of a gun, and not one of them get away?

The phone rang again, this time a cell phone on the kitchen counter and Clark rose to answer it. I busied myself jotting notes, but mostly pondering a nine-year-old boy remembering nights he spent in a bedroom that became the scene of unspeakable carnage.

I glanced at my watch. I'd taken more than the hour of Clark's time that I'd requested. He was home for another week and then back to the Middle East for six weeks, a schedule he'd told me that would allow him to retire in a few more years. Then he and his wife were going south.

If someone had told him back when he was young that someday he'd go halfway around the world to make his living, he wouldn't have believed it, he said when he came back. Yemen. Dubai. Far away in every way from the old house and his life in Stettler. He said he could remember frost on the nails in the walls in winter. Sitting by the kitchen stove, an old coal stove converted to gas, and when it was really cold the mattresses came out and everyone slept there on the floor. Hard times. Macaroni and tomatoes because there was no cheese. But everyone was fed, no one went hungry.

That was life in the Cook's house as well. The house itself was boarded up for years, then finally moved a few blocks away and rebuilt. I wondered who would want to live in that house, knowing what had happened there.

We chatted another few minutes about the divided opinion on Cook's guilt.

Bobby Cook left people feeling guilty, Clark said. In spite of his criminal record, and his lies, people warmed to him. The people who were there when he hanged shook his hand. They wept. They couldn't imagine that a character like him could have committed such an act. Hard to imagine anyone who could do such a thing. Hard to fathom what could happen in one night to a family that was well and alive and playing.

The Boy

January, 1996

It's Jonathan's appointment for his six month check-up this afternoon, and Louise is trying to wash down a mouthful of soda cracker with flat ginger ale. This time the symptoms are familiar enough that she hasn't wasted time speculating on the "flu." She's hoping she'll be able to make the short drive to the public health unit without stopping to puke.

The outside thermometer showed minus forty-two this morning and she doesn't have to bother converting. The two scales meet at minus forty and it's bloody cold no matter how you measure it. The church budget didn't cover any upgraded insulating of this old parsonage; the window sills are furred with frost, and cold radiates from the outside walls. Louise worries every time Jake is ten minutes late getting home from work. She imagines the car stalled on the highway, shrouded in ice fog, Jake's cell phone dead because he never remembers to recharge it. What would she do without Jake? How did she go from being a self-reliant, capable city woman to a quaking, dependent wife for whom even the short winter drive to Edmonton has become a trial? Hormones, she tells herself firmly.

But then there is Danny. When the phone rings, she's tempted to let the machine pick it up, sure the message will be another request from the school for her and Mr. Peters to come in and talk about Daniel. Jake has taken so much time off work for talks with the school principal and visits to the coffee shop and store where Dan has been caught swiping magazines and candy that he's begun to worry about his job.

It's one thing to pop home in the middle of the day when you live in the same city, but an hour long commute turns the same errand into a three hour lunch break, and even with his seniority and sales record, the dealership is not pleased.

Maybe this time, Louise can deal with the problem, give Jake a well-deserved break. But when she picks up the phone, it's Phyllis, and on impulse, Louise confides that she's pregnant again.

"Oh my," Phyllis says with her usual candor. "So close together."

Louise has already decided that she won't tell anyone this was an accident. She'd agreed with Jake who thought two children would be enough for this family, even though Jon will be as much an only child as Daniel has been. There's Jake's age to consider too. He's ten years older than Louise, says he's taken some ribbing at work already for being a new papa at fifty. Louise, though, is secretly delighted in spite of the prospect of puking for another eight months.

"Are you sick with this one?" Phyllis asks.

"All day long," Louise says. "But it's okay. Worth it in the end." She won't whine to Phyllis.

"Of course it is, but still I'll send Marcy to you after school every day for a while so you can at least have a nap. We'll let her have the car instead of taking the bus for a week or two." Louise is sure Phyllis's Marcy could easily run a household even though she's just sixteen. Getting Daniel to clear the table and clean his room once a week involves more energy than Louise is willing to spend.

"It's about time Daniel started doing some real helping around the house," Phyllis says as though she's reading Louise's thoughts. "But for the love of God don't let him babysit. Call me when you get home from the clinic."

- 116 -

Louise puts the phone down and scoops Jonathan out of the playpen where he's been cooing and trying to get his foot to his mouth. As if she would even consider leaving the baby with Daniel. Even Jake, she's noticed, watches closely. One Sunday afternoon though, he came into the kitchen where Louise was cutting up a chicken for supper and beckoned to her with his finger on his lips.

They stood together in the doorway and peeked into the living room. Jon was on the sofa in his baby lounger, Dan beside him with a skateboarding magazine splayed open between them.

"Okay, now look at this one, Bro," he said, "this is how it feels," and with his hand as the board, he swooped past the baby's nose, flipped, and came back to land on the terry cloth tummy of Jon's sleeper. The baby crowed and waved his hands, feet pedaling, one of his rare smiles lifting his face in delight. The flip of a few more pages, and then Dan took Jon's small fist in his hand and pressed it to the magazine. "See that one? That's the one I'm going to buy for you when you're big enough to skate, 'kay? I'll have a job, and my own place and you can stay over sometimes."

When Louise turned to look at Jake, his eyes were clenched tight behind his glasses. She closed the door softly and put her arms around him, her face pressed to his chest. He took a deep breath and she could feel him nodding. "That's the boy I want him to be, you know?"

"I know," she whispered. And she vowed that she would do her damnedest to see Dan that way, as a brother, not as a threat.

They plan to wait a month or two to tell Daniel about the new baby they are expecting, but now that Phyllis knows and Marcy will be coming over after school, he needs to be in the loop. By the time Jake walks through the door for supper, it's past eight, and blessedly, Jon is asleep and likely to last through the night. The school *has* called again, and an RCMP officer has dropped by to let them know that if Dan is caught stealing cigarettes again, the woman who owns the coffee shop is going to ask for charges to be laid.

"I'll look after it," Jake says, and thuds down the basement stairs to the corner they've carpeted and furnished with a sofa and television for Dan and the friends who've never appeared.

Now the pizza Jake picked up on the way home has been on hold in the oven for so long, the kitchen so rank with the smell of cheese, Louise has to stand on the back step and breathe the cold night to keep even the weak tea she's sipping from rising in her throat. When she hears the scraping of kitchen chairs, she steps back inside.

Jake and Daniel are silently chewing the rubbery cheese. Both of them look up at her as though the misery of this moment might be her doing. Or so it feels to her. She pulls her chair far enough from the table that she doesn't have to look at the pizza sweating its grease onto the paper napkins they've thrown down instead of plates.

Jake swallows, mops his lips with the napkin and leans back in his chair. "Okay, we've got this sorted out. There's going to be no more shenanigans. Right, Dan?" The boy ducks his chin. This will have to pass for a nod. "What do you have to say to Louise?"

Daniel grabs up another piece of pizza and crams half of it into his mouth, chewing with his eyes on Louise, his lips shiny with grease. Mouth still half full, he mumbles, "Sorry I embarrassed you by getting in trouble."

"Embarrassed me? This is not about me, Daniel." She

looks to Jake for help, but how can he, when this seems to be coming from him?

"All right then." Jake stands up and brings a mug and the pot of lukewarm tea to the table. "Now, Dan, we've got some other news here. All the more reason for you to behave. You're going to have another little brother or sister in the summer."

It's all she can do to keep from groaning and covering her face with her hands. How can a man with the impeccable timing that makes him a top salesman miss all the cues at his own table?

Daniel spits a chewed mouthful of pizza into his hand, tosses it onto the cardboard tray and pushes away from the table. The raw mix of disgust and fury on the boy's face hits her like a fist. His lip curls and he is looking only at her. "Great. You can just be fat and ugly forever that way. Can't you guys find anything else to do?"

Jake is out of his chair so fast, Louise grabs his arm. But he's stopped, just as she is, by the sudden crumpling of Danny's face. The boy is up the stairs and almost to his room before they hear a choking sound halfway between a sob and a shout. Then the bedroom door slams.

Jake, surprisingly calm, begins to clear the table, shoving pizza box, leftover slices and all into the garbage. "He'll get it over it," he says. "He's still new at being the big brother. He'll learn."

By the time Lauren is born, the big brother is no longer living with them. Daniel is on probation, and has been literally farmed out to another of Jake's kin, this one the brother of Phyllis's husband, Paul. These relatives have grown children, all of them off living in the city, and it's been agreed that it would benefit both them and Daniel if he lived with them and provided an extra hand around the place. Their farm is twenty miles from town, and Dan has not been allowed to take his bike or skateboard with him. Once school starts, the trips into town and back on the school bus every day will be his only outings for the next four months, except for Sunday dinners at home, for which Jake will pick him up. This is the arrangement Jake came up with without even talking to Louise. She didn't attend the pre-court visit with the social worker, but she can imagine the cold white cast of Jake's face when he agreed to the foster home arrangement. Louise doesn't doubt for a minute that her presence as "stepmother" is considered an obstacle to Dan's rehabilitation, treatment, whatever the hell these people feel he needs to stop him stealing. And lying. And spying. She wonders if the social worker knows that all of this began long before Louise's entry into the family. But then why would Jake offer that information, unless someone specifically asked? Jake volunteers nothing. He hates these people peering into his home, taking charge of his son.

Louise and Lauren have been home from the hospital for two days when Jake drives out to the farm to pick up Daniel for his Sunday visit. Louise, exhausted from feeding Lauren every two hours, puts Jon in the playpen with a pile of toys and curls up on the sofa with the baby. Fortunately, Jonathan is a placid child, still content to crawl, to sit for long periods quietly examining the toys around him. Daniel is the one who can elicit the most enthusiasm from the wee boy, but his interest in Jon seldom lasts through more than five minutes of rolling a ball across the floor. Still, he asked for a picture of his little brother and Louise knows, from emptying the pockets of his jeans to do laundry, that he carries it in his back pocket in a plastic folder with the learner's permit Jake reluctantly agreed to the day after Dan's fourteenth birthday. The thought of Daniel driving, even with adult supervision, horrifies Louise, but she kept her mouth shut. Always, it seems, it's the stepmother protesting. And really, the piece of paper makes no difference. Permit or not, supervised by an adult or not, it's only a question of time and opportunity. Dan has already been allowed to drive the tractor at the farm, and is pressing to practice on the truck. That, Marvin, his "foster father," told him, is a privilege he can earn by staying out of trouble for two months. What are the odds? Louise wonders.

She hears the slam of the car door, and sits up on the sofa, pulling down her t-shirt, tucking her daughter's small fists into the receiving blanket. Daniel comes through the door and straight to Jon. He lifts his little brother, tosses him into the air. And barely catches him.

"Hey, careful there!" Jake shouts. Danny shrugs.

"He's getting big. I didn't expect him to be so heavy." Awkwardly, he lowers Jon back into the playpen, and starts toward the hall, but Jake takes his arm and turns him toward Louise.

"Aren't you going to say hello to your sister?"

An exaggerated pause, then Dan takes three steps forward and leans in to peer at the swaddled bundle in Louise's arms. He looks bigger, Louise thinks. Since last Sunday, his jaw and forehead seem heavier, more masculine. But surely it's just the contrast with the baby's button nose and rosebud mouth.

"Cute," he mutters. He folds his arms. "How come you're calling her Lorne. That's a boy's name."

"Lauren," Louise says. She smiles, trying to inject the welcome she is not feeling into the moment. "L-a-u-r-e-n. You're right, she'll probably have trouble with that. We didn't even think about people hearing it wrong."

"You could give her a nickname," Danny says.

"Laurie?"

He squints at the baby. Comes closer still. Lauren opens her eyes suddenly, her tiny mouth puckering into what looks for all the world like a kiss. Danny grins. "Sweetie," he says.

Louise hears Jake's sigh of relief, can almost see him relax, feels the tension in the room melt. Jake claps a hand on Dan's shoulder. "I like that one," he says. He nods at the playpen. "Bring your brother. We boys will make lunch."

In the afternoon, Danny rattles his skateboard up and down the driveway. The sound of the wheels and the slam of the board each time he tricks and catches the board wears on Louise's nerves after five minutes, and she retreats to the bedroom and closes the window. Still she can hear the noise. Any minute now, Henry from next door will come out and shout at Dan. In fact, she suspects this is Dan's goal.

Finally, Jake calls to him. "Put that thing away, and let's go for a milkshake." Over and over again, Jake takes Dan into the places the boy has ripped off, to show the locals that his son has a good side. Sometimes he succeeds. Louise has been assured by several kind people in town that this is just a phase, boys being boys, and with their patience he'll get over it. Heck, these boys often turn out to be the real successes, the ones who take risks and make something out of nothing. She just nods, no point in telling these people she isn't holding her breath for the miracle.

She watches them leave, Jake pushing Jon in his stroller, Dan on his bike. Lauren is asleep in her arms and when tears drip onto the pink blanket, Louise is astonished to realize that they are her own. Hormones, she thinks. Because really, what on earth does she have to cry about?

So she was busy with those babies who kept com-ing one right after the other, I imagine. Didn't have much time to worry about her stepson. Daisy I'm talking about here.

Once he left when he was fourteen, he really never came back again.

Out of sight, out of mind? Doesn't work that way, I'll have you know. Sometimes it's even scarier if you can only imagine what they're doing.

Roads Back

Robert Cook's record of incarcerations was, in Jack Pecover's words, "a dreary recital." After the first sentence of eighteen months in the Lethbridge jail, he rejoined the family briefly, but then was sent by Social Services to live with foster parents. The first family moved to British Columbia, and Robert was moved to another home, another farm family. When Jack Pecover talked to that second foster mother, Mrs. Henry Stucke, she told him in her heavy German accent, that Bobby Cook was a good boy. Another boy had spoiled things for him—another boy from jail placed on a farm near theirs. The two boys stole money and stole a car and left for the States. She and her husband would have happily taken Bobby back when he was apprehended, she said, but he was sent to jail.

> "I can't say one wrong word about him. If I told him to do something, he'd do it. We could hardly stand it that he should be hung. My son died four years ago; he was caught in a cultivator and bled to death before they could get him to the hospital. It wasn't as hard as when Bobby died." (*The Work of Justice* pg. 167)

Bobby Cook's first foster family, the Larsons, who had moved to B.C., felt equally sure that he could not have committed the crime for which he died. Their daughter, Lila, became Robert Raymond Cook's advocate when he was sentenced to death.

In December, 1953, when he was sixteen years old, Robert Cook was charged with car theft in Winnipeg and sentenced to one year in the provincial jail, but after an additional three charges of breaking and entering were added, he graduated and went directly to the federal penitentiary at Stony Mountain for two years. He was barely out again, and charged with breaking and entering and theft in Hanna, Alberta, sentenced to two years in the Saskatchewan Penitentiary at Prince Albert. From there he was in and out of Prince Albert, caught in a revolving door of repetitive crime. Nineteen offenses in all in those years from 1951 to 1957. Although Cook told the RCMP later that for every offense for which he was sentenced, he had committed at least four more.

Meanwhile, back at home?

More babies. Christopher was born while Bobby was in foster care. Then two little girls born in 1954 and 1956, Kathy and Linda.

I don't imagine they looked forward to his visits home. I know I wouldn't.

No. You wouldn't. But there are conflicting stories about how Daisy and Ray felt about Bobby. Or mostly about how Daisy felt. Ray seemed to maintain a strong loyalty to his delinquent son.

In jail, exactly as he did outside, Robert Cook seemed to impress some, to leave others with Clark Hoskins' assessment that he was an affable liar. But a liar nonetheless. From the Manitoba Penitentiary classification officer's report of May 9, 1955:

This young man... has failed to improve sufficiently to warrant a parole. His general conduct and attitude towards his work is not too good. He is still quite the smart Alex type with big ideas of getting even sooner or later. (*The Work of Justice* pg. 35)

A report by another prison official recorded the same day:

This man is a quiet inoffensive worker, tries hard, does the best according to his ability. His instructor advises that he is a good worker. The young man appears to be a good risk re a ticket of leave. (*The Work of Justice* pg. 35)

The classification officer's report trumped the other, and parole was refused.

Then a classification report from June 27, 1957:

Cook has been in attendance [in vocational education] 43 days so far this term. His work, especially in math, is good. He isn't particularly interested in English subjects, but is nevertheless doing fair work in this subject. He is cooperative, reacts to kindness, and has never given any trouble in class. He has the ability and is capable of learning any shop math he will require. (*The Work of Justice* pgs. 35-36)

Jack Pecover recorded other reports which together form an impression of a young man who was occasionally fractious, generally cooperative, but by no one's estimation a hopeful prospect for rehabilitation. There is no doubt, though, throughout the reading of *The Work of Justice*, that as he uncovered this portrait of Robert Raymond Cook, Pecover's sympathy grew.

Meanwhile, it's hard to imagine that Ray and Daisy, back home, looked forward to Bobby's next release. After the murders, the information about a plan Ray had to buy a service station was conflicting. The Hoskinses said Ray and Daisy had their house listed for sale and talked about relocating, but there was no indication that they were going anywhere immediately. Someone in Ray Cook's family claimed that they were intending to slip away without telling Robert they were leaving, but were taken by surprise when he was released early.

But the surprise was not sudden. They knew about the amnesty well enough in advance that Daisy sent a new red tie and a pair of yellow socks for the journey home. The day he arrived back in Stettler, Leona and Jim Hoskins stopped in for a visit and later said the mood in the house was upbeat, everyone looking forward to Bobby's arrival, wondering what could be taking him so long. Yet surely they were wondering how long this bit of freedom would last, and what disgrace he would leave them to deal with when he was gone again. According to Lila Larson, Bobby's foster sister for a short period, "he loved his dad, but didn't like his stepmother." According to Mrs. Henry Stucke, at his second foster home, he "said that Daisy was all for her children and he was nothing in her eyes."

The transcript of a psychiatric evaluation dated March 15, 1960, says that Robert Cook stated: "My father he was remarried in 1949, I think it was 1949 to Daisy Gasper. She was my school teacher. Oh she was good. She was just the same as Mother. I called her Mum. Couldn't have treated me better."

Right. He was on trial for murder. He'd admit to bitter resentment of the woman and children who usurped his place with his father? The victims?

From what I've found about him so far, I doubt he was smart enough to have thought that strategy through. Maybe he did have positive feelings for Daisy.

But what about Daisy, what did she feel for him?

A member of Ray's family, Mrs. Mae Reamsbottom (who told the RCMP officer who interviewed her that she had never liked Ray's son) said she was sure Daisy was afraid of Bobby, even though she had never exactly said so. She maintained that Ray and Daisy were making plans to leave Alberta in order to get away from Bobby. That Daisy was trying to get Ray to understand that Bobby could not come near the house nor the children because he had ruined their reputation wherever they went. That Daisy feared that Bobby was going to wind up killing someone.

Mrs. Joe Reilly, sister of Marion Anderson with whom I spoke, told Jack Pecover that in spite of the fact that Bobby had stolen $100 from Daisy's trunk when she and Ray were first married, she said, "We get along fine. He babysits for me and Ray. He's real good to the kids."

After Bobby hit the big time and was sent to the federal penitentiary in Manitoba, Ray and Daisy lost track of him, and he was seven months into his sentence by the time his dad tracked him and wrote one of the few letters that he sent to his son. According to Pecover that letter did not survive, but Bobby's reply said:

"You also asked me to come home which makes me feel wonderful and love you all the more after all the trouble I've given you."

And indeed he did go home, after a brief foray into the world of professional boxing. Bobby Cook had his first boxing experience in Hanna when a man who owned a local gym spotted a boy he felt was bound for trouble. When Bobby wandered into Gordon Russell's gym one day, Russell decided to take him in hand:

> "I encouraged him because I thought he could use it. He seemed to me to be emotionally troubled; emotionally there was something wrong with Bobby. He was beating up on kids 13 and 14; when he got them down he would take the boots to them. He was a mean, small kid. Perhaps he did it because of his size, I don't know, but he was tough. Yet none of the guys he beat up seemed to bear him any grudges. They all liked him." (*The Work of Justice* pg. 40)

Ray Cook, however, was not pleased with this new activity and when Bobby came home from the gym one night with a black eye, he visited Russell and told him that Bobby was not to be allowed back at the gym.

> "That was the end of it. I think if he'd been allowed to stay he wouldn't be [dead] today. Even then I could see he was a natural...He

would have made a good pro." (*The Work of Justice* pg. 40)

That was not the end of it. When Cook ended up at Stony Mountain Penitentiary, he again wandered into a gym and the trainer there recognized a natural ability as well.

> "Right from the beginning...I could see the heart and other things this boy had. He could take punishment but he could hand it out. Later, when we had him on the cards if he had a guy in trouble he'd turn to the referee. Like if he had a guy with a lot of staying power, rather than pound and pound at the guy he would turn to the referee. He was no sadist. He had a sort of code of the west, a sort of do unto others... He had tons of potential... He had a punch... He was the champion of his division in the pen and he could fight in heavier classes." (*The Work of Justice* pg. 41)

It seems there was a window of opportunity for Bobby Cook, at the tender age of sixteen, to have made a career for himself as a professional boxer. While he was in Stony Mountain, Alex Turk, a boxing and wrestling promoter in Winnipeg who was also a Member of the Legislative Assembly in the Manitoba government, used that position to gain access to Stony Mountain where he funded a major part of the athletic program, and provided a place for cons to go when they were released from prison. He spotted Cook on one of his visits and invited him to contact him when he got out.

Jack Pecover devotes ten pages of his book to Robert Cook's boxing ability and "career." Cook did contact Turk, who did send him out on the boxing circuit but Turk told Pecover he couldn't remember what happened to Cook.

"He drifted away, just sort of disappeared."

> *And the point of all this is…? I'm a teacher. I know all about identifying a child's gifts. Self-esteem. Please don't have either me or Jake talk about growing grass instead of weeds.*

> Hardly. I don't think we need any clichés or folksy wisdom. But how about "the writing was on the wall"?

> *You mean Bobby Cook got back in trouble? What a surprise.*

He may have disappeared in the boxing world, but he ended up back in Hanna. He broke into a garage and scooped up a measly $1.50 for his effort, and then into the government liquor store where he found $17 in the cash drawer and helped himself to a drink, replaced the bottle and left his fingerprints behind. When he got to Stettler, his dad had a 1940 Chev and a job waiting, but the RCMP were not far behind him.

> *And Daisy? She got to say, "I told you so"?*

Daisy was the one who kept in touch with Bobby during his time in the Saskatchewan Penitentiary at Prince Albert. Or tried. From a letter she sent July 15, 1957:

> Could you kindly let me know about Robert Cook? We haven't heard from him for some time and we are anxious to know how he is. He

never said if there was anything we could send him. We would be grateful for any information. Thank you for your trouble.

Respectfully, Mrs. Ray Cook (*The Work of Justice* pg. 171)

And the reply from the warden, T.W. Hall:

Replying to your letter of January 15, 1957, I had your boy in front of me today in the matter of his non-writing to you. He admits that he has not been writing home, but from what I can gather this lack of writing is not due to any thoughts on the part of Robert that he does not wish to have anything more to do with his family, but simply that he feels ashamed for bringing his family into disgrace.

I impressed upon Robert the fact that no matter what he has done or where he was, his mother would always have the same thoughts for him, and asked him to consider that his mother would worry over him and for him to write as soon as possible.

As far as your son's health is concerned, he looks very well and is working every day. His conduct is such that he is entitled to full privileges.

Yours faithfully, T.W. Hall (*The Work of Justice* pg. 171)

Letters that sound like they could have been written about a boy away at school.

The Boy

Louise knows as soon as she hears the slam of truck doors in the driveway that the idyllic Sunday morning she and Jake are enjoying with the babies—strong coffee, scrambled eggs and thick toast Jake put on the table while she was feeding Lauren, sunlight flickering through the gold leaves on the poplar, framed in the wavy glass of the kitchen window—is just another illusion of the peaceful family life they will never have.

Jake opens the back door, and they watch Marvin march Daniel across the grass, Hilda following behind.

"Well now, Jake," Marvin begins before his feet touch the first step on the porch. "This boy of yours seems to think riding into town with me a few times is enough of a lesson that he can drive a truck." They are crowded in the doorway now, all three of them. "He might have got away with it, too, except for a little black and white striped cat that ended up in a mess on the bumper."

Jake moves aside and ushers them into the kitchen. A strong whiff of skunk follows them in. When Jon catches sight of his big brother he squeals and holds out his arms, but it's Hilda who steps forward and lifts him out of the high chair. "I think the little one doesn't need to be here," she says. She touches Louise's arm as they pass, and jerks her chin toward the living room before she bumps the kitchen door open with her hip.

Louise looks down at the sleeping baby in her arms, and sits back in her chair. No. She is not going to follow Hilda, leaving this to "the men," even though the smell is sickening.

"Sorry about the stink, Louise," Marvin says. "That was

what tipped us off this morning. Hilda got a whiff as soon as she walked by Dan's bedroom. He threw his clothes in the trash barrel. I wondered why that thing was smoking this morning. But it takes more than a bath to get the stench off your skin when you been that close."

Danny's gaze has not risen from the floor. Jake grabs his arm. "Look at me, Daniel." Slowly the boy's head tilts sideways, and he squints up at his dad.

"I'm sorry," he mumbles.

"Sorry?" Jake's voice booms and Lauren twists in Louise's arms. Still, Louise is determined to stay in the room. "Sorry doesn't cut it. You know that. What the heck were you thinking, stealing a truck?"

"I wasn't stealing." Danny stands up straighter now, defiant. "I just borrowed it. I figured there wouldn't be anyone driving around at night so it was a good time to practice." He jerks his head in Marvin's direction. "He told me he'd teach me but he keeps changing his mind. How long am I supposed to wait? I hate it out there."

"Apologize," Jake says.

"I just did."

"Not to me, to Marvin."

Marvin shakes his head. "It's okay, Jake. He already said he was sorry. Let him go now."

Daniel has already twisted loose from his dad's grasp and charges for the door, head down, arms swinging, and with a sound so wounded coming from deep in his throat, that Louise is tempted to go after him, he escapes to his room.

Louise stands and passes Lauren to Jake. "I'll make fresh coffee," she says. She's relieved when Marvin nods, and takes a chair at the table. Suddenly Hilda and Jon are in the doorway, Jon's eyes huge, his small hands clasped over his ears. He is upset by loud voices, their little son. Hilda sits, holds him on her lap, patting his back.

Louise wishes this were one of the social calls Jake has been yearning for. Sunday morning, Marvin and Hilda dropping in for coffee after church. She wishes she had something freshly baked to feed these two, and that her husband could sit down now, chat about the weather, the harvest, while she arranges cinnamon buns on a plate, brings butter and paper napkins. The tray of the high chair is littered with toast crusts. She wipes it clean, takes Jon from Hilda's lap, settles him in the chair and refills his sippy cup with milk. She brings two more mugs to the table. Everyone, it seems, is listening to the burbling coffee maker, waiting to have something to occupy their hands and lips.

"You know, it's not the pranks, or the mischief," Marvin finally says apologetically. "Hell, we all cut up a bit when we're young guys. It's the lying I can't abide. We're standing out there at the truck with skunk guts all over the wheel well and he tells me he doesn't know how it got there. I'm sorry, Jake. If I can't trust him, I can't keep him." He stares down at his heavy socks and shuffles his feet under the kitchen chair.

"And Hilda…" He looks up at his wife, and when she shakes her head sternly, he puts up his hand. "No, now, we need to be honest here too. You want to tell, or should I?" Hilda purses her lips, head still shaking. "Okay, then. The fact is the boy seems to be spying on her. She's caught him at the window, and…not just the kitchen window either." Hilda's face has gone red.

"Listen," she says. "He's a good boy. I wouldn't speak bad about your son, Jake. First Brenda…my God, what a sad story all of this turns out." She holds her hands open as though in an offering. "No offense intended to you, Louise.

You have your hands full with the babies and it's not so easy becoming a mother to a boy this age."

It doesn't get any easier. Later that Sunday afternoon Danny pleads with his dad to please never send him away again. The reason he took the truck, he says, was that he desperately needed to learn to drive so that he could get home. The two of them go for a long walk after supper, and Louise, watching from the kitchen window notes the slump of Jake's shoulders and the swagger that seems to have returned to Danny's step. Then she takes her two babies to her bed and naps with them, waking briefly to the sound of movement in the kitchen, the sky through the frosted painted bedroom window a deep indigo. She closes her eyes again, and sleeps until Lauren begins to fuss for a feeding. Jon wriggles up, rubbing his eyes. The door opens, and Jake tiptoes in.

"Come on, little man," he says quietly, and lifts Jon from the tangle of quilt. "Your big brother needs some company."

When Louise carries Lauren downstairs to the kitchen, Jake has bundled into his parka, and is caught in the circle of back porch light at the barbecue. He almost disappears in the smoke and ice fog when he lifts the lid. The table is set with mustard, pickles, ketchup, a bowl of raw onion slices. Danny watches her from the corner of his eye while he slaps down plates, knives, clumps a litre of Coke next to his place. They seem to be celebrating. What? His homecoming?

While they chew their way through the burgers, the three of them focus on Jon and Lauren, both fresh from sleep and chirping their delight when Danny pulls faces and pretends to snitch the bits of meat and bread on Jon's tray. No mention of trucks or skunks or spying.

Louise is brushing her teeth, staring back at the violet shadows under her eyes, when Jake puts his arms around her, his face pressed to her shoulder. Her flannel nightgown, she knows, is crusty with milk from feeding and burping but the only clean ones in her drawer are summer cotton. This is no night for Victoria's Secret, even if she owned such flimsy garments.

She rinses her toothbrush and turns to Jake.

"How was the walk and talk?"

"Pretty good. He says he doesn't know why he does these things, he doesn't think about it, he just acts."

Not exactly news that Daniel has no impulse control. "What's he going to do about it? What are we going to do about it? Pretty clear that we can't ask anyone else to take on the problem, Jake."

He bends over the sink to splash water on his face, then straightens, drops falling from his chin to the grey hair on his chest. Finally, he shakes his head and buries his face in the towel.

So often in bed, the two of them talk away the day's business, plan the next one, then come together in the perfect fit that keeps reminding Louise that in spite of her feeling that she'll never have more than visitor status in this town, she belongs in the house, in the bed. Tonight, though, Jake turns on his side, away from her. When she presses herself to his back, he sighs.

There is never a good time to ask the questions. "Did you talk to him about spying on Hilda?"

He growls. "Isn't there enough with stealing the truck? That's the big one, stealing. The other, that's just a symptom that the boy is bored stiff out there. I was bored on the farm at his age too, you know? That's why I'm a car salesman, not a farmer."

Louise pulls away and faces her own wall. "Fine," she says. "I guess you'll work it out on your own." She'll get on with some interior decorating and order blinds for all the windows.

Within two weeks, Daniel is caught shoplifting again, this time cigarettes. It turns out that one of the things Marvin didn't mention, thinking Jake already had enough to deal with, is that Danny swiped his smokes during his month at the farm. The woman who owns the coffee shop shook her head when Jake offered to make good the loss and get Daniel to come in at the end of every day to empty garbage cans, wash floors, do anything at all she wants done. Too late. She called the police before she called Jake. Another talk with the probation officer, and while the court hearing is still pending, Dan steals a bike from outside school one afternoon and plays hooky. After a five mile joyride, he dumps the bike, and hitches back to town, arriving home just in time for supper, just after the call from the principal who says the janitor saw him pedaling away.

"Why!" Louise can hear Jake shouting out in the garage even with the windows closed and the blinds drawn. His own dad, he told her as he stormed through the house waiting for his son to appear, would have taken him out to the barn and licked him but good. What is he supposed to do? Louise puts Lauren into her crib, hands Jonathan a plastic cup full of Cheerios to keep him busy and leads Jake to the sofa. They don't know the answers, she tells him. There was no way to figure this out for themselves. Some intervention is absolutely necessary. She doesn't tell him that she wishes that if Danny is intent on being a two-bit criminal he'd at least become good enough at it that he isn't caught every single time. They need a break.

Two days later, when Daniel sets fire to Henry Schultz's garage, the newspaper and matches so close to the jerry can of gas beside the lawn mower that it couldn't have been a coincidence, the matter is out of their hands. The child, the probation officer tells them, is obviously asking for help himself, and help is what he'll get at the juvenile treatment centre they'll be recommending at his court appearance.

During Daniel's two year stay at a Youth Treatment Centre in Calgary, by default, she being the teacher, the one most available for day-to-day contact, the one not only willing, but anxious to acknowledge that the boy is far from ready to return home, Louise has the most contact. But only with the staff. When Danny is allowed to phone home, he talks only with his dad. The gist of all of those conversations, Louise is sure though Jake never admits it, is the plea to come home. Every three months there is an assessment meeting to which parents are invited, encouraged to attend, but always there is some reason that it is not convenient for Jake. He would rather, he says, go in his own time, not at the bidding of these jail-keepers. And so he does. Once a month, he makes the four hour drive to Calgary, takes Danny out for lunch, delivers the clothes and books and CDs he's requested, and comes home silent and angry.

"He doesn't belong there," he says, on one of the rare occasions Louise is able to draw him out. "He's just a boy who's acted up a bit, not a criminal. My God, Louise, you wouldn't believe what some of those kids have come from. And what goes on inside those *supervised* walls. Dan knows more about drugs and ...deviant behaviour than I do. He's sixteen years old next month. They say he's ready for a group home. But what does that mean? Less supervision, older kids, and back on the streets."

She is afraid, so afraid that Jake is going to suggest that they push to have Danny come home. So she offers up a visit instead. His birthday and Jon's and Lauren's are all in August. "Why doesn't he come home for the birthday party?" she says. Last year Danny was scheduled to come home for that joint celebration, but went AWOL the week before and had his privileges revoked. In fact, every time he has a visit pending, he manages to shoot himself in the foot. And every time, feeling so guilty she's sure Jake can smell it on her, Louise quietly rejoices.

To Louise and Jake's amazement, the August day that Danny strides into the house ahead of his dad, their serious little Jonathan looks up from his Lego and launches himself across the room. Louise has been telling him all morning that his big brother is coming, but she's expected his usual reticence. Whenever anyone visits, Jon retreats to a special place behind the sofa. Now he holds up his arms, and Danny reaches down to pick him up, still juggling his backpack on one shoulder.

"Danny's home," Jon declares solemnly from his precarious balance on his brother's hip.

"Hey," Dan says, "is he ever big. Yo, Bro! I think it's time for a skateboard."

"No school?" Jon asks. "Why you get to come home?"

"It's my birthday," Dan says. "Yours too." Then he looks at his dad, shrugs.

"We told him you're at school there in Calgary," Jake says. "He's got a picture of you on his dresser." Picture notwithstanding, Louise is amazed that Jon has recognized his brother. It's well over a year since anyone but Jake has seen Dan, and he's grown, in that time, from a scrawny kid to a teenager. He's still shorter than his dad, but looks more like Jake than ever. His face so much heavier than when she last she saw him, and she stares at the definite shadow of beard on his cheeks. But his eyes are the same, darting around the room, avoiding hers, except for a split second of intense scrutiny that makes her skin tighten.

Louise is tempted to add that Jon drags out that picture of his big brother every time another child comes to play, telling them about Danny who is "at school." But she remembers too, the look on a couple of mothers' faces when they heard this little boy proudly offering his brother up for adoration. How long before Jon is old enough to know the nature of Danny's school?

With Danny on the floor inspecting Jon's Lego construction, Jake follows Louise into the kitchen. The table is set for the birthday party. Thomas the Tank Engine on the balloons and all the paper accoutrements. "How was the drive?" she asks. Danny was escorted to the bus in Calgary early that morning and Jake picked him up in Edmonton. "Did you have a good talk?"

Jake rubs his face with both hands. "He wants me to take him out driving this afternoon. He figures he should get his license now that he's sixteen."

"What? Now? While he's home? He's only going to be here for three days. And doesn't he need permission for that from…" Yes, who exactly is in charge of granting permission for Daniel's activities these days?

"What harm could it do? Who's going to know that he has his license?"

Oh, Jake. This is no time for pride, for taking charge of your son's destiny. "And besides," he says, "if he's going to get in trouble with cars, better he does it with a license and some driving skills than without. Of course he's not getting his license in two days, but maybe after he's been home a few more times. Hell, maybe it's time he came back for good. The kid deserves a chance, doesn't he?"

She is spared the need to reply. Lauren wakes from her nap then, squawking in the bedroom, and Louise jumps up to get her. This one will not remember Danny. By the time they are back to the kitchen, Jon and Danny have been batting balloons around the room, all but three popped and shriveled on the floor. Lauren takes one look at the mess of the decorations she so happily helped assemble before her nap and bursts into tears. That, it turns out, will be Lauren's response to Daniel for many years to come.

Jake has taken time off work to be at home while Dan is with them. He is going to make sure the kid stays out of trouble this time, he says, even if it means sitting beside him during all his waking hours. He takes Danny out for a driving lesson two days in a row, then lets him drive back to Edmonton to catch the bus on the day of his departure.

Lauren is napping, Jon playing happily in his room. "Mommy's going to have a bath," she tells him. "Call me if you hear Sister, okay? I'm leaving the door open." With Danny gone these past months, Louise has become relaxed about doors and windows, but all weekend she locked the bathroom door behind her, and was fully dressed before she came out of the bedroom in the morning, even though she would normally enjoy her first cup of coffee in her bathrobe. All weekend too, she's been aware of the too-tight clothes she has stubbornly refused to replace because she knows that will give her permission to have moved up two sizes from her pre-pregnant days. The first day, she overheard Danny ask Jake if she was pregnant again.

She strips off her jeans and sweater and avoids the full length mirror. Pregnancy, long days at home with two small children and a full cookie jar, Jake's cooking, all those meat and potato meals; the discipline of her old life has given way to lassitude. She is still in the tub, hair drifting around her, when there is the slam of the front door.

She can hear Jake calling her, then Jon's small voice. She wraps her hair in a towel, pulls on the jeans and sweater she meant to discard after she'd padded down the hall in her bathrobe.

Danny is sprawled on the sofa in the living room, the remote control from the television in his hand. "What happened? Where's your dad." He points toward the kitchen.

Jake is at the kitchen sink, a glass of water in hand. He is so white around the lips Louise pulls him to a chair. "What happened?" She sits down next to him.

"We had the radio on in the car. Some kid in Calgary was killed at the train station the other night. I heard about it yesterday but didn't pay any attention. Today they gave the name. Turns out it's one of the kids from Dan's...school." Jake's lip curls. "They've got two kids in custody, juveniles, and Danny says he's sure they're from the place too. Somebody had it in for that poor kid. I'm not taking Dan back there, Louise. Not a chance."

She leans back in her chair and looks at him for a long minute or two. "All right then," she says, "but you be the one to make the phone call. I don't have any authority over Daniel." Neither does she have a clue what will happen if they simply refuse to return the boy.

Daniel stays. Jake says it took no convincing at all to get agreement from the social worker. Louise wonders if, in fact, this is what everyone has been waiting for. She tries to talk with Danny about the murdered classmate, but he just shrugs, says he's over it. Too bad, nice guy, and he hopes the creeps who beat him to death get locked up forever.

Sunday afternoon, and Louise is reading in the living room, but can't help keeping one eye on the window to the verandah, where Danny and Jon are building a fort out of cushions and cardboard boxes.

"We have to hide from the bad guys," Jon tells her solemnly when he comes to gather more pillows from the living room sofa.

Jake is mowing the lawn. A job he shouldn't have to do with a sixteen-year-old in the house, Louise reminds him, but he points to his two sons. Way more important for Dan to spend time with the little one, he says. By the time he comes inside, the back of his shirt is sweat-streaked and he's trying to hide his laboured breathing. He sinks into the sofa.

"Don't look at me like that," he says. "I'm fine! And yes, I have an appointment for a check-up next month." He glances at the window. "Hey, I have a great idea. About time we had a date, isn't it? Let's walk down to the coffee shop for pie."

"All of us?"

She knows the answer. For the past two days Jake's been telling her how it handy it will be to have Danny at home for the occasional bit of babysitting. Look how good he is with the kids. Scoring points, Louise thinks. Same reason he's making his bed, offering to help with dishes, brought them tea last night while they were watching the news.

"No, let them play," Jake says. "I already told Dan I'll pay him for a couple of hours of babysitting, I don't expect him to be slave labour here."

No! Louise wants to scream. He cannot do these things

without asking her first. The question is whether Louise trusts Daniel enough to walk out of her house and leave him in charge of her babies. The answer is easy. But Jake isn't asking.

"Aw come on," Jake says later in the bedroom, when he comes to see what's taking her so long. "Just half an hour? What can go wrong? He's not going to hurt the children, Louise. You know that as well as I do."

Does she? Two years ago she would have nodded, but what do they know about this boy after the company he's been in? What do they know about what adolescence has wrought? Louise feels Daniel's eyes on her whenever he's in the same room.

"The biggest worry I have is that he's going to run away again," Jake says. "But he's not going to do that while he's responsible for the kids. Danny would not leave them alone. I know this. We'll be two blocks away, for God's sake. Give him a break."

So she agrees to go, but she won't leave until Lauren wakes from her nap and is happily occupied in the playpen.

"You should get rid of this thing," Daniel says. Louise has noticed that even in the week he's been home, his voice seems to have deepened. He kicks at the edge of the mesh pen she's just filled with Lauren's favourite toys. "It's like a cage."

"We don't use it very often." Louise bristles at her need to defend herself to this croaky-voiced critic. "She's happy if she has toys and her snacks." She points to the plastic cup of cheese cubes and apple. "If she starts getting cranky before we're back, give her the food."

"Come on, come on." Jake pulls at her sleeve. "We'll be back before Lauren even notices you're gone."

And Lauren *is* happily engaged when they leave, playing peek-a-boo with Danny who's lying on the floor in front of the playpen, Jonathan on his back, shouting, "Go horsey, go!" Jake looks about as happy as a man could be.

He puts his arm around Louise's shoulders and pulls her close while they stroll down the dusty sidewalk.

Sunday afternoon is always busy in the pokey coffee shop. Even though she's tried each of the three other times Jake has dragged her down here to be sociable, Louise knows that people are probably more comfortable visiting with him when he comes alone. They slide into a booth, and for a few minutes the babble in the room subsides. A couple of Jake's old friends rise from their places at the counter and wander over to shake hands. How are they are *all* doing, is the question, and underneath it the acknowledgement that everyone knows Danny is back. They're eating cloyingly sweet flapper pie when the men in the booth behind them begin talking about the murdered boy in Calgary.

"Here we go again," one of the men says. "A couple of young thugs kill that poor bugger and all they'll get is a rap on the knuckles because they're not eighteen yet. About time we realize that if they're old enough to commit that kind of crime, they're old enough to face the consequences."

"Aw hell," another voice chimes in. "Doesn't matter if they do bump 'em up to adult court. All they get there is a few years inside and they're out on the streets again, too." On and on about the soft laws, and how "therapy" has taken the place of honest-to-God punishment. Louise notices a couple of women in the booth on the other side of them, glancing uncomfortably at the back of Jake's head. Mention juvenile delinquent and Danny Peters comes to mind? Jake's face is impassive. He stirs his coffee, cuts another mouthful of pie with the edge of his fork and stares out the window.

Louise is looking out as well, when a familiar beige car

appears at the intersection, then turns left and proceeds down Main Street in the opposite direction from the coffee shop. She sits up straight in the booth, straining toward the window.

"Jake, that was my car!" He looks toward her, startled. "My car just turned the corner down there." She tries to keep her voice down. So far everyone is tending to their coffee and pie. "We have to go." She stands, brushes past the other booths and is out the door and running toward home, at the corner before Jake catches up with her. He grabs her arm.

"Slow down! Look!" He points in the direction of their house, down to the end of the street where her car sits sedately in the driveway. Still, Louise keeps on running. Inside, all three kids are lined up on the sofa in front of the television. Jake closes the door behind them, waves his hands at the scene in the living room, and shakes his head. "You see."

"Danny!" Louise can't keep the shrillness from her voice. "Did you just drive my car around the block?" Those darting green eyes fasten on hers, and a smirk of a smile skims across his face.

"Nope."

"For God's sake, Louise," Jake speaks under his breath, "I told you he wouldn't leave them alone."

Jonathan's eyes are huge. She crosses the room and kneels in front of him. "Jonny? Were you in the car just now?"

Her small son swallows, stares at her, and in a voice so tiny she can barely hear him, whispers, "Nope." And then he bursts into tears.

After Danny storms off to his room, still insisting he's done nothing wrong, after Jake goes out to lay his hand on the hood of the car, feel the heat of the motor and come back white-faced, after Louise comforts her small son and talks about truth and why it is never okay to lie, the house settles into a crackling silence.

Jake calls Danny three hours later, after he's clanged around the kitchen making his usual meat and potatoes Sunday meal. No answer to his rap on the door, and when he opens it, the fluttering curtains and empty room tell the tale.

He insists they sit down to their overcooked pork roast and mashed potatoes and gravy. When Jon pipes up wanting to know why Danny isn't eating, Jake opens his mouth, but then closes it quickly and shakes his head. He was, Louise is sure, about to make an excuse, but even that small lie would be too much for his son's ears.

"You're going to look for him, right?" Louise is amazed that Jake didn't storm out of the house as soon as he realized Danny was gone. Dumbfounded now, when he shakes his head.

"No," he says. "If he wanted to be found, he would have made sure I saw him leave."

He doesn't tell Louise until later, when Jon is out of hearing, that his wallet is gone as well. Swiped from the top of his dresser while he was in the kitchen preparing Sunday dinner for his family. "But that," he says, "will make it easier for the police to find him. He's bound to try and use the I.D."

Now you're galloping right along. It's getting a little predictable, isn't it? Foster home, reformatory, big time jail?

No, it can't be the same. That would mean that nothing has changed since the 50s. If this were 1953, Danny would already have graduated.

For the small stuff he's pulled off? Not likely.

He would have been thrown in with the two-bit thieves and scoundrels by the time he was sixteen, and would have learned some fancier tricks.

You're not going to try and prove that Robert Raymond Cook was the victim, are you? Bleeding heart kind of story?

No, I'm not going to try and prove anything. Half a dozen lawyers, two trial judges and two juries did their job. The Supreme Court of Canada upheld the decision. Why would I set out to prove them wrong? Robert Raymond Cook is dead. We'll never know what happened that night.

But we know they were afraid. At least Daisy was afraid.

We don't know that. All we know for sure about Robert Raymond Cook is that he was a liar. His lawyer told me so.

Roads Back

Forty-six years of law. I looked up The Honourable Judge D.P. MacNaughton on the Alberta Law Society roster before I sent a letter asking if he'd be willing to give me an hour of his time. He was admitted to the bar in June, 1958, and retired as a supernumerary judge in June, 2004

Initially, I had no interest in talking with lawyers and policemen. There was plenty of information about the evidence and the trials in the written material. Cook was dead. Whether he was guilty or not, whether he deserved to hang or should have been back in the news like Steven Truscott, finally free but still trying to clear his name, wasn't the question I was chasing. I insisted to myself that I didn't feel any kind of attachment or obligation to the face staring out from the cover of *The Work of Justice.* I wanted to know Daisy Cook. I wanted to know if, when she'd married Ray Cook, Daisy had imagined herself able to love his son. If she was ever able to even like him. I wanted to know if Daisy was afraid of Bobby.

Ask me! I'll tell you she was terrified.

Ah, but so many people said he wasn't to be feared. There were no signs of violence in the boy at all, in spite of his dedication to a life of crime.

Well isn't that scary? Even scarier than if there'd been some signs? You want to find those clues, don't you? You want to prove that the writing was on the wall, but no one read it.

I wanted to find one more person who'd known Bobby Cook. I tried tracking Lila Larson, the foster sister who'd gathered signatures for a petition to have Robert Cook's sentence commuted and had stood by him through the final days of his life. I checked directories for British Columbia (the family had moved there, leaving their foster son behind), Alberta (Pecover's book said that Lila had moved back to Alberta prior to Cook's first trial), I searched across-Canada directories for her married name, "Howse," but came up blank. Who else to tell me about this young man who went to his death adamant about his innocence? How many other men on death row, I wondered, went to their execution adamant about their innocence? Was it common? Did it mean anything?

Clark Hoskins had told me, after his vehement insistence that Cook was guilty, that if I wanted another opinion I should talk with Dave MacNaughton, because through the years MacNaughton maintained that justice had failed his client. I wrote to MacNaughton.

Five days later, he called. He had an energetic voice, no hint of the old age or failing memory I had begun to expect from all of the leads I followed, and he said he'd be happy to talk with me. Timing was a bit tricky, though. He and his wife were off to Montreal for the Liberal leadership convention.

Liberals are rare birds in rural central Alberta. In the last federal election the Conservative incumbent in that Crowfoot riding where Stettler sits had won with a landslide that verged on a joke. In almost all the interviews I'd done so far, even in the casual conversations I'd had with people in that area, the talk turned inevitably to law and order, and occasionally to restoring capital punishment. The Honourable

Judge D.P. MacNaughton suddenly had the appeal of an exotic bird. We made an appointment for after the convention, the fifth of December.

In the ten days before my appointment with MacNaughton, the weather shifted from unseasonably balmy, to treacherously wet. Days of freezing drizzle, then a sudden dip to minus twenty Celsius, heavy snowfall. Finally a Chinook wind blew in, melted the roads to slush and turned them to wicked black ice by night. I wasn't meant to make that trip to Stettler, I decided. The morning I was poised to phone and cancel, Dave MacNaughton called to confirm the appointment. The roads had been a bit of a problem, he said, but he'd driven to Red Deer the day before and he was sure I wouldn't have any trouble. The man was a judge. I couldn't argue with him.

I went back to my books to re-check MacNaughton's involvement. He was a young, small-town lawyer when he took on the Cook case. According to the Anderson book, *The Robert Cook Murder Case,* MacNaughton was joined at the preliminary hearing by "the famed criminal lawyer from Edmonton, Giffard Main. It was no secret that his services were being offered free of charge and that his main interest in the case was its challenge and complexity. He loved to defend the underdog." The jury didn't share Main's empathy for the underdog. On December 10, 1959, they took an hour and a half to find Robert Raymond Cook guilty.

Every time I read the account of Cook's trials leading up to his execution, I remembered all the bad movies I'd ever seen about men awaiting execution, final moments of redemption with weeping members of the family, the walk down the long corridor. Where, I wondered, were the lawyers in those last days? MacNaughton was the only one left now.

Main was seriously ill by the time of the second trial, so his partner, Frank Dunne handled the defense. Both men died shortly after Cook was executed. But MacNaughton had had fifty years to carry this infamous case with him.

The online road report on December fifth said the route to Stettler was "fair," a cautionary yellow line on the map. At 8:00 AM the temperature was zero degrees Celsius, and expected to climb to ten. Still, I threw my parka, boots, blanket, and a bucket of sand in the trunk. Filled a thermos with coffee. Tape recorder, notebook, pens, and the two books that stuck to me like barnacles, were in the canvas carry-all I'd begun to think of as my Cook bag. Did I need the books? They bristled with sticky notes, and were dog-eared, the spine on the Pecover book cracked so it fell open automatically to the photos in the centre. MacNaughton could probably tell me more than either of these two books. Take them, I thought. At least they show you've done some work already.

The CBC usually kept me company in the car. If I grew tired of radio talk on the drive to Stettler, the glove compartment held a pile of CDs, and I could switch to music. Or, I could enjoy the four hours of silence, but that was an invitation to Louise to wake up and I had now decided on a twist of plot for her story that I did not want to divulge until the words were on the page. I wanted the reins in my own hands. Louise had seized control like no other character I'd ever encountered, but I was determined that the ending to her story was going to be mine. Non-negotiable.

It was still rush hour at 9:00 AM, and traffic on the Deerfoot Trail came to a full stop so many times I was able to pour coffee and glance through my notes. Finally, beyond Airdrie the highway opened up. As the landscape flattened, a stiff wind whipped up from the ditches and threw a veil of white over the icy stretches. After a few miles, I relaxed. I am a good driver, and I enjoy the road.

I began to pay attention to the radio, to Shelagh Rogers on "Sounds Like Canada." It was the eve of the eighteenth anniversary of the Montreal massacre of fourteen young women at the École Polytechnic. Shelagh was interviewing two women involved in establishing monuments to the slain students in their respective cities. Both of them had faced fierce opposition and even personal threats. Ironic, considering their efforts were meant to honour the lives of women lost to violence. So much attention had been paid to Marc LePine, the man with the gun who'd killed himself in the end, one of the women said, that eighteen years later, everyone knew his name. But the names of the victims were lost. I turned off the radio.

Victims. Robert Raymond Cook's name was part of Alberta lore, and his father's by association, but many of the people I'd interviewed had forgotten Daisy's name and no one but the man who'd been Gerry Cook's best friend remembered those of the children.

I fumbled around in the glove compartment, randomly chose a CD and listened to the Rankin family for the next hour. By the time I got to Red Deer, the right-hand lane of the highway was snow-covered and it seemed no one else had noticed that it might be a good idea to adjust speed accordingly. I cut over on one of the secondary roads and hit ten miles of snow, an icy rut of tire tracks on each side of the road the only guide to staying out of the ditch, and those veered occasionally and then recovered the path. By the time I finally got to the intersection with Highway 21, I had begun to lose my driving nerve. Fortunately, the snow thinned, a weak sun poked through the clouds, the temperature rose, and there was so little traffic I drove for miles without seeing another car. Occasionally a truck sailed by, sending a sheet of brown slush over the windshield, slowing me to a crawl until the windshield wipers recovered the view.

I'd allowed an extra hour of driving time, and arrived in Stettler forty minutes early. The judge had given me directions to his home in the country and said it was only five minutes from town. I pulled into Tim Horton's, emptied the dregs of my coffee in the snow beside the car and took the thermos inside. I'd had plenty of coffee, but I'd fill it up for the drive home. I knew I'd need the caffeine later. Over a bowl of soup, I watched people come and go. Almost everyone who walked through the door seemed to recognize someone else and the place was buzzing.

When I got back into the car, Louise's presence was so strong she may as well have been sitting in the passenger seat. Apparently I had conjured her in that crowd of coffee drinkers.

Oh tell me about it. The joy of the small town coffee shop where you don't need to worry about people overhearing your conversation, because they all know your business already.

The pretty prairie town I remembered from summer was bleak in its dirty coat of snow. The landmarks seemed to have disappeared and I drove in circles getting out to the northbound highway.

Lost in Stettler. And I'm counting on you to find our way to the end of this story?

Finally, I was out of town, and found the turn-off in minutes. I was to look for a sign that said "MacNaughton

Ranch." There was no missing it. The sign was big enough to declare itself even in the deep snow, the house was set on a rise, the driveway wide. I drove slowly up the snowy road and parked in front of a three car garage. Beyond the sprawling bungalow there was a smaller house set into a grove of trees. A collie resting beside the house got stiffly to her feet and shambled up to the door with me. It was opened within seconds by a man in casual slacks and a golf shirt who looked as though he could have been in his sixties. Right on time, said the judge, with a brisk nod, and I was glad I hadn't lingered over a donut.

Women's voices drifted up a staircase to the left of the entryway. His wife and daughter were making Christmas decorations downstairs with some other women, he said, and he ushered me around the corner into a living room that seemed designed for family gatherings. Two big groupings of comfortable-looking chairs and sofas and tables, a piano, and a window with a view to miles and miles of snow-covered prairie that in the summer would be a soft watercolour of greens and browns and big big sky. The judge sat across from me, a coffee table between us, his chair just a little higher than the sofa I was on, so that I found myself looking up to him.

This was beautiful property, I told him, a lovely home that felt like a good place to raise a family.

It had served their large family well. Five lawyers in the family, he told me with obvious pride. Two of his children had followed in his footsteps, two more had married lawyers. The smaller house out back had been his wife's studio for years. She was a potter, but now that she'd retired from her craft, the studio had been renovated as a guest house.

We talked about the trip to Montreal, politics. He'd gone to support Stephane Dion in the leadership bid and was pleased to say the job was done. He'd been to many Liberal conventions, but this was one of the best. I asked if he'd grown up in this area, still wondering how Stettler had come to breed a Liberal. He was originally from Saskatchewan. Now that, I thought, helped to explain his political leanings. He'd come out here, he said with the hint of a smile, as a missionary. Actually he'd moved here in March of 1959 because he wanted a law practice that would leave him time for his family. He had five children by then and knew that a position in Edmonton, where he'd graduated from the University of Alberta, would mean long hours, high stress. It was the right move, he said, a good town.

I mentioned that Stettler seemed to have had more than its share of grisly crimes for such a peaceful looking corner of the country.

Again that bit of a smile. Some claimed it was the water, he said, and there had indeed been some "dandies."

And then we were finally onto the topic of his first murder defense. He was an easy man to talk with. Warm and informal, in spite of his being perched just slightly higher than I. He watched and listened as though he was as curious about me as I was about him. He told the story as though he'd told it many times before. But, he qualified, it had been a while now. That same refrain I'd heard from everyone. It was so long ago.

The first Dave MacNaughton heard of Robert Raymond Cook was a phone call on Saturday night, June 27, 1959. Cook was being held at the Stettler police station and was trying to engage the services of MacNaughton's associate who was not available. So by default, Dave MacNaughton took on what seemed to be a relatively simple case of false pretense charges. There was a problem about a new car, some unfinished paperwork, identification that belonged to Raymond Cook Sr., not the son who had picked up the 1959 Chevrolet Impala convertible in Edmonton. When MacNaughton visited Robert Cook in cells that evening, Cook told him that his dad was out of town but would be back in a few days and everything would be straightened out.

From all accounts, including Dave MacNaughton's, there was no way to explain Cook's return to Stettler as the actions of a guilty man. He drove up and down Main Street, showing off his new car. When he was asked to come into the station, he obligingly turned the car around and drove on down ahead of the police car.

At the station, he said he was sure his dad's friend, Jim Hoskins, would post bail for him. Hoskins refused, saying he needed to talk with Ray Cook first. On Sunday morning, Dave MacNaughton had a phone call from the RCMP telling him he'd best come to the Cook residence before returning to his client.

Half the town was there, he said. They were taking out the bodies.

Dave MacNaughton went back to the cells with one of the RCMP officers. When they told Robert Cook his father was dead and they were charging him with murder, he broke down. It was claimed afterwards that he didn't show much emotion, MacNaughton told me, but in fact, Cook broke down and cried.

Dave MacNaughton was two years fresh from law school when he met Bob Cook. He'd never handled a murder case, and he decided he wasn't going to risk someone's neck on his shortcomings. So he enlisted Giffard Main as senior counsel. Still, Cook ended up with his neck in the noose, MacNaughton mused. If he'd been tried a year later, he would have been sentenced to life imprisonment. He was the last man hanged in Alberta and only two others in Canada after him.

I remembered from Pecover's book that one of Cook's lawyers, MacNaughton, Main, Dunne, or perhaps all of them had said they couldn't help but like Bob Cook. MacNaughton told me Cook was polite, respectful, all the way through from the preliminary hearing to the trials. After the first trial he thanked his lawyers even though he'd been found guilty. He couldn't understand why the jury convicted him. He wrote a poem about it all. Dave MacNaughton said he had a copy of the poem. When he left the room to find it, I looked out at the snow. The sun was bright now, and the sky that milky blue of winter. I imagined walking the dog down to the mailbox. I had no idea if there was a mailbox but it seemed like a good thing to do on a winter day. I imagined children growing up here, building tree forts in the big grove of aspen I'd glimpsed as we'd passed the doorway to the family room and kitchen with large windows looking to the back of the property. I remembered that Clark Hoskins had built tree forts with Gerry Cook. I wondered if they'd ever ridden their bikes out of town and down this road. I remembered the large families, the small houses, and wondered if they had bikes. I wondered what Daisy Cook would have said about this house.

Then Dave MacNaughton was back, and pulled a faded photocopy from the file in his hand. I scanned the first page. Robert Raymond Cook was no great poet, but there was a sad poignancy to his attempt to convince the world of his innocence. Waiting for execution, he declared his serious doubt that there was such a thing as justice.

The file folder also contained newspaper clippings, one

of them with a photo of a row of children's shoes. One of the RCMP officers had lined the shoes up for the picture, MacNaughton said, and the prosecution tried to get the photo admitted as evidence. As if it was necessary to wring more sympathy out of this case. There were enough photos, MacNaughton said, that were positively horrific.

On the same newspaper page as the shoe photo there was mention of numerous confessions to the crime over the years. MacNaughton waved his hand dismissively. There had been confessions from England, from the United States. None of them at all possible, and a common occurrence in a "big murder" with wide publicity. The rumour most commonly cited locally was that Bob Cook's uncle had confessed on his death bed. Nothing to that one either.

That brought us round to family. Did Robert Cook talk about his family, I asked. About his stepmother? Daisy?

Finally!

He talked about his dad, MacNaughton said. They seemed to have a good relationship. Dave MacNaughton hadn't known Ray Cook at all, but knew one of his former employers very well. The father had a reputation for being light-fingered. Missing tools from the place of work, car parts, that sort of thing. MacNaughton said that when the white shirt found under the mattress turned out to be a mystery, he'd wondered if the answer was something as simple as Ray Cook having lifted it from a car he was fixing. And he just took it home because nobody had ever worn it.

The origin of that filthy white shirt hidden under the blood-soaked mattress, along with Robert Cook's suit, had remained a missing piece of the puzzle. There were some other pieces of evidence that were never explained.

Yes, MacNaughton said, and those pieces had caused a lot of trouble. Bob claimed that when he came back to Stettler he dropped in at home, had a beer, picked up some suitcases his folks had left behind, and put them in the trunk of the car. But one of the police officers who'd stopped him in Camrose earlier that afternoon had searched the car, claimed there were already suitcases in the trunk. Yet another witness from Edmonton who'd ridden briefly with Bob Cook in the old station wagon before he traded it in said there had been no suitcases in that trunk. Who to believe? Bob just made things up as he went along, MacNaughton said. They all do.

Yes, they do. All of that legion of liars to which Danny belongs.

A merry band of men? Bob Cook told MacNaughton that he never robbed individuals. Just Treasury Branches. The lawyer had a twinkle in his eye, almost a note of admiration in his voice when he talked about this young man he'd defended. That same fondness that seemed to spill into all of the comments from people who'd known Robert Raymond Cook, from prison guards, to his jailmates, to the pastors who were with him at the end.

And such loyalty from his colleagues in crime. Jim Myhaluk was a good friend of Cook's. He came to MacNaughton's office after Cook was charged and asked what he could do or say to help. When MacNaughton pressed him as to what evidence he could offer, he said he'd come up with whatever would be best for his pal. Just tell him what to say. That's the kind of guys they were, MacNaughton said. Whatever they could come up with to get out him of the jam.

Bob Cook, he said, had an answer for everything as quick as you could ask the questions. When he was captured after the escape from Ponoka, he told the police Myhaluk had helped him. MacNaughton discovered that Myhaluk had been in jail that night so he asked Cook what the real story was. Cook said that when he was in the lock-up at Ponoka, standing there at the window, he noticed that the bars moved a bit. The grout was loose. He just waited until it was dark, and he had no problem breaking out. And of course no problem getting a car started when he found one. His rationale for making up the story about Myhaluk? The police seemed to really want him to say that he had help. He told them what they wanted to hear.

On my trip to the Hanna cemetery, I'd wondered who stood there at the graves the day the seven were buried. Dave MacNaughton had no idea who'd arranged the funeral. He'd never spoken with anyone in the extended family. Not Ray Cook's family, nor that of Josephine Cook, Robert's mother. No one in the family came anywhere near Robert Raymond Cook after the murders.

I'd been to the cemetery, I told him. And he, with a grin, said I probably didn't find anyone there who could tell me anything. Bob had sent him on a wild goose chase through a cemetery too.

One of the unresolved pieces of evidence was around money Cook claimed to have dug up from a buried stash somewhere near Bowden—the loot, or swag, they called it variously in court—from the Vegreville Treasury Branch heist that had landed him in the Prince Albert penitentiary on his last incarceration. Cook told MacNaughton the can was still buried. If MacNaughton would just arrange a bit of a leave of absence he could take him there. To the exact spot. That, of course, was not remotely possible, so Cook supplied directions instead. MacNaughton said he went out with a shovel and the map, and ended up in a cemetery. He didn't find the money.

He was quiet for a minute, waiting for me to ask another question, but I was still back in Hanna, staring at the stone on the grave. Thinking about the funeral.

Did Cook ask to see them? I was thinking out loud, I realized suddenly. Did he see their bodies?

Dave MacNaughton raised an eyebrow, that same twitch of a smile. No, he said quietly, not afterward anyway.

I sat up a little straighter.

He shifted slightly in his chair. Bob told them what they wanted to hear, he said. He could have taken a lie detector test and I'm sure he would have passed it.

About the escape from Ponoka?

That too. About any of it.

About the murders?

Yes. Because he didn't believe he did it.

Do you? I asked.

He barely hesitated. Yes, he said. But he felt it was the same sort of situation he'd seen where someone had been raped or suffered some other brutal experience and then totally blotted it out of their mind. Cook had been in a fight with another prisoner just a few months before, and still had the scar on his forehead. He was a boxer in prison too. That was an angle MacNaughton said they followed. They thought the blow to his head in the prison brawl or the boxing matches might have caused brain damage. But Cook wouldn't even consider an insanity plea. He didn't do it. He wanted to take the stand.

I'd heard that MacNaughton had remained a staunch

defender of Cook. Did he think, from the beginning, that his man was guilty?

The evidence came together slowly, MacNaughton said. Cook had a good story about the car and he wasn't acting when he broke down and cried when he was told about the deaths. There was very real anguish when he cried for his father. Dave MacNaughton was sure that so far as Robert Raymond Cook knew in his own mind, he had not killed his family. But the evidence was so strong neither jury took any time at all in reaching their conclusion.

Bob Cook was a good liar too. He could have said his name was Dave MacNaughton and passed a lie detector test, the real MacNaughton said.

But in the end, it was the lies that did him in?
Did you ask him that?

It was the death penalty that did him in, MacNaughton said. Look at Colin Thatcher. He's out. Bob would have been out in twenty-five.

Colin Thatcher had spent twenty-two years in jail for the murder of his wife in Saskatchewan in 1983. He maintained his innocence throughout. I remembered with a jolt that Joanne Thatcher was shot and bludgeoned to death. But throughout Thatcher's imprisonment, members of his family stood steadfastly behind him.

Mrs. MacNaughton came upstairs then, and into the living room with a smile and a welcome. We chatted a minute about the weather and the roads. I wondered if they had prearranged signals, these two, whereby she would interrupt after an hour as my cue that it was time to go. But after she'd left the room, her husband settled back into his chair. Who else had I spoken with, he asked, and what other information was I looking for? Possibly he could find some other contacts for me.

I hadn't found any members of the family, I told him. There had been a number of people who'd suggested that poking around in someone's tragedy was in bad taste.

Murder is in bad taste.

All these wry comments, I wished I'd had the chance to hear him on the bench.

The thing about capital punishment is that there's no comeback if you are innocent, he said now. Look at Milgaard.

For a few minutes he talked about David Milgaard who'd been imprisoned for the murder of a nurse in Saskatchewan in 1969. Twenty-two years later he was finally released and DNA evidence proved him not guilty. During those twenty-two years, David Milgaard's mother never gave up the fight. She was still beside him during the long inquiry into what went wrong in the case. There was no one left to stand beside Robert Raymond Cook. Not one family member who ever made contact.

But then Joyce Milgaard believed in her son's innocence.

Ah yes, and she was his real mother. There is a difference.

MacNaughton said he'd never understood the Milgaard case. Why Milgaard's counsel, who later became the Chief Justice in Saskatchewan, never called him to the stand. The reason you don't call someone to the stand, he said, is that you know he's guilty. If he's confessed, but you're hoping to get him down from murder to manslaughter.

Or he's guilty but by reasons of temporary insanity?

That was an interesting twist as far as Ponoka was concerned, he said. Up until the day Cook escaped, the psychiatrist maintained that he hadn't finished his assessment, but when it came to court, there were complete reports.

His escape brought them to the conclusion that he was sane?

Apparently. It certainly brought him to a conclusion.

The judge was beginning to look tired, I thought. It was time to finish. I asked him if he'd visited Cook in Fort Saskatchewan. He had. Had he been there at the end? He shook his head slowly. He didn't have the guts he said, and had regretted it ever since. There were two pastors with Bob Cook when he was executed. They'd spent several months visiting him, and had come to know him well.

We both looked toward the window. It was only 2:30 but the sun was getting low.

When I was back in the car, I drove onto the main road, and then pulled over to write a few more notes. Although it would be there on the tape, there was one thing I wanted to be sure I remembered. There was no one, he'd said. Nobody. Bob was strictly on his own.

The Boy

Louise's past contacts with lawyers have involved no more than a few quick office visits to close a real estate deal, and the gentle guidance of the family friend who was her dad's lawyer and helped her when she was executor of his affairs. Some day she'll have the same kind of somber appointments over the probate of her mother's will. It's beginning to seem, though, that her mother is going to live forever in the fairyland she inhabits inside her head.

Now, Louise and Jake are in steady consultation with criminal lawyers over Daniel's latest charges. Juvenile hearings were humiliating enough, Jake says, always someone looking at them as though they were the problem. But now that Dan is eighteen and has graduated to adult court, there's no more pretending that he'll outgrow these boys-will-be-boys activities that get a little out of hand. They've entered a world of serious theft, break and entry, assault, and God knows what else they're going to have to listen to in the corridors of the courthouse. There's the expense as well. Legal Aid is a joke. After one attempt to get Dan hooked up with that service, Jake threw up his hands and said he'd rather pay a stiff fee for a bit of empathy and some real effort than beg for the free services of someone who was overworked and indifferent. At the end of the last hearing, the one that sent Daniel to Bowden for his current two years, the lawyer came to them with a long face and expressions of sympathy. Minutes later as they were leaving, they saw him down the hall, slapping a colleague on the shoulder, laughing, arranging a golf game. Well why not? Louise asked, when Jake bristled.

Wouldn't he be doing exactly that if it wasn't his son who'd just shuffled out of the room en route to jail? She struggled to hide her relief that Danny would be out of their lives for another two years.

No one asks about Dan anymore. Louise is sure there's a consensus down at the coffee shop that the judge made a good call. The scrawny boy with the feral look has turned into a lanky teenager with a bad attitude, someone other parents warn their own kids to stay clear of. Not that any young people in town ever sought him out.

At least the last break-in was in Edmonton, not the general store up the street, or Henry Schultz's garage or some farmer's machine shed. Still a loner, but Dan seems to run into the boys he knew at the treatment centre every time he goes to Edmonton. Is it any wonder, Jake said, that he hangs out with a bad crowd? A boy needs friends, and if the good kids will have nothing to do with him, well then he'll look for company somewhere else. Unfortunately, the last company he hooked up with enlisted Dan's help in breaking into a video store in a small strip mall. According to Dan. According to one of the other boys, the only one who was still a juvenile and ended up back at the centre in Calgary instead of in jail, Dan was the mastermind behind the plan.

Louise groans when she hears this. "Does a mastermind leave a calling card?" Dan's wallet was found on the sidewalk outside the store. No doubt it slipped out of his jacket when he was stuffing electronic games into his pockets.

"Well what do you want, Louise?" Jake snaps back at her. "A sophisticated bank heist? This is kids' stuff. It always has been."

"And always will be? You really believe that, Jake?" She can hardly speak. He is going to continue denying that Dan is in serious trouble. Her affable, reasonable, good citizen of a husband, still believes that the world is ganging up on his kid? She takes a deep breath. "It's going to get worse, Jake. Now there's drugs, alcohol."

He holds up his hand, head shaking so vehemently his face is a blur. "Dan says he does not do drugs. Maybe there's booze, but what teenager doesn't get drunk enough times to teach himself that the party isn't worth the morning after?"

"And you believe him? About the drugs?"

"I have to." He looks away from her, lips like a ridge of ice. "The rest of you have given up on him already. He's eighteen years old!"

Exactly. Danny is eighteen now and shows no sign of the maturity she's prayed would turn him around—everyone in town had cited some local kid who'd been "turned around" at the magic age of eighteen—nor does he show any interest in the jobs his dad keeps finding for him, or the counseling of a whole army of social workers and probation officers.

So far as Jon and Lauren are concerned, Danny, the big brother who flitted in and out of their life, is an adult now, no longer in "school." But how much longer, Louise wonders, before someone tells her five-year-old son that his brother is a jailbird.

Louise gave up on convincing Jake to move back to the city while he was so torn up with Danny's troubles, but she re-opens the debate, this time with the other two children's futures at stake. "There are more school options for them in the city," she argues. "More options for me too." She could get a job at either the elementary school in Valmer, or the high school in the neighbouring town to which the Valmer students are bussed, but she does not want to teach children whose families she knows, nor does she want to run into her students at the coffee shop. Jake doesn't get it.

"You still don't understand, do you?" he asks, genuinely puzzled, she can tell. "That's the advantage of living out here. Your life doesn't have to be compartmentalized. I'm sure that if Danny had grown up out here with cousins and people he knew around him from the time he started school, things would have been different. It's about growing up with people who care about you."

"It's possible," she says carefully, slowly, "for people to know you too well, and to fail to really see what's happening. Haven't you noticed that horrendous crimes happen in small towns, too, and that when something awful happens within a family, everyone claims they were just ordinary people?"

"If it's any comfort to you," Jake says, his voice chilling her in spite of the warm June day, "Dan says you couldn't pay him to come back here and live with us. He doesn't feel welcome. I'm going to visit him on his birthday next month, but don't feel you have to come along."

She feels her face redden. She has never visited Danny in his incarcerations. Not in juvenile detention, not at the group homes, and she can't imagine sitting in a grey room at Bowden trying to make pleasant talk with her stepson. She's talked with Phyllis about this, and Jake's cousin shakes her head. She doesn't see any point to it, she says, and then waffles around trying to find a tactful way of saying that Danny would probably rather have his dad to himself, even in these pathetic circumstances. No, Phyllis assures her, she shouldn't feel guilty. Bad enough a father has to go to such a place, and perhaps she'll suggest to Paul that he offer to go with Jake, just to let him know that he isn't alone in all this.

So Louise buys birthday presents; running shoes Danny requested, books, chocolate. Jon wants to give his brother a deck of cards. Danny, Jon reminds his mom, just loves playing Go Fish with him, and maybe some of his friends like playing too. He and Lauren spend an hour making birthday cards. At the end of it, Lauren asks, "Who's this for again?"

When Louise reaches up into her bedroom closet to find the wrapping paper she keeps there, her hand lands first on the scrapbook full of Brenda's clippings about the Cook murders. Just for a second, she flips through the pages, and pauses on the photo of a row of shoes; a tiny pair of mary janes, a little girl's party shoes, three pairs of generic-looking boys' running shoes, a mother's scuffed pumps, and the worn work boots of the dad. Who, she wonders, thought there was artistry in lining up the footwear of a dead family? Surely the murderer didn't amuse himself thus. When she hears Lauren's chirpy voice in the hallway, she stuffs the file under the heap of laundry on the bed and takes the wrapping paper out to the living room. No balloons or birthday cakes for Dan, Jon tells her seriously, and chooses instead a slick sheet printed with red racing cars.

Later, when the kids are settled in front of the television watching *Blue's Clues*, Louise goes back to the bedroom. She folds and puts away the pile of clothes on the bed, and finally sits down to look at the clippings again. With her eye on the clock, Jake due home in another hour, she skims through articles, barely able to read the account of the discovery of the bodies, and finally stopping at the story of Robert Cook's escape from the Ponoka mental hospital. A stepson, so jealous of the new family that usurped his father's love, that he flew into a rage and murdered them all. But did he? Because the articles also offer up dissenting opinion, doubts about the conviction. "Hometown still divided on guilt" one headline reads.

"Mommy?" Louise looks up, startled, at Jon. "Can we make a cake for Danny?"

"A cake?" She glances at her watch. "I don't know, sweetie." She's about to say that she doesn't know if they're allowed to send a cake. Isn't that the old movie cliché, the file baked into a cake? She imagines Danny escaping from Bowden, running barefoot through the countryside the way Robert Raymond did all those years ago. Except he wouldn't be barefoot; he'd be wearing the expensive pair of running shoes his dad brought along with the cake. A far cry from the plain sneakers worn by the little Cook brothers. "We'll ask your dad," she says. "He'll be here any minute, so I'd better get the spaghetti on."

At dinner, Jon mentions the birthday cake again. "I don't know, buddy," Jake says. "It's a nice idea, but this place where Dan's staying it's kind of ...there's a lot of guys there, so maybe it would be better if I just took a piece of cake instead of the whole deal."

"Can I come?"

"Not this time, son."

He sounds so weary Louise doubts he's even registered what Jon was asking. Not this time, not ever. She's sure Jake can't imagine taking this sweet boy inside the walls of a prison any more than she can. Jake came home from the last visit to Bowden white-lipped and furious. The visitors were kept waiting for almost two hours for no apparent reason. Little children waiting to see their dads, cranky and tired and hungry by the time they were allowed in. "Helluva way to run a railroad, is all I can say," he muttered, and remembering that now strengthens Louise's rock solid conviction that neither she, nor Jon nor Lauren will ever make that trip. She will make sure they never visit the scummy world of their half-brother.

"But here's an interesting coincidence," Jake continues, looking at Louise now instead of Jon. "Remember Alice? My old neighbour in Edmonton?" It takes Louise a minute to dredge up the memory of the old woman who lived next door to Jake when she met him. The one who was happy to come over and sit with Danny if Jake had to go out, the one who gave Louise such scowling scrutiny the couple of times they met, that she was sure she failed the test of whether she was worthy of entry into the family. She nods.

"She came to the salesroom today with her grandson. The kid's just graduated from university and he's got an engineering job up north. Twenty-four years old and a big enough income to finance a brand new Tundra." Louise shrugs. "A new truck, Louise," he says impatiently. "Imagine a kid like that with a six digit income? Anyway, Alice is proud as punch, and wanted to make sure he got a good deal." He twirls spaghetti around his fork, pauses with strands dangling over the plate. "When the kid was off doing the paperwork Alice asked me about Dan. She heard he was having a hard time." Always Louise has to bite her lip when Jake talks about Dan having a hard time. Aren't they the ones having a hard time with their son? And what about the people he robbed? "To make a long story short, I told her I was going down for his birthday and she asked if I'd take a present for him, and then all of a sudden she decides she wants to come along." All of a sudden, Louise suspects, was when Alice heard that Jake was going alone. "I'm going to make some calls and see if we can get her on his visitors' list."

Louise nods and nods, because there is no other response. An old woman with no more than a brief connection as a neighbour will make the effort to visit Daniel in prison, and she, his stepmother, can't make herself even consider that trip.

"Good," she says finally. "We'll send a piece of cake with the presents. And a piece for Alice too."

In the night, Louise lies awake thinking about Daisy Cook, wondering if she ever went to visit Bobby in prison.

On the day of Jake's trip to Bowden to visit Dan, Louise packs the two kids into the car and drives out to the farm to visit with Phyllis.

Before she married Jake, Louise had close friends, most of them teachers, with whom she went to movies, out to dinner, to the pub for a beer after staff meetings. Occasionally, a couple of her old friends drive out to see her in Valmer, shaking their heads over the change in her lifestyle, the old house with its smell of Pledge furniture polish and the lingering kitchen aromas of decades of Sunday's roasted meat.

Jake keeps urging her to hire a babysitter once a month and go into Edmonton to shop and meet a friend for lunch. But she's reluctant to leave Jon and Lauren for more than an hour or two. Her city friends are all single and Louise has moved off the common ground—men, travel, work—that consumed their conversation before. She suspects, too, that her friends feel sorry for her. Though no one has ever said as much, she knows they think she made a serious mistake, marrying a man with a problem son, and although she's kept her mouth firmly shut about Danny's further adventures, by now someone will have heard how much more deeply into trouble he's descended.

Phyllis, on the other hand, loves both Jake and Danny fiercely but is still able to listen sympathetically to Louise's outpouring of frustration. She is the kindest and most honest woman Louise has ever met.

Jon and Lauren are out of the car and halfway across the farmyard before Louise unbuckles her seatbelt. Phyllis bobs up in the garden beside the house, waving. "Let them go," she calls. "Paul's in the barn. He'll herd them back if they get into trouble."

Louise hesitates—she doubts she'll ever be relaxed enough to "let them go" without worrying—and then joins Phyllis at the tap where she's peeled off her gloves and is splashing water on her face. "Good timing," she says. "I've had enough sun." She nudges the pail at her feet with her boot. "I pulled some carrots and onions for you to take home. Let's put them beside the car so we don't forget."

They go inside then, to the cool kitchen that always smelled slightly earthy to Louise. Root vegetables with the dirt still clinging, strong coffee. Phyllis sweeps a pile of papers off the table and grabs a cloth to wipe away the lunchtime crumbs. For all her saint-like Mennonite ways, she is the most casual of housekeepers. A pleasant surprise to Louise who expected to be judged by Jake's family because she didn't bake her own bread or churn the butter.

"So," Phyllis sighs, after a long drink of the iced tea she's poured for them. "He's gone to visit Danny in the jailhouse again? You told me before, I'm sure, but how long this time?"

"Six months, but the lawyer said he'd likely be out much sooner."

"Well that's good, isn't it?"

"Is it?" Louise says. "Will he have changed?"

Phyllis fishes a slice of lemon out of her glass and nibbles it off the rind. "What do you think it will take? They give him schooling in there, not? Maybe if something interests him…"

"We've tried to find something that would interest him for the past four years, and he says there's nothing. Absolutely nothing that appeals to him. Or no, what he says is there's nothing that's worth his while. All he wants is to make enough money to buy a car and have his own place. How likely is that for someone who's barely finished grade nine?"

"I guess he could go north. Lots of the young guys are making big money in Fort McMurray." Phyllis frowns. "I hear that's the worst place of all to get in trouble. Drugs and alcohol and I wouldn't let any of mine go there because of the sheer danger of the work. One of the Plett boys was only up there a month before he lost three of his fingers. He's lucky it wasn't the whole hand."

"Jake wouldn't even consider letting him go."

Phyllis raises her eyebrows. "You think Daniel's going to let his dad make those decisions for him now he's eighteen?"

Louise looks out the window for the third time since they came inside. Jon and Lauren are at the back of the house now, playing on an old board swing that hangs from the branch of a huge laurel leaf willow. They are almost hidden under the canopy. She smiles at the idyllic picture. Then she turns back to Phyllis. "No, I don't think we have much of a say anymore." She's glad, actually, that Danny is eighteen and there'll be no more hauling him back home. It would be easier if he moved to another city, another province, and yet she knows that would be disastrous for him. Without the touchstone of home, what hope would he have of going straight? She sighs. "He'll have to come home, though, because where else would he go?" From her chair, she watches Lauren's feet soar past the window with each push of the swing. Jon is so good at looking out for his little sister.

"Jon's present to Dan was a deck of cards," she says

to Phyllis, "so he can play Go Fish with his friends. He wrapped them up himself."

Phyllis claps her hand over her mouth. "Oh dear Lord, you have to laugh or you're going to cry, right?"

"I wish I could laugh," Louise says, "but the truth is I'm scared half to death."

"Scared, why? You're afraid for Daniel? We all are, Louise."

She bites her lip, knows she should bite her tongue. "I'm afraid *of* him, not *for* him, although there's that too. I'm afraid…" She remembers that scrapbook of Brenda's, the picture of the white clapboard house, the smiling children. "I found some newspaper clippings in with a bunch of recipes and quilting patterns of Brenda's that Jake had packed away. A murder story from a long time ago, but it seems it was someone Brenda knew."

Phyllis's hand flies up before Louise can go on. "Cook, right? Robert Raymond Cook. I don't know why that girl was obsessed with Cook, but you should throw the stuff away. She met him once at a party when she was in high school, and she never got over the whole bloody deal. I refused to talk to her about it." Phyllis leans forward, her work-worn hands flat on the table. "Listen, Louise. That's all past. It's nothing to you and Jake. There are plenty of folks around here who are sure the son didn't kill the family. They say an uncle confessed on his deathbed about ten years after young Cook was hanged. Stop scaring yourself without reason. There are enough real troubles to worry about without swimming around in other people's sorrows."

"You remember it then?"

"Of course. Everybody does. Stettler's not far away and that was the biggest thing that happened when I was growing up. My God, when he escaped from Ponoka, they had every policeman in the country and the army too out there stomping around. As I remember it, he gave himself up. Just walked out of somebody's pig barn with his hands in the air, meek as could be." She shakes her finger at Louise. "Didn't I just say you should put it out of your mind? Daniel Peters is no Robert Raymond Cook. In fact, people who knew him said Robert Raymond Cook couldn't have killed his family. Paul's aunt worked at Ponoka. She said he didn't look like any monster to her." She stands up. "Come on. Let's go take the children for a walk. The saskatoons are ripe, and if they help me pick we can bake a pie. You'll stay for supper."

Of course they will. Louise is not anxious to go home to the empty house.

Isn't that what they always say when someone flips out and goes on a bloody rampage? He couldn't have done it. There were no signs?

I guess it is. But who understands why a child kills his parents.

You must have some clues by now. You've been reading those creepy stories about the child murderers for long enough. And don't you dare put that book in Brenda's box of treasures!

No, Brenda wouldn't have gone looking for other stories. She was only interested in Robert Cook.

And you? Isn't that where your obsession began?

Yes, and that's where it will end, but meanwhile I keep wondering what leads a child to murder. There are the obvious answers. He was abused. He was crazy. Neither of which fits Robert Raymond Cook.

Nor does either fit Daniel, but that's no real comfort. And aren't you forgetting that Bobby Cook escaped from the mental hospital? Someone thought he was crazy enough to be sent there.

No. He was sent there because remand for psychiatric assessment to determine if he was fit to stand trial was automatic.

Exactly. Someone who murders his parents and five little brothers and sisters is definitely in need of psychiatric assessment.

Roads Back

Whenever I asked people if they remembered the Cook murders, they either shook their heads, or landed on the subject like magpies on roadkill. So many opinions on Cook's guilt, whether or not he got a fair trial, capital punishment. And a big fence down the middle, which no one straddled.

Some of the memories of the summer of 1959 affirmed my own, others conflicted. I remembered hot weather, someone else remembered weeks of cold rain. I remembered being grounded for the full two months of vacation, someone else remembered biking across town to the swimming pool every day. Another friend remembered that the swimming pools were closed. It was the summer of the polio epidemic. His youngest sister died. How could I have forgotten the other fear that hung over us? Poliomyelitis, polio, infantile paralysis, my own father had been left with a paralyzed right arm in the 1937 outbreak when he was twenty-four years old. In that last epidemic of 1959, 1,887 cases in Canada resulted in paralysis. By 1955 immunization in the form of injected inactivated polio virus vaccine had begun, and by 1962 the use of oral polio vaccine containing live weakened virus was widespread. I remembered lining up at school for both the injection, and later the oral vaccine. Possibly the Cook children were immunized as well. Safe from at least one peril.

It was no wonder that memories of that time were vivid for some, shadowy for others. Not surprising, considering the Cooks and their infamous son had been dead for so long, that many of the people who knew them were also long deceased or too frail of mind to recall anything other than the sad shame of it all. Finally, my good friend, Shirley Black, put me in touch with one of her old school friends, Doreen Scott, who happened to have been the head nurse on the psychiatric unit at Ponoka where Robert Cook was held.

She would be happy to talk with me, Doreen said, but doubted she'd have much to offer, because she'd only actually seen Robert Cook once. Doreen was seventy-two years old, still working a few shifts a week in a nursing home, and serving a couple of Anglican parishes as well. She'd gone from nursing to theology, completed a PhD just a few years earlier, and had recently been ordained as an Anglican priest. She and her husband used to own race horses. Even if she had nothing illuminating to offer about Cook, I was sure her company was worth the trip to Lacombe. Doreen suggested we meet for lunch on a day when she had a small window of time between duties.

I asked Shirley if she would come with me. She'd watched me dig myself deeper and deeper into the story of the Cook murders, and in the years I'd been writing, Shirley had been one of the best critics I knew. Six hours of conversation in the car was bound to lead to insight.

Lacombe is just five kilometers off the main corridor between Edmonton and Calgary, the Queen Elizabeth II Highway which I travel often, but I had never had a reason to visit. I found a town that was movie-set pretty. Tree-lined streets, stately old homes, parks, and an "Edwardian" business section refurbished under the Alberta Mainstream program in 1987 with a view to preserving historic buildings. Another idyllic place to raise a family. But Lacombe is in Central Alberta, only an hour away from Stettler, and I'd been told many times that the region had more than the infamous Cook murders in its criminal history. In 1956, the Social Credit Member of the Legislative Assembly for the area gained infamy when he murdered his wife, three children, and a sailor who had the misfortune of being a visitor to the home that weekend, and then waded into a slough and committed suicide. John Clark had had a history of mental illness. So, too, did the man who murdered the Weltys, a farm couple a writing colleague, Faye Reinberg Holt, spoke of when I talked with her about the Cook murders. She grew up on a farm near Stettler, just a few miles down the road from the Weltys, who also became part of the homicidal history of the area. That farm couple made the fatal mistake of leaving their living room drapes undrawn, and were shot and killed by a young man well known in the community. He, it was discovered, had made a list of prospective victims, and Faye's dad was among them. So many people in that area with memories of violent crime, but many of them reluctant to dredge for the kind of details I was seeking.

As soon as Doreen strode into the restaurant, I was sure there would be no problem with failing memory or reticence around talking. A statuesque woman in flowing black cassock and cape and clerical collar, she swept through the room greeting people on every side, turned a warm smile on me as she approached the table, hand extended.

Doreen settled into the booth next to Shirley, and the two of them took a moment to catch up on news of their mutual friends. They'd been girls together, classmates. Then Doreen turned to me. This is so interesting, she said. She dug a book out of her bag and placed it on the table. The same one I had in front of me; *The Work of Justice*, by J. Pecover. In spite of the fact that not everyone I'd interviewed agreed with Mr. Pecover's conclusions, he'd sold a lot of books.

Now tell me all about you and what you're doing, Doreen said. She leaned toward me, and I had the feeling I'd be telling her my own story rather than getting hers if I wasn't on my toes. The restaurant was full. Working people, lots of jeans and a scattering of cowboy hats. Doreen seemed to know them all.

She pulled a single sheet of paper out of the book and passed it to me. She'd kept notes during her years at Ponoka, she said, thinking she might want to write about that experience some day. But she'd recorded nothing on Cook, and this was all she remembered. The short paragraph seemed a précis of what I'd already gleaned from newspaper clippings, and that one bit of information that kept surfacing as a rumour:

> "It is worth noting, that about fifteen years later, after of course Robert was hung, his uncle gave a death-bed confession saying that he had committed the murders of the family."

Doreen said she didn't know the details of the confession, but she'd heard about it many times. She hastened to qualify that most of what she could tell me wasn't based on the small contact she had with Robert Cook, but on the assessment of a psychiatrist whose report she'd read.

So we chatted over lunch, Doreen pausing frequently to wave and smile at people who entered the restaurant. To put it plainly, she said, the psychiatrist thought Cook was a "punk," a "bad boy," with a string of petty crimes his only accomplishment. But he didn't think that he had committed the crime. In fact, none of the staff did. It was "weird," she said, this sense they all had of him as a young man who was just foolishly joy-riding.

Even after he escaped?

She nodded. There was such terror in the community when he was on the loose, she said, and she thought that fear was a big factor in Cook's being convicted. Even the escape, she said, wasn't his own doing. She was sure someone on staff had helped him, someone with a grudge against the administration and problems of his own. That man was dead now—and so was Robert Cook—so she didn't think there was any point in naming him.

As for her own impression of Cook, she said that because she was a supervisor, she had less direct contact with the patients than the other staff did. "A big shot with long sleeves and cuffs and a cap," she said with a smile. A woman on a unit that was traditionally all male, and not very popular on the unit because she was trying to make some changes. She only met Cook once, and her lasting memory of him was of "a gentle little fellow."

She pulled her copy of *The Work of Justice* alongside her plate. A good-looking young fellow, she said, but the photos all gave the impression of a husky man, and he was really quite a small person.

Perhaps it was the suit in that particular photo that made him look more substantial, I suggested. What had he worn at Ponoka?

Pyjamas. White flannel pyjamas, and slippers made by one of the patients. His name was Ben, she said and he worked for Cy Bedard, the tailor, and made the most wonderful melton cloth slippers. The staff all bought them for twenty-five cents a pair. Robert Cook wasn't allowed to wear day clothes. His blankets were probably made out of canvas sturdily sewn together out of strips—so he couldn't hang himself. She winced. What irony. Meals came with plastic spoons and cups. Two staff members with two keys were required to open the door and hand him the metal tray of food.

Doreen's memory of the facility, of the room Cook occupied, was vivid. It was all tiled, she said, with squares of white marbley material and the window in the door was made of Georgian glass, very expensive, but it would break with enough force. He would have had to sit on the floor. The rooms relied on the heat coming in under the door from the hallway. In the winter there'd be frost on the insides of the windows in the rooms. Terrible. Oh those times, she said. When she thought about them now, she was ashamed. The nurses were treated royally; fresh cinnamon buns and butter, and coffee with real cream for their coffee breaks. On a silver tea service no less. She shook her head. The patients got their coffee in plastic cups with sugar and milk already added whether they wanted it or not.

But to get back to Robert Cook, Doreen said, she didn't believe he was guilty. There was no definitive evidence. He requested reading material and writing paper and a pencil, and every single magazine came back with a message written on it: I did not kill my family. He believed that so fervently, she said, that she had to believe it as well. This wasn't a sophisticated criminal. He wasn't that bright. He knew how to steal cars.

We both looked down at the picture of Cook on the front of *The Work of Justice*. Such an ordinary-looking young man. I guess he was never bound for glory, I mused.

Well, no, Doreen answered, but she was certain he deserved a better ending.

Suddenly she asked about my children. How many did I have, and what did they do. I told her about my three, my librarian daughter, conservationist son, and our youngest, an aspiring musician. When I said that he was a drummer, she patted my hand. A good way to get rid of aggression, she said. But what about you, she asked, what is it that's compelling you to spend months—years, I could have corrected—tracking the dead? This was a question I'd been trying to answer, trying to justify the time spent poring over newspaper clippings and gory details with an interest that dumbfounded me. Trying to justify the expense in time and travel and distraction from the other writing that would have come easily, and probably would have yielded far more gratification by now. Memory, I told her, seemed to be the root of it. There were scraps of memory that I was struggling to connect, not necessarily to reach a conclusion of any sort, but to weave them into enough of a story that I could feel a sense of personal resolution. I had become bound to the story as well, I told her, because of the number of people with whom I'd spoken who believed Cook was innocent. Not that I was trying to establish either his guilt or innocence or even come to a conclusion of my own, but that uncertainty left so much room for discovery.

She nodded slowly as though she understood perfectly, and I believe she did. She was sorry her information was slight, and her memories so shaky, she said.

Mine, I told her, because they were childhood memories, were even less reliable.

Oh, but she hoped that I had good childhood memories too. Memories were so important. She and her husband had owned race horses, and when they won her husband would have lobster served for forty or fifty people at the McDonald Hotel in Edmonton, or the Palliser in Calgary. Roses for all the women. When they lost he did the same thing. She had wonderful memories. So important.

Then she suggested I speak with someone else who'd worked at Ponoka and had been on duty the night Cook escaped. She would call Gary Anderson for me and ask his permission to pass along his phone number.

Shirley and I walked out to Doreen's car with her.

Good luck with this, she said. Do a good job for Robert Raymond Cook.

Funny, isn't it that he was always Robert Raymond Cook in the news? Never Bob or Bobby.

She put an arm around me. Oh, I'm sure he was, somewhere, she said. Somebody had to love him, somewhere along the line.

On the way home, Shirley and I talked about the shadowy figure of Robert Raymond Cook, about how there wasn't a single impression I'd gleaned from anyone who'd come in contact with him that suggested the kind of violence that had wiped out the entire Cook family that summer evening. And yet. Weren't sociopaths charming liars? Deceitful? Shallow? Egocentric? Did the fact that Bobby Cook wasn't cunning enough to get away with any of his crimes overrule that possibility? Was the affection he had for his dad real? How could he show remorse, or lack thereof if he truly didn't believe he'd committed the crime? What if he didn't commit the crime? Who did? Was that something I would pursue, Shirley asked, if I became convinced that he was innocent? No. I wasn't interested in detective work of that nature. Then what was this investigation in aid of?

That sure seems to be the question, doesn't it?

It was three months before I was able to talk with Gary Anderson. On a sunny day in February, I picked up a bouquet of tulips on my way out of Calgary, and drove the Queen Elizabeth II Highway once again, this time to Ponoka. I would go on from there to my old hometown of Camrose where I was reading from a new novel that evening. That first book, *Running Toward Home*, is the story of a young boy lost in the child welfare maze. I'd left the story open-ended, to the dismay of some of the readers I'd been hearing from. But what happens next? Is there finally some hope for Corey and the people who care about him? I maintained staunchly that I didn't know. I didn't believe in fairy tale endings, but liked to offer up a bit of redemption. I pondered as I drove, how I'd left Corey's mom and great grandfather on a street corner. How I'd discarded another ending as too maudlin, too unlikely for the characters given their history. How relieved I'd been that I wasn't going to follow them into the next chapter.

The problem with the Cook story was that the people in it were real. The ending was written, and there was no redemption.

So, that's the purpose of my story. Epiphany! We must be on the road to Damascus!

No, we are on the road to Red Deer, far from any epiphany. Go back to sleep and let me concentrate on the scenery.

During the writing of *Running Toward Home*, I had spent hours, days, months hanging out at the Calgary zoo where the story was primarily set. Now, this central Alberta landscape I was driving through had taken on a new persona in the months that the Cook murders occupied my thoughts and

. my writing. These were roads that Robert Raymond Cook drove in June, 1959. If his explanation of his hours between his release and his return home to Stettler were true, then he drove this same highway to recover the loot he gave to his dad. It was the $4100 he gave to his father that set in motion the sudden trip to British Columbia to look for a service station, the father and son opportunity they'd both spoken of. Robert had said that after taking the midnight bus from Saskatoon, he and his pal, Jimmy Myhaluk, arrived in Edmonton at 7 A.M. on Wednesday, June 24. Myhaluk went to his parents' home, and Cook checked into the Commercial Hotel. He washed up, had breakfast, and then made the first of his three trips to Hood Motors where he found the Impala convertible, the object of another of his dreams. He told the salesman he was a mechanic, in business with his father. He said he'd return with a car for trade-in on Friday. Then, according to a story that stayed constant through the trials, and in a document he called "Murder by Infernce" that he wrote while he awaited his execution, he walked south on 104th Street until he came to a used car dealership on the outskirts of the city. He hot-wired a car, drove away undetected and headed south for Bowden. There, he dug up a tobacco tin he said he'd buried in April 1957, the loot from the string of break-ins for which he had just served his time. With $4300 in his pocket, he drove back to Edmonton, returned the car to the lot and went off to find Myhaluk or any other of his cohorts for a night of partying before his return home the next day. This was the same Bowden landscape Dave MacNaughton had scoured with Cook's directions, trying to corroborate the story, but ending up in a graveyard instead. No one, it appears—from Pecover's book which looks at the "Bowden caper" in detail, and from the court transcripts—attempted to pin down the car lot and establish the probability of Cook stealing and returning a car in broad daylight. His own explanation from his testimony in the first trial when he was asked why he didn't just abandon the car:

> It is much better to leave it where I took it from and then it isn't reported stolen and the guy doesn't miss it. Nobody is hurt and nobody knows different. (*The Work of Justice* pg. 195)

Nobody hurt, by Cook's assessment, in any of the crimes he committed. And a theft that would seem all in a day's work to Robert Raymond Cook who'd been stealing cars since he could peer over a steering wheel. After he broke out of Ponoka, Robert Cook hot-wired a car and drove these same roads. As I passed the hamlet of Morningside, looking for a sign that said Spruce Road that would signal the turn to Gary Anderson's acreage, I was only about ten kilometers away from the Ponoka mental hospital. I imagined this countryside in July, 1959, swarming with police cars and army. I imagined Robert Raymond Cook, the "gentle little fellow" Doreen Scott had described—or was he the killer with "the coldest eyes ever seen" as a *Red Deer Advocate* reporter described? He said one look at Cook had chilled him "to the bone."

The offering of tulips was a good impulse. Gary Anderson and his wife were gardeners. We sat in the sunroom of their acreage home and looked out at the large garden, stalks of last year's perennials poking through the snow. After working as a psychiatric nurse at the Ponoka hospital, Gary had gone on to university to take a degree in Education, then a Masters degree in Psychology. He was now retired.

Since my phone call, he had been looking for information on the Cook case on the internet. He said his memory of the case was sketchy, and it had been a long time since he'd even thought about Robert Raymond Cook.

Gary Anderson was nineteen years old when he started work at the mental hospital in April, 1959. That fall, he would start a three year course in psychiatric nursing. It was a practical arrangement; a decent wage while he earned this credential.

On June 30, 1959, Robert Raymond Cook was admitted to Male 6, the admission ward at Ponoka, and a few days later, Gary had his one and only contact with Cook. Disturbed patients or dangerous patients, Gary told me, were held in "side rooms" on the admissions ward. They had their meals in their rooms, while the other patients ate in a common dining room. Gary and some of his fellow staff members wondered why Cook had been sent to Ponoka and not to Alberta Hospital in Edmonton where most of the forensic cases were confined and assessed. Ponoka did have a unit for the "criminally insane" who he said it seemed to him were often there for "years and years" without review.

There were always three staff members on duty on the admissions ward, usually one psychiatric nurse and two attendants. Gary remembered Robert Cook as looking very much like the newspaper photos; sandy-haired, clean cut, probably no more than five foot six, and not particularly muscular, but "agile-looking." On the day of their one contact, Cook had asked to use the washroom and Gary and another staff member escorted Cook from his room to a toilet across the hall. The staff members, Gary said, were understandably wary. Here was someone who was believed to have savagely murdered seven people. Yet here he was, pyjama-clad, quiet, polite when he did speak. There was no door on the washroom, so he was led there and back under close watch.

On the night of July 10, Gary was again on duty on the admissions ward, this time on the night shift. Staff who lived in residence at Ponoka took their meals there, and supper for the night shift was at 11:30. Gary was "second junior on the totem pole" that night. After the 11:30 room check, the senior staff member passed the "check key" for the side rooms to Gary and left to have supper in the staff dining room. The most junior member, a university student working there for the summer, was in another corridor, checking dormitory rooms.

At midnight, Gary peered through the observation window in the door to Cook's room. He had a flashlight, but said he didn't need it tell that the room was empty. The green night light illuminated the small room well enough to show him that the inside mesh screen from the window was on the floor amidst splinters of glass from the outside pane. He tried to peer down to the base of the door and along the wall to ensure that Cook wasn't crouched there, waiting, but could see nothing. In retrospect, he says, he knows he should have called another staff member but he was immediately struck with the huge significance of the empty room. He said he had to confirm that Cook was really gone before he sounded the alarm, so he opened the door and went inside. The screen, which required a wrench to undo the deadbolt that kept it in place, had been removed and the window punched out. There was blood on the shards of glass remaining in the frame. In mental hospital vernacular, Robert Raymond Cook had "eloped."

The opening through which Cook had wriggled was eight inches by eleven inches, slightly smaller than a sheet of letter paper. When the RCMP tried to re-enact the escape, their officer became wedged in the opening with his head and one arm outside the window, unable to move either forward or backward. He had to be pulled back into the room by his colleagues.

How could Cook have managed this escape on his own? Gary hesitated before he answered. There was a fire escape outside the window, he said, and it would not have been difficult for someone to come up those outside stairs, break the glass, and hand through a wrench or some other tool for liberating the screen. Cook could not, Gary was sure, have drawn back the bolt that held the screen with his bare hands. Not even with the rush of adrenaline that must have propelled him through the glass-barbed window. There had been a lot of speculation among the staff as to whether or not the assistance, if there was any, had come from the inside. While Doreen Scott had mentioned a staff member, Gary said there was also a patient in the discharge unit who was very close to release, a man who may have felt sympathy for Cook, and could certainly have found his way to that window because he had the run of the hospital grounds in the last stages of his stay. Perhaps he'd talked through the window with Cook, and planned what was necessary to remove the screen, then come back with the tool in hand. The patients knew the schedule of nighttime rounds and between the time Gary and the departing day staff made the shift-change check of the room at 11:30, and Gary's return just after midnight there was time.

With the full alarm sounded, the manhunt was on, but even after Cook's capture, the question of how he got away was never answered. Cook told Dave MacNaughton he'd given the police the story they wanted—he had help—but that he'd really broken out on his own, and forty-five years later, none of this, Gary and I agreed, was more than an interesting riddle. What remained was the fact that even before the trial, there were some among the staff at Ponoka who were convinced that Cook was not guilty. It seemed extraordinarily unlikely, though, that anyone would have been sympathetic enough to have helped him escape.

Dave MacNaughton had spoken to a psychiatrist at Ponoka the day before Cook eloped and was told that the assessment would not be complete for several days. After the escape, though, a report was provided saying that Cook showed no psychotic signs and was fit to stand trial. Ponoka was done with him. Looking back, Gary Anderson said, Cook's actions after the murders, his joy-riding and the return to Stettler, were exactly the sorts of irrational actions that would point to illness. So, too, was Cook's rationale for his escape—his wish to attend a funeral that was already over. Or maybe the confinement at Ponoka pushed him over the edge. He is quoted in a report by one of the psychiatrists, Dr. Edwards, as saying, "If I'm not crazy now, I will be by the time the 30 days are up."

I went on to Camrose after talking with Gary Anderson, and that night met several old schoolmates at the reading. Over drinks afterward, someone asked what story I was working on now. I hesitated, always reluctant to talk about a project too early, and in this case so unsure of my motives for pursuing the story that I felt a little foolish. The mention of Robert Raymond Cook brought a chorus of "I remember that!" Stettler is close enough to Camrose that several people had older brothers and sisters who'd either met Cook, or knew someone who knew someone who had. There was dissent over his guilt, which I'd come to expect, the invoking of the rumour of the uncle's death bed confession, and finally the childhood memories we all seemed to have of adults whispering about the pit full of bodies and the rampant fear after Cook's escape. It was a hot summer, someone said. The hottest one she remembered.

You think he was innocent! You've become sympathetic!

I don't know if he was innocent or guilty. But yes, I'm becoming sympathetic. Too many holes in the story. Questions that were never answered.

Oh so now this story is about the son, is it? What about the family? What about Daisy?

Yes, Daisy. Let's go back to Daisy. And you.

The Boy

Louise and Jake have been circling around the topic of Daniel's homecoming like a couple of cats stalking the same bird. He's served fourteen months of the two year sentence and is due to be released in another month. No one wants to ask, "What next?" Until Jon comes home from school in such a deep pout his lower lip stretches almost to his nose.

He throws his backpack across the kitchen floor, a burst of aggression so unlike him and yet becoming so much more frequent that Louise's throat tightens.

She sits him down at the kitchen table with a plate of cheese and crackers, then pulls a chair close to his and puts her arm around him while he munches. "What's up? Bad day?"

He looks down at the plate, traces a trail in the cracker crumbs with his finger. Looks up at her with pleading eyes. "Can you come to school tomorrow and tell the kids Danny's not a jailbird. Mommy, what's a jailbird?"

Ignorant parents! And what about the teacher? "Does Mrs. Ferguson know the kids are teasing you?"

He nods. "She said I have to talk to you and you should come see her. She said it means Danny's in jail."

Which Jon has known for months now. They dropped the pretence of "school" when Daniel graduated to Bowden. "Did she say Danny's trouble with the police has nothing to do with you?" By now both Jon and Lauren know that when a policeman comes to the door it's because of Dan. Even with Dan locked away, the police keep coming. Did he ever hang out with this one? Known to associate with that one?

Do they know where he was on the night of some date two years ago?

"When does Danny get to come home?"

Louise has a blinding flash of memory, of Jon on Danny's back. Go, horsey! Yo, bro, it's time for a skateboard! Wow, did this guy ever grow!

Jake is barely through the door two hours later, when she takes his arm, pulls him into the bedroom and closes the door.

"So what's the story on Danny? Is he coming here, or what? Every time I've asked you just shrug and say they haven't worked out his plans yet. Jon just told me the kids are ragging him about having a criminal for a brother. He wants to know when Danny's coming home. What do I tell him?"

Jake pulls the sheer curtains aside and braces his arms on the window sill. Not much to see out there, just the wall of Henry Schultz's garage, the corner charred from the fire. Maybe, Louise hopes, that reminder will inform Jake's decision. She presses on. "You must have talked about this the last time you went up there. What does he want?"

Jake gathers a handful of curtain and holds it away from the window, contemplating as though he's redecorating rather than facing a family crisis. "I don't know, Lou." He sighs and finally turns, shoulders sloped, his arms at his sides as though there are impossible weights tied to his wrists. "You can probably stop worrying, because he doesn't want to come home. He says there's nothing here for him." He looks at her thoughtfully. Trying to imagine her through Danny's eyes? She gave up that game long ago, how to be the good stepmother. "He says he's nervous around you.

Always sure he's going to make a wrong move. And then he always does."

"Like what? Asking him to take his shoes off when he comes inside makes him nervous? Put the lid down on the toilet after he uses it?" She tries to keep the whiny tone out of her voice but it's impossible. Lately it isn't her image through Danny's eyes that troubles her, but how Jake must see her. What would Brenda have done these past eight years? Jake must ask himself that question as well.

"I'll go talk to Jon about the gossip the kids are spreading," Jake says. "What about Lauren? She upset too?"

"Jake, it's not gossip. Everybody knows where he is. We can't make it out to be the fault of the kids. That's what kids do. Lauren's okay, I think. She's way better at telling them to get lost and she's the queen bee of grade one so the other kids want to be in her good books. It's Jon who's wounded every time." Jon, she doesn't say, who keeps trying to defend his brother.

Jake opens the bedroom door, words coming back to her over his shoulder. "Then it's time he toughened up a little," he says. "Don't worry. I'm not going to tell him to duke it out. My pacifist upbringing is still too strong for that."

What he does instead of talk, is to take both Jon and Lauren to the coffee shop for milkshakes, treat a couple of their friends as well, and make sure he tells everyone in the place that Dan is getting out soon, and he and Louise are optimistic. The boy has surely learned his lesson and it can only get better from here on in. Jon comes home with a smile on his face, swinging hands with his dad on the way up the front walk.

That night, spooned into the curl of her husband's warm body, Louise keeps hearing the replay of the words he whispered before he fell asleep. "We have beautiful kids, Lou. So beautiful."

She lies there, trying to feel reassured, feel everything right in her small world, and yet that cold hand clutching her stomach will not ease off. She shifts slightly, then widens the gap between them and finally slides away from Jake and out of bed.

After Jake stormed at her to get rid of Brenda's Cook murder files, she stashed them in the laundry room in the basement in a box filled with quilt squares that belonged to her predecessor. Not that she had any intention of stitching together Brenda's abandoned project, but the neat piles of colour and texture-coded squares seemed too precious to be thrown away.

The concrete floor is like chipped ice on her bare feet. She pulls a pair of Jake's socks out of the dryer along with the sweatshirt he wore around the house on Sundays. When she's warm again, and the creaking of the basement steps and all the other sounds of the old house that she stirred when she made her way down the stairs have settled into silence, she opens the scrapbook to a clipping from the *Red Deer Advocate*, July 3, 1996, the Cook case brought to light again because of the publication of Jack Pecover's book.

Under the headline, "Did He Do It?" the newspaper article includes a collage of faded photos: Robert Raymond Cook's RCMP mugshot; a snap of the five Cook children squinting into the sun; a formal portrait of a bespectacled Daisy looking every cell the school marm; the white frame bungalow with the truck parked next to the garage; and finally a crowd in the street in Bashaw waiting for a glimpse of Robert Cook after his capture following the Ponoka escape. Louise holds the photos close and looks hard into

Daisy's eyes. A serious face, but is she only imagining fear? She can't bear to look into the children's faces. She closes her eyes, leans her head against a garment bag of winter coats hanging on the wall and wills that scrapbook out of her hands, into the trash barrel, incinerated somewhere far away. Daniel Peters is Jake's son, a boy she's known since he was twelve years old, the brother of her own children. He is not Robert Raymond Cook. She is not Daisy Cook. There is no connection here. None.

Is that clear enough? Can we burn those clippings now? Donate the books to the next used book sale? I'm sure someone out there will find them morbidly fascinating. Can you tell I'm tired of this and I have a bad feeling about the way it's going?

I'm not sure why. I know now how your story will end. You are not Daisy. But do we dare to imagine Daisy's ending?

That's the problem, isn't it. Neither of us wants to go there?

You mean into the white bungalow on the night of Thursday, June 25, 1959?

Exactly. Why don't you just write that story and cut mine loose?

Because no one knows what happened?

You're a writer. Make it up.

I've tried. I can't, because I don't know the truth. And anything less dishonors these people.

But we can imagine it, to a point, can't we.

Not me. Not even to a point. But I can give it to you.

All right then. This is how I've dreamed it.

Daisy, splashed by a blood-red setting sun, leans into the window. The air in the kitchen is soupy, not even the sigh of a breeze.

She lifts a corner of waxed paper covering the plate of sandwiches, pokes at a crust of bread. Mustard has dried marigold yellow on a protruding grey bologna tongue. She re-wraps, and presses the plate to the counter. Too late for the fridge? Lock the barn door when the horse is dead?

"Mommy?"

Kathy, cheeks flushed, kitty-cat pyjamas twisted, droops in the doorway between kitchen and bedrooms. Then Linda toddles to her sister's side, blanket trailing, thumb corked between her lips. Daisy huffs the fringe of hair off her forehead. "Back to bed, babies!"

"Thirsty!" Kathy's toes click on the linoleum. From the living room, the voices of her brothers are muzzled by the heat. "Bobby here?" she asks.

"Not yet." Daisy scoops one pudgy girl onto each bare arm. She waltzes slow around the kitchen, sets the fly paper spinning. Then swoops over the grey arborite table. Linda's diaper snags on the chrome edge. Daisy lifts, then bops her around the table, one damp print at each place. Deposits her finally on Daddy's spot. Shifts Kathy to sit beside her baby sister. Lifting the corners of her apron, she fans a breeze for two flushed, up-turned faces. Reminds herself to take off the tatty apron. Berates herself that she cares. Touches her hair, self-consciously. Relives the plucking of a coarse strand of white from the red this morning. And feels that sting all over again.

From the living room, the opening music to 77 Sunset Strip snaps its fingers. Daisy winks at Kathy. "Kookie, Kookie, lend me your comb!" she sings, tickles her fingers through the little girl's hair. "Turn it down!" she calls to the boys. "Your dad will be here any minute." Ray can't stand the show. Kookie too much like Bobby, she thinks. So why isn't Kookie in jail? And where is Ray? Where is Bobby, now that he's been sprung?

Then loud voices in the garage, sharp as the edge of a shovel, the scuff of feet, the hard bark of a laugh, scrape of the door as it opens into the kitchen. Ray and Bobby, husband and stepson, drag the smell of grease and garbage into Daisy's kitchen. She encircles the little girls, and calls the boys from the living room.

How am I doing? Is that you how you imagine it?

Yes. Almost exactly. And then …?

I can't go any farther.

And neither can I.

Oh, I know that. You're having even more of a problem going there than I am.

The Boy

After Louise burned the Cook files, after she agreed to take Daniel in once again, after Jake arranged to pick him up the day of his release, the boy disappeared. Jake phones from Bowden to say that the time Dan had given him for the pick-up was late by two hours. He was let out in time to get the morning bus to Edmonton. Jake's going to drive on to Edmonton and check out a few possibilities.

"No," Louise says. "Please don't do that." There's such a long silence, she's sure they've been disconnected.

"Why? I thought you were willing to take him back this time."

"Don't you get it?" she says. "If you go looking for him and coax him back home then he's in control. Anything goes wrong, it was your fault for making him come back."

Another silence. And then to Louise's surprise, "You may be right. I'll see you in a couple of hours."

Jon, at the table doing his homework, doesn't look up, and for a moment Louise thinks he must be was talking to himself. "If anything goes wrong if anything goes wrong if anything goes wrong it's gonna be bad." His voice winds tighter and tighter. "Mom?" eyes still focused on the map of Canada he's colouring. "Is Danny coming home with Dad?"

"No," she says, and walks over to the table to look down at the neatly printed city names. Edmonton. Regina. Saskatoon. Winnipeg. In a few days Danny could be anywhere.

"Good," her son says, so softly he's an echo of the voice in her own mind.

The months with no trace of Danny are the most restful Louise can remember in the years since they moved to Valmer. People stop asking about him. In August, just a week before the collective birthday that seemed always to end in disarray, the phone rings on Sunday morning and it's none other than dear old Alice. She asks for Jake, and Louise feels the familiar Dan-induced tightening of her jaw as she listens to Jake's side of the conversation. When was he there, how long did he stay, did he say where he was going, how much did Alice give him?

After he hangs up the phone Jake stares out the window for at least a minute before he faces Louise. "Danny showed up at Alice's a little while ago. Just out of the blue. She said he looked a little rough. She tried to get him to stay and eat with her, even spend the night, get a good rest, call me to pick him up."

"What did he want?"

"He wouldn't stay. There was a guy waiting for him outside."

"What did he want from Alice, Jake? How much did she give him?"

"I think I'll give Paul a shout and see if he'll come to town with me. I'm going to check out some of Dan's old haunts. Two can spread out and cover more territory."

"If he wants to see you," Louise speaks slowly, each word a labour, "he knows where to find you. He always has, Jake."

"Are you saying I should ignore the fact that my son who's been missing for six months turned up a half hour drive from here, and made contact with the one person he could be sure would phone me?"

"You think that's why he went to Alice?"

"Of course. Why else would he go there?"

"Because she's a vulnerable old lady and he needs money."

"Jesus Christ, Louise!" He slams his fist down on the kitchen table, breakfast dishes flying, and Lauren, who appears around the corner from the living room at that very minute flies wailing to her bedroom. "Don't you run to her!" Jake shouts at Louise. "She's fine! It's tears over everything and she'll get over it in a minute."

She stares at him. "Is this our fault? Mine and the kids? Go then. Track him down at one of the shelters, or maybe you'll find him if you check every greasy coffee shop on the south side. Fortunately, it's too early in the day for the bars to be open. And then you'll bring him home? Shall I bake the birthday cake today instead of on Wednesday, just in case he takes off again by nightfall? Write welcome home on it?"

She can't stop herself. "Daniel is not a little boy lost, Jake. The reason he hasn't come home is that he knows what he needs to do to live here, and he's not buying it."

Jake grabs a kitchen chair and spins it around. He sinks onto the seat and leans on the back, his face in his hands. When he looks up at Louise she takes a sharp breath. His skin is chalk white, sweat beading his forehead. He opens his mouth to speak but all that comes out is a gasp, and then again he drops his head and slumps forward.

"Jon!" Louise wrenches the old phone from its cradle on the wall. 911? Out here, almost an hour away from ambulances, fire stations, hospitals? She doesn't know who to call. Phyllis and Paul. Without pause, her fingers have already found those numbers but there is no answer. Of course not. It's Sunday. They're at church all day.

Jon, in the kitchen now, his head whipping back and forth, looking first at Louise who stands there pounding the phone into her hand, then at his dad who has managed to straighten up in the chair, still breathing hard but steadier now. "It's okay," Jake whispers, his hoarse voice stopping both of them where they stand. "I'm okay."

But he is not. This Louise knows. Within minutes she has Jake in the back seat of the car, Jon next to him holding a cold towel to his dad's face, his own pinched and tear-streaked. Lauren in the front passenger seat gibbering, "What, Mommy? What's wrong? Where are we going?"

By the time they pull into the University Hospital Emergency entrance, Jake seems to be breathing a little more easily. But when the attendant asks him if wants to walk in, he shakes his head, squeezes Louise's arm for a split-second and then transfers his weight to the man in the white coat who helps him into the wheelchair.

Three hours in the waiting room before Louise is called to the treatment area. But only she is allowed, not the children and she searches frantically around the crowded room, all those sick people, the coughing and the sagging bodies. Next to her, a young woman holding a listless toddler shrugs. "I'll keep an eye on them for you, but who knows how long I'll be here."

Louise shakes her head. "It's already too long for you," she says. "You'll be going in soon." The nurse is standing there, waiting for her. "I can't leave my kids alone. Please tell my husband that's why I'm not with him. I'll be there soon." She's been calling Phyllis since they arrived, but in a house that eschews technology there is no answering machine. Finally, on this desperate try, Paul answers. And yes, he says, they will be there within the hour. Hold on. Tell Jake to hold on, they're coming. Again, she encircles Jon and Lauren with her arms. "Aunty Phyllis is on the way." Meanwhile, she will feed her children. There must be a coffee shop close at hand. "Come," she says, lifting them to stand with her. "Daddy's going to be fine. I feel much better now. Let's go find some food."

Alone in her bed that night for the first time since she married Jake, Louise imagines him in the hospital bed. He is asleep, she's sure, because when she leaned over to kiss him before she left, he struggled to open his eyes, the whites showing a tracework of red.

"He seems awfully weak, "she whispered to the nurse who was fussing with an IV pole."

"Not bad," she said. She put a hand on Louise's shoulder. "Look at his lips. They look plump and pink as rosebuds compared to when we got him up here."

More like undercooked liver, Louise thought, but the flesh on Jake's face had settled into the familiar lines around his eyes, and the two vertical grooves over his nose on the high smooth forehead. She brushed back his hair, and grabbed a tiny piece of reassurance from the warmth of his skin.

"He's groggy from the meds," the nurse said. "We'll keep him quiet for a few days and he'll be back to you soon. You go on home now and get a good night yourself."

How likely that she'll ever have a good night again, she wonders now, the darkness in the room leaning a heavy hand on her chest. Jake laughed when they first moved here and Louise told him the house was too dark for sleep. Maybe they should use the bedroom at the front of the house even though it was smaller, she suggested, and she would leave the blinds rolled high so that the lone streetlight on the corner could dance a few shadows around the room. Maybe, he said, they could put on music for the dance as well. A CD of traffic sounds and noisy neighbours to really make her feel as though she was back in the city.

She finally relaxes, is slipping into sleep when she feels the tilt of the mattress beside her and warm breath on her cheek.

"Mom?"

She lifts the quilt so that Jon can slide in, then turns on her side. She pulls him close, breathing the funky smell of his hair. She sent the kids to bed without baths. "Can't sleep?" She feels the back and forth of his thick hair on her throat. "Me neither," she says. "I'm worried too."

He pulls away slightly, his elbow caught in the neckline of her nightgown. "I heard noises," he whispers. "Are you worried about Daddy?" She frees him from the fabric, his bones so small in her hand. "But *he's* going to be okay, isn't he?" Jon says, his voice croaky.

Jon's breath is stale, garlicky. After Phyllis brought the kids home, she fed them a cheese and sausage snack while they waited at the living room window for Louise to arrive back from the hospital. They would not budge from that window, Phyllis told Louise when she phoned to say she was on the way.

"Yes of course." She nods. "The nurse told me when I was leaving that Daddy needs a few good days of rest and he'll be home."

He sniffles and pulls a handful of sheet to wipe his nose.

"Go to sleep," she says. "Things always look better in the morning. Honest."

"It's not Daddy I'm worried about," he says. "It's Danny. Why won't he come home?" She sighs, too weary for this discussion. She cannot force herself to parrot Jake's forced optimism, tell this little boy his brother is going through a bit of bad behaviour that some young people try out, that he's going to grow up very soon. And he'll have learned his lesson. And he'll stay out of trouble for good.

"I don't know," she says. "No one except Daniel knows, and he's not ready to tell us." Jon is quiet, and for a minute she thinks he's fallen asleep.

"I'm so scared," he says, "cause Danny doesn't have anyone looking after him. He could get hurt really bad."

"Shhhhh," she whispers. "Go to sleep."

As his weight settles against her and he begins to snore softly, she thinks about Jake and what he would say if he walked into this scene. He would say that Jon is too old to be coming into their bed. That she's coddling the children. She wonders if Brenda faced the same criticism, or if Daniel was a more independent, thick-skinned boy than this little brother of his. Daniel was only ten when his mom died, just two years older than Jon is now. She can't imagine the boy in her arms motherless. Nor fatherless. She simply will not let her mind move in that direction. Not imagine herself alone forever in this creaky old house with her children.

By the time Louise feels her bones begin to settle into the warm sheets, she can see reassuring streaks of dawn around the edges of the blind, and sometime later, she's pulled briefly out of a fretful dream by the sound of a car in the driveway. Then she's back in the misty hospital corridor, running from room to room, looking for Jake.

Phyllis surprises Louise, calling softly to her from the bedroom door. Louise sits up in bed, Jon struggling up next to her, rubbing his eyes. "What time is it?"

"Eight o'clock, but don't hurry. Go back to sleep if you need to. You probably didn't get much."

Louise eases around Jon and slides out of bed. Her nightgown twists around her thighs, she tugs it straight with a crackle of static, a whiff of her own tired body. "I'm sorry I didn't hear you knock," she says. "Did Lauren let you in?"

Phyllis shakes her head. "I just knocked once and tried the door. It was open."

"Which door? The back?" None of Jake's kin ever come to the front door. Always through the kitchen. But Louise went out that way to the car yesterday afternoon, and surely she locked the door behind her even though she was in a panic to get Jake to the hospital. Locking doors is instinct to her. She came in through the front door with the kids last night when they got home, left the car out front because she knew she'd need it first thing this morning. She locked the door behind her last night.

Phyllis looks unconcerned. A door left unlocked is small when someone she cares about is lying in a hospital bed. "I'll fix breakfast," she says. "I put the coffee on already. I imagine you want to get away quickly. What do the kids like? Toast? Cereal? Or do you just want to have the donuts for now?"

Donuts?

"You made donuts already this morning?" Louise says. "You must have been up around the time I was going to sleep." She slips on her bathrobe, ties the sash, looks up.

Phyllis has her hands on her hips, lips pursed in the wide pale bowl of her face. "I don't make donuts these days," she says. "Too much for Paul's cholesterol. He'd eat a dozen straight out of the hot fat. There's a box of donuts on the kitchen table. Did you forget about your late night run past Tim Horton's?"

Did she? Louise barely remembers the drive home last night, just the sense of being strung like a wire between the hospital and home, not daring to leave Jake and yet wanting to hold her children close so desperately she felt as though her skin would slide away without them. Tim Horton's? No, not even in a state of confusion would she think it a good idea to bring home donuts. She shakes her head. "I didn't buy donuts."

"Somebody must have heard about Jake and dropped them off then, so you and the kids could have a sweet snack when you got home."

Where were they when Jake was stricken? The kitchen, in the midst of preparing Sunday breakfast, Jake frying sausages, a tea towel tucked into his shirt to protect from grease splatters, Louise dipping bread for French toast when the phone rang. "The kitchen must be a disaster," she says. "We left in the middle of breakfast. Don't you dare clean it up. I'm going to shower and come right down."

Jon is between them now, rubbing his eyes and snuffling. Phyllis turns him toward the doorway with a gentle smack on the bum. "You go wash your face and hands and you can have a chocolate glazed and a glass of milk." She closes the bedroom door behind him. "The kitchen is fine, Louise. A bunch of dishes soaking in the sink, but that's all. You must have tidied up when you got home?"

"No." She did not tidy anything. She did not stop at Tim Horton's. And though a neighbour might have done her the kindness of cleaning her kitchen, they would not leave dishes soaking, nor would any woman in Valmer bring store-bought donuts to a family in crisis. "I left the kitchen in a mess." And she wrenches open the bedroom door, Phyllis right behind her.

The table is still set except for one plate and fork. In the fridge, there are five cooked sausages, unwrapped on a plate. A bowl full of soggy bread slices. And on the far end of the counter, an empty beer bottle. She picks it up and waves it at Phyllis. "Someone was here while we were gone. Do we have to ask who?" Her hissing anger sends a spray of saliva into the air, and she stops, embarrassed. Phyllis does not need this. Neither does Louise want Jon and Lauren rushing in to find her in another state of emergency.

"I wondered about the beer bottle," Phyllis says softly. "Thought maybe you needed it after the day you'd had. Come." She takes Louise's arm and guides her to the table. "Sit down. Have a cup of coffee. Is it such a bad thing if Danny came home? It's just too bad he didn't know why you were away. Maybe he would have stayed."

One deep breath, then Louise crosses the kitchen to the basement door. She doesn't hesitate at the bottom, kicks open the door to the room he hasn't inhabited in over two years, and exhales. He is not here. But he was. The new clothes Jake took to Bowden six months ago are no longer folded on the bed and the dresser drawers are open. She doesn't need to go upstairs to the desk in the den and slide open the cubbyhole where Jake keeps emergency cash. It's gone. She is as sure of this as she is that Daniel did not come home with any intention of staying.

Jon heard a noise in the night, and she had heard a car pull away in the early hours of morning. Either he was in the house, hiding in the basement room, or standing in the dark kitchen when they came in last night, or he came in while they slept, puttered about in the kitchen, gathered his things, and crept away quickly. Or he might have come and gone earlier, before they returned, the noises just the usual creaking of the house, the car outside of no relevance to this house and family. Louise sweeps all those bits of evidence aside. She will not dwell on them, nor will she tell Jake that Danny came home. For now.

Why the dirty dishes?

Stuck in my mind, I think, from Pecover's chapter on the unproven alibi and clues left dangling. Bobby Cook said he came home on Thursday night, had coffee and sandwiches with his folks, and then left soon afterward. There were coffee cups stacked beside the sink, but no one counted them.

That's a serious omission?

It might for once have validated something he said. Jim and Leona Hoskins had coffee with Daisy and Ray before Ray went out looking for Bobby. Four cups. If there were only four cups when the police searched the house, then Bobby's story about the welcome home refreshments was probably a lie. If there were five cups, or maybe seven if Ray and Daisy indulged in a clean cup to join him, just a fragment of truth wouldn't have harmed his case.

No matter who drank coffee and ate sandwiches, or how many cups were left for next morning's dishes, the rest of the night is still a black hole.

Not if Bobby's story that he was helping Sonny Wilson break into Cosmo Cleaners in Edmonton at 1:00 AM had been proven.

That was the only thing standing in the way of an innocent verdict? Where did you get that idea.

From Jack Pecover. He told me to re-read Chapter Twenty.

Roads Back

Two years after I'd walked away from the Hillhurst Sunday flea market with Jack Pecover's book in my hand, I had reams of newspaper clippings, audio files of interviews, random notes scribbled after long walks in which thoughts churned and clotted into ideas. I had also applied to and been accepted in the Master of Fine Arts program in creative writing at the University of British Columbia, something I'd been contemplating for some time. Now I had a purpose beyond earning another degree. If I was to do justice to this piece of history, I needed strong guidance in the area of creative non-fiction. I was convinced, after several aborted starts on the book that I could not separate the story of the Cook murders from the fiction that was growing even faster in my mind. My goal was to write a story that reflected the human side rather than the legal twists and turns and infamy of the Cook case. But the discomfort I felt in delving into the personal lives of people who'd met such a horrible fate was close to stifling me. The first summer residency at UBC liberated me from that sense of privacy invaded. Truth, Terry Glavin, the non-fiction instructor with whom I was to work through another full year course and an independent study, insisted, would validate my intent. And Truth was only attainable, in so far as it is ever pinned down, through fact. Do the research, never depart from the facts, and remain humble in admitting inadequacies. Let the unproven remain unknown, and bring what you can to the page with respect and honesty.

So many people remembered the Cook murders, so many still wondered at the outcome, several had written about it, likely others would as well. There were, I was sure, no answers to the big question of whether Robert Raymond Cook was guilty, and if he wasn't, then who was, and if he was, had his guilt been proven beyond the shadow of a doubt, and even if it had was the death penalty warranted? Even less likely that there was an answer to my own quite different question: Who were these people, and how did this horror befall them? Out of my interviews I'd begun to extract almost cinematic images of Father, Mother, well-tended children, modest home, small town life. In my mind, I could see children spilling out the back door of the white bungalow, Daisy Cook at the kitchen counter buttering sandwiches, Ray Cook tinkering in the shadowy garage. I could imagine life in that house, but I could not make myself go beyond 9:00 PM. on the Thursday night of June 25, 1959. While my quest had been to bring life back to the images of Ray and Daisy Cook, Gerry, Patty, Chrissy, Kathy, Linda, I'd found an even clearer image of Robert Raymond Cook emerging— Bobby, the cocky delinquent stepson who stole from the family the benign description of "ordinary folks."

In the reading and re-reading of Jack Pecover's book, I could get so far as the meeting of father and son on Main Street, Stettler, at around 9:00 PM, conjure the scene around the kitchen table, coffee cups in the hands of the adults, five children circling shyly around the prodigal brother. But from what I'd read and been told about Robert Cook, I could not put the shotgun in his hands or imagine him swinging through the house in the bloody massacre of his small brothers and sister. I could not put his face to the image of the man heaving bodies into a pit, pouring kitchen garbage over those remains. And I could not see him scrubbing the splattered walls. The jury had been able to imagine exactly that scene, though, and I admitted to myself that if I'd been confronted with all of the evidence and the stumbling, prevaricating Cook in the witness box, I too might have been convinced of the ending.

Took you a while. I knew a few chapters into this that you didn't want Bobby Cook to be guilty. That's why I'm here. You want to change the ending. But I'm leery of where we're headed. Changing the endings doesn't necessarily mean happy endings to you, does it?

Of course not. Ultimately every story has to end sadly, doesn't it?

Only in real life.

Roads Back

Pecover's exhaustive exploration of the Cook murders had become my textbook. He had so thoroughly peeled back the messy layers of the criminal case that even had I been inclined to follow that thread in my own obsession with the Cooks the work was already done. Pecover's wit, the deep irony of the story, made fascinating reading. I had read the chapters titled "The Suspect" and "The Seven" so many times the pages had separated from the spine of the book. I'd begun to wonder what Pecover would think of my unsure feet following the trail he'd laid, and finally picked up the phone one day and called him. The Canada 411 listing did not give an address for Jack Pecover, but from the area code, I'd assumed he lived in Edmonton. An easy destination for me, and family in that area always added another purpose to my trips. Yes, he would be interested in hearing about what I was up to, he said, but he lived near Westlock, another hour and a half's drive north of Edmonton. He went to Edmonton, he said, only when absolutely necessary and two days hence would be such a day.

I arranged to meet Jack Pecover at a bookstore on the far south end of the city, and once again drove through nasty weather, this time a wet day in July with the temperature hovering around five degrees Celsius. Just north of Red Deer, a storm threw down blinding curtains of rain. When I tried to pull over, wait out the worst of it, there were so many cars following close behind I was afraid I would lead several more in the same direction, none of them expecting me to stop. I was sure I would remember the pursuit of this story as fraught with treacherous driving and cold feet.

There are two photos of Jack Pecover in *The Work of Justice*. In one he is standing in a stairwell at the Fort Saskatchewan Correctional Centre in front of a door through which twenty-six men and one woman passed on their way to the old gallows in the exercise yard. In 1954, a new Superintendent of Prisons for the province of Alberta, E. E. Buchanan, proposed moving the hangings to an indoor location. Previously, tarpaulins had been slung over windows that gave some of the prisoners a view of the execution site, and people in the community had been known to seek out high vantage points so that they could watch the show. In the second photo, Jack Pecover crouches on the floor of the room that became the indoor death chamber. The trapdoor in the floor is now filled in with plywood. For six years after it was constructed, the gallows in the room was unused, and after Cook fell through the trapdoor into the autopsy room below—another photo in the book—it was never used again.

I arrived at the bookstore with just enough time to check my tape recorder before I splashed across the parking lot. So far no one had objected to my recording their words. I am a poor note-taker, caught up too easily in conversation, depending on memory. But notes it would have to be with Jack Pecover, because the slick digital device was dead, and not even fresh batteries revived it.

He was easy to spot, a tall slim man in a trench coat, his face familiar from the photos. We sat at a small table crowded into the coffee shop corner of the store, and I found myself babbling nervously about my interest in the Cook case. I did not need to explain my fascination to the man who had written a 449 page book on the trials of Robert Raymond Cook.

Jack Pecover was still in law school when Robert Raymond Cook was executed. He become engrossed in the case, and one day, about a year after Cook's death, he was walking in downtown Edmonton and found himself outside the office of Giffard Main. On a whim, he went up the stairs, asked to speak with the famous lawyer and to his surprise was escorted into Main's office. He wanted to write a book about the Cook case, he told Main, and to his even greater surprise, the man agreed—on the condition that he, Giffard Main, would write the first and last chapters of the book. Jack Pecover said that at that point, he would have agreed to any condition to be given Main's blessing. Main helped carry the files related to the case down to the car, and Pecover drove away with the pieces of a story that would take almost twenty years to emerge as a book, and even then would remain an unfinished puzzle.

Over the course of several years, Jack Pecover saw Gifford Main a number of times, but said Main never berated him for his slow progress on the book. Before it was completed, Main died, and the ending was left to the author.

I had read *The Work of Justice* so many times, and it is such a complete compendium of the facts related to the Cook case, that I found myself with few specific questions for Jack Pecover. I found myself, too, feeling nervous, a little awkward throughout our conversation, and later I would discover that the notes I made were sketchy, and felt as though they had been directed by Mr. Pecover himself.

Mainly, I wanted to hear about his experience, about the years spent poring over records, talking with more than two hundred people, and about the image of Robert Raymond Cook that must surely have become a presence by the time he reached his conclusions. I was curious, too, about his conclusions, despite the disclaimer in the introduction to the book:

> My purpose is not to second-guess the jurors, they concluded what they did based on the evidence they heard. Nor is it to criticize those who investigated or those who tried the case – although some such criticism, occasionally severe, will be found here. Rather, it is simply to present the complexities of the case, allowing readers an outsider's view of how and why a man was sent to death by his community. Readers will be left to decide for themselves whether his guilt was clearly established. (*The Work of Justice* pg. xxiv)

Jack Pecover may have left it to the reader to decide if Cook was guilty beyond the shadow of a reasonable doubt, but it was clear that he himself had considerable doubt. And he made it clear almost as soon as we sat down with our coffee that he believed Robert Raymond Cook was innocent. So sure, that he and a journalist who had written one of the other books I had used in my research—Alan Hustak, author of *They were Hanged*—had seriously discussed pursuing a posthumous pardon for Cook. Why, I asked was he so sure? Chapter twenty-one, he said. Read chapter twenty-one again.

Chapter twenty-one is titled "The Second Newspaper." In it, Pecover does an analysis of the possible whereabouts of the copy of the Friday, June 26, 1959 *Calgary Herald* that was delivered to the front porch of the Cook residence at around 6:30 P.M. on that date, so the paperboy told Dave MacNaughton. So, too, was the Saturday, June 27, 1959 *Calgary Herald* delivered, but when the house was searched on Sunday, June 28, only the Saturday paper was on the floor where the paperboy had dropped it. Among the items listed as found in the grease pit in the garage with the bodies, were "three newspapers," only one of them identified as the issue of Wednesday, June 25. If one of the blood-soaked papers was Friday's, then the bodies—or at least the five bodies in the layers above those papers—were not placed in the pit until sometime after 6:00 P.M. on Friday. If the Friday paper was not among those in the pit, then someone removed it from the house between Friday at 6:30 P.M. and Sunday morning. Cook's whereabouts had been documented by the prosecution, almost to the hour from the time he arrived at the car dealership in Edmonton at about 8:00 AM Friday morning until he returned home to Stettler on Saturday evening. If it was he who removed the Friday paper from the house, he either took it with him on his joy-ride down Main Street after his quick stop at the house on Saturday but the paper was not found in his possession, or it was in that one hour that he pulled the Friday paper from beneath the Saturday issue, threw it into the pit, hauled the bodies out to the garage and scrubbed down the premises. Jack Pecover's view of the likelihood of that possibility:

> The clean-up alone invites awe. Seven maids with seven mops couldn't have accomplished in half a year what Cook carried off, along with everything else, in a little hour by way covering his tracks to seven bodies. (*The Work of Justice* pg. 359)

On a copy of the preliminary inquiry transcript, there is a note by Dave MacNaughton: "Where was Friday's paper?" and further notes, and there is a memorandum prepared by

MacNaughton to question the milkman as to whether he saw the Friday paper when he went into the porch on Saturday around noon, found no bottles, and concluded that the family was away. The question was not asked in the first trial, and by the second, the milkman had died. The paperboy told MacNaughton that he did not see the Friday paper when he delivered Saturday's, but he was not called as a witness.

Chapter Twenty-one talks as well about the discrepancies in the description of several other pieces of evidence:

> The salient characteristic of a good part of the physical evidence which played a part in the Cook trials was its ability to materialize or vanish at will as if some psychic dimension enconjured from the intoxicating philosophy of the New Age hovered over the case extruding some things and swallowing others.
> (*The Work of Justice* pg. 351)

Then who had murdered those seven people? Did he have a theory? Of course. But he would not be following that trail any further. And neither, I decided as I listened, would I. The one thing I knew for sure from the months of digging through information about the Cook family murders, was that I was no investigative journalist. Over and over again, I realized that I was leaving fragments of information behind. By the time I met Jack Pecover, I was desperate to be finished with the story, to return to fiction.

Ha! You think you're desperate? Was it really necessary to drag me along this bloody trail? Yes.

That's the one thing I know for sure.

Jack Pecover turned over every pebble he could find on the twisted path that led Robert Raymond Cook to the gallows, and in the process, he said, he felt he'd come to know young Cook very well indeed. He'd visited the Cook family grave in the Hanna cemetery, and the room where Robert Cook was hanged at the Fort Saskatchewan Gaol. He'd spoken with the two Lutheran ministers who, at the request of Lila Larson, Cook's foster sister, had given him spiritual counsel in the last month and attended his execution. In his epilogue, Pecover says:

> I have purposefully omitted a discussion of Cook's religious conversion being unqualified to offer any opinion—assuming one is called for—on its genuineness. As a non-believer, I saw myself as running the risk of dismissing it as a foxhole conversion without having the credentials to pronounce on it in any way. Being unqualified to have an opinion however rarely operates as a bar to having one, and mine is that it was genuine. If a man's last words are a call for forgiveness of those who have trespassed against him, as much as one can do is grant him the moment and stand back in silent and contemplative respect. (*The Work of Justice* pg. 435)

Unlike all of the other people I had interviewed who had begun by saying it was so long ago, it seemed to me that for Jack Pecover, the Cook case had not receded into any past. Cook was long dead, but the questions that the courtroom had failed to even ask remained unanswered. As for the book, he said there were chapters he would like to rewrite.

We talked, at the end of our conversation, about the political implications of Cook's death sentence and the subsequent efforts of his lawyers and Lila Larson to have his sentence commuted. The timing, however, was terminally bad for Cook.

Jack Pecover asked if any of my work was on the shelves of this bookstore we sat in. It was not, but I had a copy of my first novel in the car and gave it to him in meager exchange for the book that had given me the strong bones of the Cook story. I found myself, as I drove back to Calgary that day, feeling the weariness that I had sensed in Jack Pecover. I, too, wanted to be done.

Two weeks later, I had a letter from Pecover. He had read my novel and said that he believed Cook had now "fallen into good and eminently competent hands, which I welcome. He did not deserve the fate he received at our hands, and his shades now deserve the perceptiveness you'll bring to them." That confidence felt misplaced. I feared that I would end with even more questions than Pecover. I would have to rely on fiction, on Louise.

I am not reliable. And I am not a credible stand-in for Daisy. Everything you've found about Daisy makes her out to be the good step-mother. She never stopped trying. Doesn't Pecover mention that the prison incoming mail records are full of "Mrs. Ray Cook"? And those yellow socks and the red tie that she sent for his release. Surely she had a smile on her face when she chose those.

Is that what you imagine?

Ah, that's right. You want me to do the hard

part for you. Yes, I can imagine Daisy sending
packages to prison. To a boy, who's turned into
a man in a place that is beyond her imagining.

Daisy takes the cardboard backing out of the shirt to fold it in two, slide it into the cracker box—Ritz—the only small box she can find. She rolls the socks into a yellow ball, wraps tissue paper around the tie. Still there's room to spare. What else? Five cent pack of Kleenex, Juicy Fruit gum. Bar of soap? Are they allowed to use their own soap? She doesn't want to think about this, about where men shower. The steam, wet bodies slick with hair. Thick arms reaching for the soap, armpits dripping. Is the water hot or do they shiver in lukewarm? Are the towels thin and grey? Does he pull on the same sweat-stained shorts and undershirt, or clean clothes every day? No. Not every day. What is there to dirty outer garments in those locked rooms?

The sound of boys' voices in the yard. Now Daisy imagines Jerry, Chrissy, Patty in that shower room. Small, cold. Naked. She slaps the lid closed on the cracker box. Tapes it over and over around and around.

On the table, on top of the pile of letters home, the details of Bobby's impending release. Daisy skims through the pages. A letter from Bobby to Ray, July, 1955:

> Here's the way I figure it. Am going to be 18 in a few days and its just about time to smarten up. If I get into trouble again, don't write me or anything, just forget I am your son. Dad, Im really sincere this time. I mean everything I say for if I get into another jam, it will go on and on until I kick the bucket

in a pen or some dirty provincial jail, but if
things work out the way I plan, I'll be home
for Christmas.

Bobby did not make it home for Christmas. He was
barely released that time when he was picked up again and
charged with breaking and entering in Hanna. Two years in
the Saskatchewan Penitentiary. How long this time?

She hears the car, slam of the door, Ray's quiet voice
midst the shrill children. Where does Bobby fit in all this?
Nowhere. Tell him! Tell him we are going away!

Well, you seem to have taken over. You're going to write the ending for me? She sends the cheery socks and tie and then has Ray tell Bobby, when he arrives home, that they were really a farewell gift? That he and Daisy and the kids are leaving town, no forwarding address for errant sons?

Isn't that what happened? He found out they were moving away without him? And then he flew into a rage, some kind of dissociative state, killed them all, dumped the bodies, drove away, and when he came to all he remembered was that travel plan. They were gone to B.C. to find a service station, a father and son opportunity.

That's the theory. That's what people in town believed, if they believed he did it.

Why would anyone believe anything he said to the contrary? He was a liar. He was wearing the yellow socks when he was arrested. That red tie, we both know, ended up under the mattress, "blood spattered." So much for Daisy's gift.

The Boy

As soon as Louise turns the corner, off the main drag and onto their own tree-lined street, she wants to drive right past the house and out the other side of town, straight to the farm. Too late. Jake has spotted the police car as well.

He groans, sits up straighter in the passenger seat. "Now what?" The lines around his mouth and between his eyes, etched even deeper after three days in hospital, look like scars against the pallor of his skin.

"Whatever it is this time," Louise says, "you're going in to bed. I'll handle it." Louise feels the back of her throat tighten against the sour tide rising from her gut. She's tried to ignore the burning in her chest these past few days, Jake's wounded heart eclipsing all other concerns. She's glad Jon and Lauren aren't home to welcome their dad. Phyllis offered to come in and wait with them, but Louise wanted time alone with Jake. She'd bring them to the farm if that was all right, she told Phyllis. And come pick them up after their dad was settled at home.

Against Jake's protests, against the assurances of the two RCMP officers that they have just a few questions, Louise puts her arm around her husband's waist and glides him through the door and onto the sofa before she goes back onto the front step to invite the two men into the kitchen. There, she leaves the door open so that Jake can hear the conversation but not engage. No matter what they have to say, he will need to know, but she wants him sitting down, and she wants to provide the answers. When the questions begin she's gladder still that her children are innocently soaring on the swing in Phyllis's garden.

Alice has been robbed and assaulted. She is barely conscious in a hospital bed, unable to offer any clues as to who forced their way into her house on Sunday night, beat an old woman in her nightgown, and made off with a paltry few dollars from her purse. Alice's daughter and grandson found her on the kitchen floor.

"The daughter says she can't imagine anyone wanting to hurt her mother, and there's nobody in their lives who'd take advantage of an elderly woman all alone. But the grandson informs us there is a person of interest. Can you tell us about your son's connection to Mrs. Kelly?"

No doubt Alice's grandson—that successful young man who bought a new truck from Jake—has remembered the car salesman's jailbird son for whom his grandmother seemed to have a soft spot. He may have remembered, too, that his grandma went to Bowden with the father to visit the guy. That she talked about what a poor lost little boy Danny had been, his mother dying, father remarrying, the new kids grabbing the attention.

Before Louise can answer, she hears the thump of Jake's feet, and he is off the sofa, the effort of the walk to the kitchen enough to leave him leaning on the door frame.

"Jake! For goodness sake go back and lie down. I'll handle this."

"Now, Lou." Jake looks like he's pulling up every molecule of energy in his slumped body just to speak. "I think I should just tell these men what they need to know and get it over with."

"No." She takes his arm and this time steers him slowly down the hall, into the bedroom and closes the door. That he offers no more protest, just turns on his side on the bed and waves her away makes her as sad as anything that has happened in the six years they've been married.

When she returns to the kitchen, she motions to the two men to sit down, offers to make coffee but they politely decline. She tells them she's going to make it anyway, her husband needs a cup of strong coffee. She needs Jake in the kitchen with his coffee mug in his hand as soon as she can get rid of these two.

They look at one another, nod and sit down at the table while she measures coffee into the basket, grounds spilling from the spoon because she cannot control her shaky hand. "You *are* Daniel Peter's mother?" one of them finally asks.

"Yes," she says. "The only one he's had since the real one died, so I'll have to do." She takes a deep breath. "You want to know his connection to Alice. We were neighbours. Danny and Alice were pals back when his mom was still alive. The year I met them, Dan spent part of his Christmas money on a box of chocolates for Alice without anyone telling him to buy her a gift. He was twelve years old." She looks back and forth at the two faces, neither of them obviously impressed with young Dan's generosity. "Alice went with my husband to visit Dan at Bowden a while back. Jake said Danny was so surprised and pleased to see her he looked as though he was going to cry." She's making this part up, but dares anyone to ask for proof. "Daniel did not hurt Alice. I am positive of this. Our son is a thief, but I know he would not lift a finger against that old woman." She can hear Jake's words coming out of her mouth, but for once, she believes them. She knows this is true. "Dan was here, at home on Sunday night."

Another glance passes between them. When did he arrive, they want to know, and how long did he stay? Now she has to admit that she didn't actually see Danny, just evidence that he'd been there. No, she has no idea what time he would have arrived, or how long he stayed. And no, she has no idea where he is now. No direct contact with him since he was released from Bowden. No familiarity with his "associates." Yes, should he come home she will be sure to call them. Yes, they can count on this. And yes, she is absolutely sure that her husband's health will not permit him to talk with them today. For a split-second, she thinks they are going to insist and she feels such a rage rising in her that she grips the edge of the table. Raging at Danny. Then they stand up so precisely in tune that she wouldn't be surprised if they turned smartly on their heels and galloped out of her kitchen.

When Louise takes coffee into the bedroom, Jake seems to be asleep. She is about to turn and tiptoe out of the room, when he lifts a hand and pulls himself up on the pillows. "He didn't hurt Alice. Did you tell them there is no way that Danny would lift a finger against that woman?"

She smiles and feels every muscle in her face tremble with the effort. Sits down on the edge of the bed and holds the cup out to him. His hand is steady, steadier than hers, when he takes it, raises it to his mouth. "God that tastes good after the slop in the hospital," he says. "You should have let me talk to them. I'm okay now."

"No," she says. She takes the cup from him, sets it on the bedside table and leans close to put her arms around him. "You didn't need to. I told them exactly those words." She pulls away so she can look into his eyes. "I believe it too, Jake. Dan might have robbed her, but he would not hurt her." Not intentionally, she thinks. This is not in him.

But now she has to tell Jake that Danny came home that night. Even though she's kept it to herself, not a word to Jon and Lauren, asked Phyllis not to mention this to Jake.

"Aw no. He finally comes home and I'm not here to tell him I'm so glad he made that choice."

Louise fights a sudden urge to pull away from Jake. As well as the smell of hospital still strong on his skin, his breath is foul. In his face, she can see that he is imagining the same thing that horrifies her—Alice, a cowering rag doll, a man with a blank face towering over her. But Louise finds herself imagining her own mother on a kitchen floor. Or her father. What if her dad were alive, and *someone* went to his house in desperate need of cash. Someone he knew well enough to have opened the door. No! The boy is a sneak and a liar and a thief. But not this.

The next day, Jake talks with Alice's daughter. He says she sounded wary on the phone, but relaxed enough, when he told her how fond he and Brenda had been of her mother, how worried he was now about his old neighbour, to tell him that Alice has recovered sufficiently to talk with the police. All she can tell them, though, is that the man who rang her doorbell late in the night was wearing a knitted mask over his face. He didn't speak, just pushed his way into the house, knocked her to the floor. Beyond that, she remembers nothing. Can Jake and Louise visit Alice? A long pause. Perhaps in a week or so, give her time to rest. She won't be going home. Arrangements are being made to transfer Alice to an assisted living facility. Surprisingly, the daughter says, her mother is offering only token resistance.

The day they visit, they find Alice in a wheelchair in a small lounge, watching television.

"I can walk," she says, "but they insist on wheeling me down here. They say I'm too brave for my own good, even though I promise them I won't try to march out of here if they'd just give me my shoes." She waggles a slipper-clad foot at them. "Ha!"

Alice looks better than Louise expected. Apart from purple bruises beginning to yellow on her nose and forehead and black stitch marks in a gash at her hairline, she seems as steady and sharp-eyed as always. She purses her lips, and stares at Jake with one eye squinted shut. "You look like you've had a rougher time than me," she says.

Jake pulls up two chairs, and he and Louise sit facing Alice. "Getting better," he says. "I had a bit of a cardiac upset the same day you had your…"

How to describe something Daniel is still suspected of committing even though Alice has doggedly refused to implicate him.

"But I'll be good to go again in no time," Jake says. "I'm taking a month off work to lie around the house and drive Louise nuts."

"Still no sign of Danny?" the old woman asks. Louise can't read her face, something there besides concern for either Jake or his son. Jake shakes his head. Alice seems to be working her jaw, rearranging dentures. She shifts in the chair as though she's suddenly less comfortable than she's led them to believe. "Well for what it's worth," she says, "I've seen a few bad apples in my time, even had a brother who turned a little rotten, and I don't think Danny's the bottom of that barrel. But you, you look like death on the back burner, and the best you can do is just try not to think about that boy for a while, Jake." She winces and leans sideways slightly. "Maybe it's time to make some tough choices for your own sake. That's all I've got to say."

Then, she says she's tired, nothing serious, just in need of a nap before her grandson shows up. Maybe better if they leave before he gets here.

At the car, Jake insists on driving. "I'm not going to

behave like an invalid, Louise. I feel a lot better now that I've seen Alice. She didn't look too bad at all, don't you think?"

No, Alice doesn't look as damaged as Louise expected, but she's sure that neither she nor Jake can really imagine the terror of that night.

"Anything else we need to do before we head home?" Jake asks, but when Louise shakes her head, he pulls into the donut shop, parks, and opens his door. "Stay here," he says, "I'm going to get us some coffee."

He's back in a few minutes with two large coffees, an apple fritter, a French cruller, and a box of mini-donuts. He hands the tray through her window, and when he gets into the car, he slides his seat back. He taps the box. "I figured we'd better take something home to the kids if we're going to have a treat."

A treat? "Jake, apart from nutrition and the fact that I'm trying so hard to watch my weight, I don't even like donuts. And the kids would never know."

He shrugs, grins at her and for a moment looks like the man she met in a bar years ago. "I guess I'll have to eat both of these. And don't you dare give me the cholesterol lecture today. I need this sugar, Lou."

As he bites into the fritter, flakes of icing dislodge and sift down onto his lap. "It would have been a lot to easier to eat this inside," she says. She struggles with the lid on the coffee, finally gives up and sips from the plastic rim. The coffee will not sit well. Already, she can taste the backwash of acid. When they get home, she'll call for a doctor's appointment. Just a check-up is all she needs, she's sure, but it's suddenly imperative that she stay well. What if something were to happen to her? Who would look after Jon and Lauren? The obvious answer is Jake, but with a jolt that almost makes her gasp aloud, Louise feels Jake's impermanence beside her. She wants to grab him and wrap her arms around him, but instead she sits quietly and watches him eat a donut.

After he's polished off both the fritter and the cruller in no more than three bites each, Jake grabs a napkin, wipes his lips and hands. "I wanted privacy. I don't even want strangers to hear me talking about Dan." He wriggles the lid off his cup, sets it in the cup holder and holds out his hand for hers. "It's downright dangerous trying to drink hot coffee from a spout. Here. Go careful." After two long slurps, he looks at her over the rim of his cup, his thick brows clamping down over eyes still veined with pink, baggy with fatigue. "What Alice said in there, Lou, about not letting him come home again, even if he shows up, is that what you think would be best too?"

Louise swallows. She wishes she had peppermints in the bag, the way her mother always carried them, so that she could suck away the bitterness in her mouth. "You mean turn him away? Are you sure that's what she was saying?" A sharp image springs to her mind, she and Jake barring the door, Daniel unkempt and angry on the step, pleading with his dad. "Surely you don't think I'd ask you to turn him away."

Jake still has a dusting of icing sugar around his lips. "How many chances have we given him? How many do I owe him? He's an embarrassment, Lou. And I can't help wondering about Alice ...God, if he's responsible ...I don't know what I'd do to him if he was standing in front of me."

"I don't think so, Jake. Like I told the police, I'm sure he was in the house that night likely even before I got home and he stayed until it was light. Alice said it was dark when she opened the door."

"And that doesn't make me sick to my stomach, him creeping around the house in the dark while you and the kids were sleeping?"

"Jake, this is Danny we're talking about."

"No, it's not," he says. "This isn't the kid I raised, this is some man who grew out of that one and I feel like I don't know him anymore." He stares straight ahead through the windshield, his lips grey, frost-tinged. "I'll do whatever you want, Lou, to make sure you and the kids don't have to stand in the path of all the shit he kicks up."

Louise rolls down her window on the pretence of clearing the muggy smell of coffee, but really it is Jake's breath puffing out all those words that makes her stomach churn. The day is overcast, not a hint of breeze. She stirs the air outside the car with her hand, trying to create a freshening current. When she looks back at Jake, he's picking at the rim of the cup. "Just once I'd like to win," he mutters.

"We can't turn him away, Jake." She takes a deep breath. "In fact, I think that would be the very worst thing we could do. You're the only sure thing he has, and if you take that away from him, what does he have left?"

A long ragged breath and then he grabs her hands. "Thank you," he says, before he starts the car. In the half hour drive home, there is nothing more to say.

Jon's voice, loud and then even louder, "Mom, Mom, Mom," now he's tugging on the pillow. Louise drags herself awake. She automatically moves over, makes room for her son. Another nightmare.

"No. Come," he says, "I heard this awful noise. In the bathroom."

Louise sits up, but knows without turning or patting

the sheet behind her that Jake is not in bed with her. She races down the hall ahead of Jon. "Bring me the phone," she shouts, even before she opens the bathroom door. Even when she sees Jake on the floor, the absolute stillness of him, she shouts again for the phone. Get help.

If she hadn't been so sound asleep. You were exhausted, and understandably so, Phyllis tells her. Jake was probably careful not to wake you when he got up to go to the bathroom. If she had heard him cry out, if she'd gotten to him more quickly. Probably a massive coronary, the emergency room nurse tells her, nothing she could have done to save him. If she hadn't let him eat that donut. She looks at Phyllis and the two of them break into guffaws that become barks of laughter and then sobs.

Oh.

I'm sorry.

Roads Back

After the interview with Jack Pecover, I felt that I had done as much gathering as I needed. All of his files, he'd told me, had been donated to the Stettler Public Library, and if they needed his permission he would ask them to grant me access. As it turned out, the files had been accessible enough to the public that some items had gone missing and out of concern for preserving the archives, all of the material had been moved to the Stettler Museum. The curator of the museum told me that I could examine whatever I needed to see and read, but to keep in mind that these were artifacts, and must be treated as such. I imagined donning white gloves and holding documents with my fingertips. There would be no photocopying, no borrowing of material. My friend, Shirley, agreed to come along to Stettler, she, still puzzled by my obsession with the Cooks and curious, too, about this town with the bloody history.

> *Wait a minute. Wasn't that an awfully abrupt ending to my story?*

Why do you assume that's the ending?

> *Well even if it's not, that's all the words you're going to spend on Jake's dying? Jake is dead, right?*

That is correct.

> *Short shrift! Two paragraphs?*

In emotion-charged scenes, sometimes what's

left unsaid is more powerful than trying to find words.

And…?

Yes. And I'm finding it hard to write this ending.

Not just the ending to my story. You're struggling with the whole of it. That's why it's taken five years. What are you afraid of?

Just a minute here. Let me finish writing this chapter, and then I'll try to answer that question once and for all.

The Stettler Museum is an historic village with ten buildings including a courthouse. The September day I chose to scan the evidence Pecover had examined in the writing of his book was again unseasonably cold and wet—the parking lot at the museum site almost empty.

In the reception office, a small group of people sat around a table behind the counter drinking coffee, eating donuts. They were volunteers, the director told me, when she introduced me as someone interested in the history of the Cook murders. As always, they remembered. Bobby Cook was a mean child, one of the women said, beating up on everyone else, the children, even some of the adults afraid of him. But, no, someone else piped up, I wasn't afraid of him, and he was always kind to the girls, it was just the other boys he picked fights with. I was anxious to get to the archives, not inclined to hear any more divided opinions on Cook's innocence, and I had decided that I was no journalist eager to follow every lead, so I left them to their coffee and their own re-hashing of the crime. A summer student was sent to sit with us in the old courthouse while I examined the archives, to supervise my handling of them, safeguard against theft, I presumed. The building was unheated, and Shirley and I shivered in our thin fall jackets. Behind the bench, a mannequin who looked like a clothing store dummy from the boys' department was clad in judicial robes which the curator told me later had been donated by Dave MacNaughton. We sat at a table at the front of the courtroom where decades of lawyers and accused must have made their cases to the bench. The supervising student sat on the other side of the railing in the spectator seats, reading. First, though, she used a key to open the glass cabinet at the front of the room into which the files had been crammed. Folders and folders and folders of court transcripts, letters, newspaper clippings, envelopes of crime scene photos, the familiar photos of the family and the white bungalow all crammed into a piece of furniture that would have been no obstacle to either theft or natural disaster. I did not need white gloves to handle the disorganized mass of material that literally fell off the shelves when the doors slid open, but I did handle all of the pages, and the pictures with the care their aged state deserved.

So much of the material was familiar; the same newspaper stories, transcripts from which I had read the salient bits in Pecover's book. I looked for new information, missing pieces to my own wonky construction, and found myself wandering off on tangents.

I pulled photos out of an envelope. Crime scene; the familiar newspaper photos, pictures of every room in the house, every piece of evidence, different stages of the removal of the bodies from the pit. Everything sharper, more real. Cowboy scenes on the wallpaper in the boys' bedroom, a plastic tablecloth on the kitchen table, worn upholstery on the sofa in the living room. Seven pairs of shoes. Real photos of a real home.

In another envelope, a scrap of fabric from the blue suit tailored at Saskatchewan Penitentiary for Cook's release, found bloodied under the mattress in the master bedroom, a cuff from the mysterious white shirt to which ownership was never ascribed, a swatch of the wallpaper someone had scrubbed in an attempt to remove the spatters of blood. Real pieces in my hand.

Shirley leafed through clippings, letters, pausing now and again to slide something across the table to me. How sad, how horrible, the two of us sighed and murmured in that icy cold room.

Too much to copy, so much I'd already seen or read about in one form or another. We adjourned, finally, made our way to a warm restaurant on Main Street and watched the ebb and flow of the town around us. If I'd walked down the street, stopping people and asking about the Cook murders, I was sure I would find another dozen people with a dozen similar versions of what happened in the house on 52nd Street.

When we went back to the old court room it was even colder, and for three hours I read into my tape recorder: transcripts of interviews, letters and telegrams. I felt guilty, making the young student sit in that icy room, but she, at least, was dressed in toque and heavy jacket, turning the pages of her book with mittened fingers.

Now, the voice of Robert Raymond Cook seemed to fly loud and clear off the pages. From the cross examination in the first trial:

Q: A thing that gives me some pause – why do you suppose Constable Bell would say he saw two suitcases and a metal box in the truck of your car at 4:30 in Camrose if they weren't there.

A: Well Sir, I have done a little bit of thinking about that myself and the only conclusion I could come to he didn't mention it at the preliminary until he found out there were suitcases in it when I was picked up. I can't state for sure, but I think he's been reading too many newspapers.

Here, finally, in a psychiatric report from an interview at Fort Saskatchewan Provincial Gaol, March 15, 1960, Robert Cook responds to questions about his siblings:

Yes they all got wiped out, Gerry nine years old, Patty eight, Chris seven, Kathy five, Linda three. Yes, I knew them all except Linda I didn't know her very well she was so little and she didn't know me one night when I was home before the murder. Yes real cute, that's all. I have pictures of them. They're real cute kids. It's hard to figure out how anyone could have done that only one person I know.

There was a break in the interview after which the psychiatrist noted:

On prisoner's return he had snapshots, several including the whole family, father, mother and stepsiblings. Seemed to take normal pride in showing me them and in particular in speaking about the kids and his father. He himself was not included in any of the groups and possibly he had taken the snaps.

No, more likely that Robert Cook was in prison when the photos were taken. During the short lives of the young Cook children, Robert was simply not part of family life.

The interviewer asked Cook if he read. He replied that he liked historical novels, stories like *Ben Hur.* He said he didn't read mysteries although he had read *The Anatomy of a Murder.* For now, he thought he had enough mystery on his own hands.

Here was the handwritten note from Cook to Dave MacNaughton pleading to be allowed to attend the funerals, and here was MacNaughton's sincerely regretful reply.

Here was the letter from Dr. J. M. Byers of Ponoka, after Cook's "elopement," declaring him "fit to stand trial."

The letters were filed chronologically and as I read through Cook's many notes and telegrams to Giffard Main and Dave MacNaughton, I found myself growing as tense as if I didn't know the outcome of the story. Over and over again, Cook analyzed the evidence, offered advice, tried to come up with new information. When Main suffered a heart attack just before the second trial, his partner, Frank Dunne, took over and it was clear from the letters that followed that neither Cook, nor his former foster sister, Lila Larson, felt comfortable with the replacement. Lila became a frequent visitor to Fort Saskatchewan, and in a letter to Main just before the Appeal in March 1960 said she was "anxiously waiting. May God help you see that justice is done."

Mrs. William Hanson from Streamstown, Alberta sent cigarettes and books, small amounts of cash and corresponded with both Cook and the warden of Fort Saskatchewan, finally sending a plea to the Prime Minister's office. The final note in her communications was a letter to her from the warden, returning her money order of two dollars that had arrived on November 17, 1959, "too late to be cashed."

Nora Gall, Astrologer, Calgary, Alberta had written to Cook's lawyers offering to plot Cook's horoscope. No one is this country, she wrote, afforded astrology the proper respect, and she was sure she could shed light on Cook's personality if someone would please provide the dates she required.

Mrs. C. Parraton wrote to Main saying she did not know the family at all but had been keeping up with the hearings. And ended with a plea: "Please do not hang him. I am a mother and I have a son."

There were letters from amateur sleuths who were sifting the evidence, discussing it in the community, speculating on the testimony of some of their own. Others advising divine intervention as Cook's only hope: "Do not know if your man is guilty or innocent but has your man asked for the help of God?"

So much material, Shirley and I passing papers back and forth across the table. I envisioned coming back again, when I could read and record without hunching into my coat.

On October 11, 1960, Lila Larson wrote to Dave MacNaughton to say that she had had a half hour visit with Bob Cook and she feared he had lost faith. An article in the *Edmonton Journal* about his lost appeal mentioned three other people who had been successful in their appeals and ultimately acquitted. Bob wondered, Lila said "if there is another sets of laws for him."

In the final chapter, Pecover's book devotes three pages to the re-appearance in Cook's life of the Larson family, former foster parents, and in particular to their daughter, Lila. The Larsons remained steadfast in their belief that the boy they had known could not have committed this crime. In the Stettler museum, Lila Larson's handwritten letters to MacNaughton, Main, the Prime Minister, the Governor General, the Solicitor General, the Premier of Alberta finally give real voice to someone with a personal connection to Robert Raymond Cook. MacNaughton, Main, and Dunne worked tirelessly on his behalf. Among the documents, there is an invoice from a firm of lawyers in Ottawa, requesting payment of fees in the amount of $77.85 for acting on Cook's behalf in the Federal Court of Appeal. As laughably small as that fee seems by today's standards, the Alberta lawyers likely received even less for their efforts. But theirs was a professional involvement, in spite of the obvious emotional nerves struck by the young Cook's plight.

There were strict rules around access to death cells in 1959: prison officials, chaplains, immediate family, defense counsel, senior police officers if there was good reason. Lila Larson put her request to visit to Giffard Main. She was directed to the Warden, who asked, "How good is your stomach?" and when she replied that yes, this would bother her, but she was not going to let it show, he in turn sent her to the Sheriff, whose responsibility it was to plan the details of the execution. A responsibility, Lila Larson told Jack Pecover, that he said he "hated." Pecover speculates that the Sheriff may have seen Lila Larson's request as an opportunity to "alleviate the agony of a condemned man." Whatever the Sheriff's motivation, Lila Larson was given the written permission she required.

Meanwhile, efforts on Cook's behalf continued. In the files, there is a copy of a letter dated Oct. 26, 1960, "Personal and Confidential" to the Rt. Hon. John Diefenbaker from Terence Nugent MP For Edmonton Strathcona:

> As you are no doubt well aware the above-named is now under sentence of death for the murder of his father with execution scheduled for the fifteenth of November. I am writing to you personally as one lawyer to another to stress one factor of this case. On Cook's first trial, my senior partner, Giffard Main, defended Cook and took the appeal. Giffard is certainly one of Alberta's outstanding lawyers if not the top one in his field with experience in many murder trials…both of my partners are very competent, sound and realistic barristers, both stress the entire circumstantial nature of the evidence in this case and both are very uneasy about the conviction. Each one of my partners has earnestly impressed on me that they have a very real doubt as to Cook's guilt. Each feels we may hang an innocent man here. For this reason, because of their real fear in this regard I ask that this sentence be commuted.

There is no copy of a reply from John Diefenbaker, but Pecover's book mentions that prior to Cook, thirty-two death sentences came before Diefenbaker's cabinet for review and twenty-six of these men on death row were granted a commutation of their sentence to life imprisonment. In this, Pecover says, Diefenbaker "exhibited political courage of a high order since his party's natural constituency knew the death penalty was the only effective deterrent to murder and the only fitting punishment for those murderers who were undeterred." The odds, then, should have been in Cook's favour, but the commutation of the sentence of a Calgary man, Ronald McCorqudale, convicted of killing a child, brought such outrage just prior to the request on Cook's behalf that "political courage" must have faltered at the prospect of "political suicide." Ironically, McCorqudale committed suicide early into his life sentence.

A telegram to Dave MacNaughton on November 14, 1960:

> Governor General in Council will not interfere with death sentence passed upon Robert Raymond Cook tried for murder in Edmonton, Alberta.

> It was signed by P.D. McDonald, Assistant Deputy Minister of Justice

At the back of this file there are some exchanges of correspondence between Dave MacNaughton and the Warden of Fort Saskatchewan gaol regarding the remaining personal effects of "the late Mr. Cook."

And a letter from Frank Dunne to The Right Honourable John Diefenbaker, dated November 18, 1960 (three days after Robert Raymond Cook was executed):

> Re: Robert Raymond Cook

> May I thank you sincerely for your courtesy

and attention to the above matter and for your courtesy to me on the telephone. This letter is to request you to give consideration to amending the criminal code to eliminate capital punishment. To my partner, Mr. Giffard Main Q.C., and myself, both of whom defended Cook, the guilt of the accused remains a matter of very serious doubt. Our suggestion is that the section of the criminal code that allows capital punishment should be eliminated or amended as cases like this which are based on purely circumstantial evidence will always be a matter of doubt and uncertainty. May I further suggest that capital punishment is a survival of the barbarism of the eighteenth century and should be abolished as it serves no useful purpose. Would you be good enough to give this consideration as I realize that you personally have had much experience in the field of criminal law.

On May 7, 1964, Main, Dunne, Nugent, and the other partners in the firm, Forbes and Babie, sent a similar letter to The Right Honourable Lester B. Pearson, whose Liberals had defeated Diefenbaker's Conservatives the year before.

In 1966, Bill C-168 was passed limiting the death penalty to the killing of on-duty police officers and prison guards. On July 14, 1976, under the Liberal government led by Prime Minister Pierre Trudeau, Bill C-84 was passed abolishing capital punishment from the Criminal Code.

We filed the letters and clippings neatly in their folders and took care to place them on the shelves of the cabinet so that the doors would close easily, the lock slid securely into place. It would be interesting, Shirley said, on our way out of the frigid courthouse, to see if there was evidence of anyone else having poked through these souvenirs when I came back again.

I shook my head. I think I may be done.

Oh no you're not! You promised just a few pages ago that you'd finally talk about what's scaring you.

Everything about this story scares me. From the very beginning I've been afraid to come to the page each time I sit down.

Why didn't you walk away? You don't have a contract with anyone. And why so scary? It happened fifty years ago. Robert Raymond Cook is dead, no threat to anyone.

That's the thing. From what I've found, he never really was a threat, except to people who forgot to lock their cars. He was just a punk, and his family was an ordinary family.

Exactly. And you write about ordinary people. They're your stock- in-trade.

They are indeed, but my people never end up as decomposing bodies in a grease pit.

Bad things happen to people.

Yes, I know that. And bad things happen at the hands of people close to them. But…

There's always a reason? Something that could have prevented a tragedy? Is that what you've been looking for?

Yes.

Did you find it?

No. Not for the Cooks. Because their story was finished when I began. No redemption.

The Boy

Phyllis and Paul broke the news of Jake's death to Daniel. They had the local RCMP do a search, and when they found him in the Winnipeg Remand Centre awaiting trial for the armed robbery of a liquor store, the two of them flew to Winnipeg. They hoped to arrange for Danny to be given an escorted leave to attend the funeral, but he wouldn't apply. He knew of someone, he said, who'd gone to his little brother's funeral in prison clothes and handcuffs with an escort of two guards. No thanks.

When they came back and told Louise he wouldn't be coming, she felt such a deep wrench of sadness for Daniel, that young boy on whom Jake had never given up, that she vowed she'd visit him. As soon as the funeral was over, as soon as she could bear to leave the children for two days, she would ask Paul to come with her and she would go. But she never did. Jake died in January, and when August was suddenly there again, and the fog around her lifted, she sent a birthday card in care of the federal prison at Stony Mountain. It was returned with a note that said Daniel had been discharged in July. She never told Paul and Phyllis, because she was sure they would try to find him, and ashamed though it made her, she didn't have energy for any more than the mailing of that card.

Now, four years later, August again, and Louise has a feeling Dan will turn up. It's time.

So far as she knows, no one else in Jake's family has made any effort to track Dan, and only twice has Phyllis mentioned hearing from him—once by way of a letter and then about a year later, by an out-of-province phone call. If Louise asked for details, Phyllis would probably provide them, but it's too hard. Louise hasn't wanted to know of Danny's troubles, because if she did, she would have to reach out. Have him back in their lives, hers and Jon's and Lauren's.

Then last year, two days before Jon's birthday, a package arrived in the mail; skater shoes, the exact brand Louise had refused to buy for her son because of the astronomical price. How could Dan have known so accurately, she asked Phyllis, what his brother was yearning for, and the size? The shoes were a perfect fit. Phyllis blushed.

"I told him," she said. "He phoned a couple of months ago and asked me what I thought he should send. He couldn't remember how old Jon was, but he said he wanted to buy something that was just right. So I asked Jon what he had on his wish list. Bless his small heart, he told me about the shoes, but he told me I shouldn't even consider buying them—he thought I was fishing for ideas myself, I guess—because they were way too much money."

When they were cleaning up after Jon's party, Lauren picked up the card that came with the shoes and asked, "Who's Dan, again?"

"He's our brother, you twit!" Jon shouted. "And he's way cool!"

Louise knew from the gift that it was only a matter of time.

Now both of the kids' birthdays have passed, and Louise has begun to relax. Not so much, though, that she isn't aware that today is August twenty-fifth, Danny's own birthday.

Late in the afternoon, she goes into the living room to open the windows for the breeze that's sprung up and there he is, standing at the end of the sidewalk. He has his back to the house, studying the street. As though there's more of interest or concern behind him than ahead? Louise peeks through the curtains until he turns and walks to the front door. He pauses before he knocks, and she's startled to see a smile she'd all but forgotten. When she first knew Danny, she would sometime catch him unawares, sitting on his bike in the backyard, or alighting from the skateboard at the end of the sidewalk, almost trancelike. A smile that played across his face like that of a child asleep, lost in a happy dream. She taps on the window, waves, and then goes to open the door. The smile is gone, his face carefully blank.

"I had a feeling you'd come today," she says. She holds the door wide. "Happy birthday."

He looks startled. "I didn't think you'd remember."

She fixes him in her sternest teacher look. "I baked enough cakes for you, Daniel Peters, that you should never have doubted me." Then without hesitation, she steps forward, and puts her arms around him. But only for a few seconds, then she lets her arms fall. His cotton shirt feels stiffly new. She's sure she recognizes the faint smell clinging to him. Jake described the smell of the jail as nothing more than layers and layers of paint trying to hide the stink of too many men in one place.

He stands there in the sunshine, blinking at her. "Louise," he says, as though having to remind himself on whose door he's knocked. "So I guess I should have phoned and let you know I was coming. I asked Aunty Phyllis to tell you, but she said I should do it myself."

So this is why Phyllis called two days ago and invited Jon and Lauren to come out for the weekend. And didn't warn Louise because she knew that too much time to prepare would only make things worse? She was right about that. If she'd had time to think, Louise would have conjured an image of Danny that was more mug shot than portrait, more like the photos in those scrapbooks about Robert Raymond Cook that she'd thrown away not long ago because she was afraid Jon or Lauren might someday stumble across them. The Daniel standing in front of her bears such a strong resemblance to his dad that she can't stop staring at him. Even his eyes have become Jake's. He looks back at her with a level, slightly quizzical look. There doesn't seem to be anything of the sly boy left in his face. But then Daniel is no longer a boy. He is twenty-five years old today.

"Now that I'm here," he says finally, "aren't you going to invite me in? You could offer me some lunch." He glances at his bare wrist. "Oops, wonder where that went. But I'm sure it must be lunch time."

Louise leads the way to the kitchen, Dan as light as a cat behind her in his running shoes. For the short while he lived here, she had him trained to take his shoes off at the door, but it's unlikely any of the places he's been since had a basket of knitted slippers at the door.

She fills the coffee pot, measures grounds into the basket, while he asks about the kids. She's self-consciously aware of her bare legs below the pair of baggy shorts she's wearing.

"They're at the farm for a couple of days," she says. "They love it out there." She turns to look at him. He shrugs, his own resistance to visits to Phyllis and Paul's likely forgotten. He seems to be scanning the kitchen, disoriented by the changes probably, and there are many. When her mother died two years ago, Louise came into enough money to finally redo the kitchen and the bathroom. By then she'd decided against moving back to the city, or rather Jon and

Lauren had out-voted her. "Do you like the new cupboards?" she asks. "I've done a bit of renovating."

"Nice," he says. "Guess you plan on staying here a while then."

She takes a can of salmon out of the cupboard, struggles with the can opener for a minute, and then he comes to stand beside her, takes it out of her hand. "Christ, Louise, I'll buy you a new one for Christmas. I think this one belonged to my granny before my mom had it." She's forgotten how many of the things in the kitchen were Brenda's. Jake wanted to throw away all of the old utensils, his and hers, and start anew, but Louise was too practical.

She spreads salmon on two sandwiches, remembers that Dan loved dill pickles and puts a whole one on his plate. Sits down at the table with him. He devours a half sandwich in two bites, shoves in the second piece before he can possibly have swallowed. She fixes her eyes on her coffee cup. Doesn't want him to know that she's noticed either the hunger or the lack of manners.

He gobbles the other sandwich as fast as the first, clears his throat. "That was great, Louise. You always were a good cook."

"Hardly," she says. "Anyone can make a sandwich. Why do you think your dad took over on weekends?" He can't have forgotten all those pot roasts and chickens, mashed potatoes, peas and carrots. Occasionally, Louise will prepare such a Sunday dinner when she's missing Jake unbearably, and always Jon says, "Just like Daddy used to make."

"Still have a sweet tooth?" Louise asks. "I think there's a banana loaf in the freezer."

"Nah, don't bother. But I sure wouldn't mind another sandwich. You don't have to fight with the can opener again.

Cheese or peanut butter would be fine." He stands up. "Hey, why don't I just make it myself?"

Because, she wants to say, I don't want you acting like you live here. When she jumps up and wrestles the jar of peanut butter from his hands, he returns to his chair.

Bravely, she takes a run at the questions that need answering. "You've been inside again, haven't you?"

He grimaces. "Yeah. Six months."

"For?"

"Possession of stolen goods."

She slumps against the counter. "Do you ever think about the promise you made to your dad the last time you saw him, Dan? You were sitting right there at the table with Jake across from you and you swore that you were finally going to make it." Oh, she hates talking to him like this. He's been in the house less than half an hour and she's ragging at him again the way she did the day he stormed out and said he wasn't coming back. She holds up her hand. "Just a minute. You don't have to answer that. Forget I even said it."

He looks straight into her eyes. "No, I probably owe you an answer. For him. Christ, Louise! I tried. I've been clean for months. I didn't steal the stuff, and how the fuck was I supposed to know it was hot?"

For years he didn't swear or use coarse language in front of them. But now he seems to have dropped any pretence of refinement. All right. If he wants to talk about it, they will talk. "Daniel Jacob Peters! You've been a thief so long you must surely have a second sense."

He laughs. He put his head back and laughs until he's gasping. "Oh that's rich," he says finally. "Problem is I'm a stupid thief. That's why I've been in the pen more than out." He rubs his face with his hands. "But I think I might finally have gotten a little smarter. This last time I did the school work. I passed grade ten. I'm going to learn welding. A friend of Uncle Paul's has a shop in Edmonton and he said he'd take me on."

Louise closes her eyes. She fears that when she opens them again she will weep. She turns back to the counter and slowly spreads peanut butter on two pieces of bread, slices a banana and layers it on top, carefully aligns the top slices of bread.

"You don't have to cut those up. We're not having a tea party here, eh?"

"I feel like we should have a party of some sort. It is your birthday, after all, and your dad," the words catch in her throat, "you know how pleased he'd have been to have you back."

He takes the plate she hands him, leans back in the chair. "Phyllis said he would probably rest easy up there now, knowing I was finally going to straighten out."

Louise sits down, and stares at him. "Is that what you believe?" He stares back, looking for a minute like the defiant young Danny. "Because I don't, you know. And your dad didn't either. He told me he was sure that when it's over, it's over, so we do the best we can with what we've got."

"You're saying it doesn't matter what I do now, because I let him down when he was alive?"

She shakes her head slowly. "Not at all. I'm saying you can honour his memory by doing the things that would have made him proud. And if that's what it takes to stay out of trouble, then do it."

He shoves the sandwich away. "You don't think I can do it. You never thought I was worth anything. Dad told me you were afraid of me."

She feels her hand fly up to her throat. "When did he tell you that?"

"The last time I came home. I asked him why you were so uptight, and he said you were afraid I was going to hurt you and the kids." His lip curls. "Damn it, Louise, I'm not dangerous. I never wanted to hurt any of you. After he died I knew you wouldn't want me around. That's part of why I didn't bother coming to the funeral. I figured it was too late for him, and I'd just be an embarrassment, sitting there with my escorts beside me. That's why I haven't come back since."

Can she deny that she's been relieved all these years? After she kissed Jake's cold cheek for the last time and walked out of the hospital, right after she wondered how on earth they would survive, she and the children, the next thing she'd wondered was how she could widow herself from her stepson.

"I should have come to see you," she says. "I'm sorry. But I couldn't. I was afraid, yes, I was. Afraid of prisons and the people in them and afraid that you'd become one of them."

"So are you still afraid of me?"

She takes a long time. She wants to tell the truth. "I think I am," she says. "But not so much as before, and if . . ." She stops short of putting the onus back on him. If you stay out of trouble, if you show me you can be trusted, if you've stopped telling lies. How could that help him? She smiles. She can hear Jake's voice. How could that help him? Think about it, Louise.

"Yeah, well." Danny pushes away from the table. "I guess I'll be going."

"Where?"

"Back to Edmonton. Don't worry. I'm not going out to the farm. I won't hurt the kids."

"Danny, don't." She stands too and puts her hand on his sleeve. "I know you won't hurt them. But how will you get back to the city?"

"Same way I got here. I'll hitch. Farmers are good about picking you up." He pulls away and turns to leave, but stops suddenly. "I want to go to the cemetery sometime. Paul said Dad's buried in the city, beside my mom. Can you write down how I find them?" He looks toward the phone desk where they always kept paper and pens.

"Give me a minute," Louise says. "I'll just change my clothes and drive you in. We'll go to the cemetery."

Mount Pleasant Cemetery is neither a mountain nor particularly pleasant in Louise's opinion. Apparently it is the highest point in this quadrant of the city, giving an exceptional view from the graves. Those were the exact words of someone in the City of Edmonton's cemetery department when Louise idly questioned the name the day she came with Paul to make the burial arrangements. She would have walked away, had Jake cremated and spread out in the fields instead, but this is where Brenda was buried, and Jake owned a plot next to her. And his family needed to bury him in their own way.

Danny has been silent through the drive. Louise finally gave up asking mundane questions. She parks the car at the entrance gate and she and Danny climb the long hill to the farthest corner of the graveyard. "I think it's about three rows from the fence," she says. "I haven't been here in a while," she starts to say, and then she takes a deep breath. "Actually, I haven't been back at all. My mom and dad's graves are on the other side of the hill, and I meant to walk over here after we buried mom, but I just couldn't. I felt so tired."

"I didn't know your mom died," he says.

"You'd probably forgotten she was still alive," Louise says. "But don't feel bad about it. Why would you?" She looks around. "Phyllis comes once a year. She has done ever since your mom died, to leave flowers."

It's Danny, not Louise, who spots the flat stones from two graves away. Louise half-expected to see flowers against the stone, but incongruously there is a plastic chrysanthemum blown against the back side of Brenda's marker. Definitely not Phyllis's offering. A runaway from some other grave. She snatches it up and stuffs it into her pocket for lack of a nearby trash barrel. Dan doesn't notice. He's standing well back from the graves, as though reluctant to tread on them. Looking from one name to the other, chewing his lip, hands thrust deep into his pockets.

He squints at her against the evening sun. "What do you figure this does to the real estate value?" he asks, waving his arms at the rather unpicturesque view of the backs of houses on the other side of the fence. There's a woman on the back step at one, pegging clothes to a line. She glances their way, then back to her work. She must see many like them, Louise thinks, standing, staring, wondering why they're here.

"Well, it's a green space. Pretty quiet."

He snorts. "Did he tell you this was where he wanted to go? I mean did you talk about that stuff? I don't remember ever coming here."

She nods. "When my dad died, Jake told me your mom was buried here, and that he had this plot beside her. He wondered what we should do about that. Whether I wanted him to get another spot for the two of us." She shudders. "I told him I didn't care, I didn't want to talk about it. Whoever was left could make sure all my useable parts were donated, and they could do whatever was easiest with the rest of me."

"Are those the orders you're going to leave the kids?" Jake asked her that day, ever so quietly.

"Not now, okay Jake?" she said. "Let's talk about it another time?" She'd had some other time in about twenty years in mind.

Dan moves now to stand in front of his mother's grave, still well back. He sighs, a deep long lonely sound and again, Louise feels like she's seeing him as he will be for the rest of his life. A man at the graves of his parents.

"Maybe we shouldn't have come," she says. She won't tell Dan that she feels nothing at all. Jake isn't here. They buried his dark blue suit here, and a white shirt and a rather loud tartan necktie that he'd loved and always worn, he said, when he needed a lift. A bit of a joke. What bones and dust there are between the clothes is of no consequence. Maybe it is of consequence to Daniel, though. Everyone has urged Louise to come back here, to cry, to let herself grieve. Don't be so stoic, Phyllis said. The thing is, though, Louise has kept right on talking to Jake in her head, and she doesn't want to stop. It's only in the past year that his voice has grown so faint she can barely hear him at times, and she will fight "closure" as long as she can. You need closure, they keep telling her, all part of the vernacular around death and loss. She doesn't need it, she doesn't want it, but maybe Danny has a right to closure of his own. She's the wrong person to be standing here with him. Maybe someday he and Jonathan will visit their dad's grave. Except that Louise has always felt that Daniel considers himself to be more Jake's child than either of her two children. In his wonky processing of information, half-brother, also means half-son.

Robert Raymond Cook was not allowed to attend the funeral of his family, never visited his father's grave. When her clandestine reading about Cook had finished, it seemed to Louise that Cook was indeed a victim of a flawed and misdirected system of justice. He was entirely right when he said he was guessed into a guilty verdict. But while his lawyers laboured to find the truth, the whole truth and nothing but the truth, Robert Cook's inability to tell the truth himself, seemed to have sealed his fate.

And that, she feared, will be her stepson's destiny. She crosses her arms, shivers. It's getting late and a sudden damp has settled over this shaded landscape. Daniel doesn't have a jacket, and no bag of any sort either, she realizes with a jolt.

As though he feels her eyes on him, he swings his head around suddenly. "No, I'm glad we came," he says, back to the question she'd all but forgotten.

"Where are you staying, Dan? Do you have clothes somewhere?"

He shakes his head. "Nah, I figured I still had some stuff at your place. I was going to throw some clothes into a suitcase. You still have some old luggage down there in the basement, don't you?"

Of course. She hasn't thrown out a single thing since Jake died. His clothes are still in the closet in their bedroom. Danny's are in the makeshift bedroom in the basement that Jake had just begun to finish when it became obvious that Dan wouldn't be back. Never permanently at any rate. She nods. "It's all down there. But look, Dan. It's getting late, and there's no point your staying in Edmonton without your stuff. Let's go back. I'll drive you out to the farm and you can spend the night there."

He doesn't seem surprised, in fact doesn't seem to have

heard her. He's looking up at the road, his jaw working. She waits another minute. "Dan? Are you ready to go?"

He sits down on the grass, legs crossed, his back to her. "No. I'm going to stay for a while. I've got some friends here on the south side. I'll hop on the bus."

She crouches behind him, her hand on his shoulder. "That's not necessary, is it? Just come home."

When he doesn't answer, she lets her hand trail across his back and stands up. When she's halfway up the hill, she looks back and he is still sitting there.

Roads Back

June 2009

We were on our way to a writers' retreat at Emma Lake in Saskatchewan. My friend, Myrna Garanis, and I had spent the night in Saskatoon. I was carrying the Cook story along with me, my goal for the week to make some progress on the rewrite. I had completed a first draft in my work at UBC with Terry Glavin, but I had a long way to go. I knew that I had to go deeper into the story. My friend and mentor, Dave Margoshes, had read the manuscript for me a few months earlier, and I was working from his comments and suggestions. Another friend, Barb Howard, had also supplied fine feedback and the consistency of the responses from all three of these people told me what I'd known all along. I was avoiding the questions that had been compelling me all these five years. Fear was at the heart of my obsession with the story. Fear kept pushing me away.

We left Saskatoon in torrents of rain, and I was tempted to forget my plan to have a quick look at the penitentiary in Prince Albert. But I needed to acknowledge Robert Raymond Cook's departure point from that prison as the beginning of the story, because I had finally accepted that I was not going to be able to trace the tragedy of the Cook family back to any other incident or event. I could not rewrite that story.

The Prince Albert penitentiary is on the south side of the river, on the perimeter of the town. Brick, windowless walls, chain link fences topped with coiled wire around an area at least two city blocks square that I assumed must be the exercise yard. There was little to see, nothing to photograph but walls, the historic guard box at the side of the road. We stopped, took pictures, stared a few minutes. Enough of this. My only sense of the place was that there were no signs of life. Few cars in the parking lots, so probably not a visiting time. Although I doubted that the parking lots of prisons were ever over-crowded with the cars of visitors.

From where we had stopped at the side of the road, we could see as far as the next bend, where there seemed to be yet another cemetery, iron gates, old trees. The day before, on the way to Saskatoon, we'd stopped at the Hanna cemetery for one more visit to the Cook family graves, and then at the Asquith cemetery so that Myrna could visit the graves of her parents. This project of mine, I thought, had become an endless circling around the dead.

Still, I turned in at the iron gates, thinking only to do a quick drive through and turn-around. As familiar as every other country cemetery, except that from the farthest graves, beyond a large area of meadow, we spotted rows of white crosses. Who was lying there, and why the distance from the other graves? The rain had begun again, so we decided to add a second visit to St. Mary's Cemetery to the return itinerary.

Through the week at Emma Lake, the rain continued, with only the occasional sunny break to distract me from my work. Louise had gone silent, and I was relieved. Her story was ended. At the end of the notes he'd sent me after reading the last draft, Dave had penned: "this closing chapter, focusing on Louise and Danny is excellent. We get no closure on the BJ story, though."

I plodded through the books, my interview notes, reams of clippings, checking dates and cross-checking facts. Looking for clues? Trying to decide whether the right man had been hanged? That wasn't even a question for me, my opposition to the death penalty so ingrained. Had justice been served? Jack Pecover's exhaustive examination had pointed to so many holes in the trials of Robert Raymond Cook that this question was purely rhetorical as well. But did it matter, these fifty years later? I knew by now that investigative journalism was not my calling, that I would return to fiction; to spinning, polishing, weaving the strands of yarn into loose endings that bore little resemblance to the tight noose around Bobby Cook's neck. If I had donned a super-sleuth's hat, gone beyond Pecover's speculation on the pieces of evidence that should have been enough to cast reasonable doubt on Cook's guilt, if I had tracked a suspect, found solid proof that someone else had committed the frenzy of shooting and bludgeoning in the Cook family bungalow on the night of June 25/early morning of June 26, 1959, would it have mattered to anyone? Not a single family member stood by Bobby Cook through his trials or at his execution. Lila Larson cared and was with him nearly to the end, but she seemed to have vanished and when I tried to take her perspective, I imagined that I would only feel deeper sadness and bitterness if I learned that someone I had loved had died for a crime he didn't commit.

The ending to my own story? Each time I'd read the descriptions of the blood- soaked mattresses, the spattered wallpaper, the tangle of bodies in the pit, I'd reared back in horror, not just for the Cook family, but because my imagination was capable of transposing the faces of all the boys I knew onto that figure in the cheap jailbird suit. The

Cooks were an ordinary family, Bobby Cook a punk of a kid, but no more so than many another black sheep. Ordinary life is full of sorrows, but tragedy of the magnitude of the Cook family murders is extraordinary in the extreme. That it happens shakes us to the core. That it happens infrequently and without warning has to be enough to allow us to move on. That is where I had to rest my need for redemption.

We drove away from Emma Lake, back to Prince Albert, on a sunny day and I could easily have sailed past the turn for the jail and the cemetery beyond. Robert Raymond Cook was not buried there. I had felt no compulsion at all to visit the Fort Saskatchewan jail were Cook was hanged. The photos and descriptions in Jack Pecover's book were enough. Nor had I tried to find out the final fate of cadavers donated to medical science. But the image of those rows of crosses we had spotted in the rain a week earlier was still vivid, and I knew that I would eventually spend unnecessary time on research to satisfy my curiosity.

We trudged across the field, making a beeline for a large stone that marked a section of rusty lichen-covered headstones in front of the rows and rows of crosses. Canada Corrections. A list of some sixty names, some of them just surnames, others initials, the occasional one a full name: Anderson, Frosty Eric; Baumont, J.C.; Rogers. And one that when it caught my eye, lifted off the grey stone in sharp relief: McCorqudale, Ronald. Here was the final resting place of the man whose sentence John Diefenbaker had commuted to the rage of the community. The political mistake that he was advised he could not make again when the request for clemency for Robert Raymond Cook crossed his desk. Here, at the Saskatchewan Penitentiary at Prince Albert, Ronald McCorqudale had taken his own life, according to Jack

Pecover's book. And the other men? How had they died? Was this a boot hill of sorts? The resting place of men executed here?

I watched Myrna walking thoughtfully through the rows of crosses, reading the inscriptions, none of them more than a surname and a number. She turned and waved at Ronald McCorqudale's grave. Someone tended this field, kept the grass neatly clipped around and between the crosses, but I wondered how long it had been since anyone had scanned these rows for a familiar name. If anyone ever came searching.

Two days later, I sent an email through the Correctional Services Canada website, asking for information about the cemetery. The quick and courteous reply:

> I am responding to your email received via the CSC Internet Website. I am limited as to what information I can share with you in accordance to the Privacy Act. The cemetary that is located next to Saskatchewan Penitentiary is the property of the St. Mary Anglican Diocese. All of the inmates buried in the inmate section died while in federal custody and their remains were unclaimed by family. No one has ever been executed at Saskatchewan Penitentiary.
>
> I trust that this information is of assistance to you.

These were the graves of Robert Raymond Cook's fellows.

Men who had died incarcerated as he had predicted for himself in the letter home just before his eighteenth birthday: "I mean everything I say for if I get into another jam, it will go on and on until I kick the bucket in a pen or some dirty provincial jail." Men who had been boys in families of one sort or another, but in the end, were unclaimed.

And this is where it ends. In the real world. In a cemetery.

But what about Danny? Where does he end?

Ah, you are still with me.

Of course. You know very well that I'll keep coming back.

I do. And that's why I will give you this closure. Danny will end in the Mount Pleasant Cemetery. But not yet. He will hold down a job in a welding shop, find someone to love, and look back ruefully in his old age on the years he wasted as a punk. In the end, his family will claim him.

Afterword

The Boy began as a work of fiction, but shortly thereafter, I recalled the 1959 Cook murders and the story of Louise and her stepson became entangled in the research I felt compelled to do around that real crime story. The chapters titled "The Boy" are purely fiction. Those titled "Roads Back" chronicle my journey through the writing of this book and adhere as closely to fact as I am capable of in the telling. The name of my childhood friend in the chapter recalling the summer of 1959 is the only one I have changed. I have had no contact with "Rose" in more than 40 years, and failed in my attempts to find her in order to match my memory of that time with hers. For this reason, I felt I owed her anonymity.

The voice of Louise, who pops in and out of the narrative, is very real to me indeed. In all my fiction, there seems to be at least one strong voice demanding to be heard. Many of my stories have female characters that bear strong resemblance to the author in either life experience or personality. Often I end up in dialogue with those characters, but never before have I allowed that conversation a place on the page. Here, it seemed the only way to tie together this braid of fiction, memoir, and investigation.

A summary of the events that led to Robert Raymond Cook's execution for the murder of Ray and Daisy Cook and their children, Gerry, Chrissy, Patty, Kathy, and Linda:

On Tuesday, June 23, 1959, Robert Raymond Cook was released from the Saskatchewan Penitentiary (more commonly referred to as "Prince Albert", for the town in which it was located, or simply "P.A.") He was serving a three year term for break and entry and car theft and was not due to be released until October. Queen Elizabeth II and Prince Philip had arrived on June 18 for the opening of the St. Lawrence Seaway, and a general amnesty was granted to certain classes of prisoners to honour the sovereign's visit. Cook and about 120 other prisoners were sprung early.

It seems unlikely that Robert Raymond Cook gave even passing thought to Her Majesty when he walked into the open air and stepped onto the bus that would take him and his fellow inmates to Saskatoon from where they'd disperse. Dressed in a prison issue blue suit and black oxfords, and a white shirt, yellow socks and red tie that had been sent by his stepmother for the occasion, Cook was bound for Edmonton. One wonders if the royal couple, during the forty-five days they toured Canada, heard anything of Cook.

After spending Wednesday, June 24 in Edmonton, celebrating his freedom with some of the friends he'd made in previous incarcerations, Cook headed for home; for Stettler, where his father, step-mother, and their five children awaited his arrival. Robert Cook was twenty-two years old, and since his first prison term when he was fourteen, he had spent all but 243 days in jail. He arrived in Stettler early in the afternoon, and wandered everywhere but home. His father, Ray Cook, was seen meeting up with him later in the evening, and the two drove off together. Later that night, Robert Cook returned to Edmonton in his father's car. The next morning, Friday, he appeared at a car dealership and traded Ray's 1958 Chevrolet station wagon in on purchase of a new white Impala convertible. Then, looking for yet another of his ex-con acquaintances, he drove to Camrose, halfway between Edmonton and Stettler, and on a vague suggestion that his friend might have gone to Whitecourt, picked up three teenagers and took them along on a joy-ride to Whitecourt and back. Finally, on Saturday evening, he ended up back in Stettler, cruising the main street in his new car. He had made a quick stop at home, he would say later, and finding the house empty, the family gone, assumed they had left for British Columbia in search of a service station that father and son were going to operate together. Saturday night, after a call from Edmonton alerting the Stettler RCMP that Robert Raymond Cook was wanted for questioning on false pretence charges for using his dad's identification to buy the Impala, Cook was stopped on the street and asked to come back to the station. He was held overnight.

Meanwhile, stirrings of unease at the convoluted story about the sale of the car, and the ever-changing versions of the family's departure prompted one of the RCMP officers to visit the Cook home. After a quick look inside with his flashlight, he determined that the house was empty, and went back to the station to arrange for a further search in the morning. By the light of day it was clear that the house had been the scene of horrendous violence and that someone had attempted to wash blood-stained walls and had piled clothing and bed linens atop the soaked mattresses under which a blood-spattered blue suit and white shirt were concealed. Finally, in the garage, under sheets of cardboard, a grease pit was uncovered and the badly decomposed bodies of the seven members of the Cook family were found.

Robert Raymond Cook was charged with the murder of his father, Raymond Cook, and was remanded for thirty days for psychiatric examination at the Provincial Mental

Hospital at Ponoka. Eleven days later, just before midnight on July 10, Cook escaped from Ponoka and set off the biggest manhunt in the history of the province of Alberta. More than two hundred men fanned out over the countryside on foot and in jeeps, trucks, armored cars, boats and planes. Still, it wasn't until Tuesday, July 14, that Cook stepped out of a pig barn in view of a farm wife, and waited to be arrested.

Cook's trial took place before a judge and jury and lasted eleven days. On December 10, 1959, after one and a half hours of deliberating, the jury returned a verdict of guilty and Cook was sentenced to be hanged on April 15, 1960. An appeal was filed and a new trial granted. The second trial took six and a half days, and the jury this time returned in half an hour with the guilty verdict. Cook was sentenced to be hanged on October 11. A second appeal was filed and turned down. An application to appeal to the Supreme Court of Canada postponed the execution date from October 11 to November 15, but the application was dismissed. A final plea was made to the federal Cabinet for an executive grant of clemency that would commute Cook's sentence from the death penalty to life imprisonment. An Order in Council was issued saying there would be no interference with the sentence. Robert Raymond Cook was executed just after midnight on November 14, 1960.

Acknowledgements

In the four years I spent writing *The Boy*, many people shared their recollections of the Cook murder case. My particular thanks to The Honourable Judge David P. MacNaughton, Clark Hoskins, Doreen Scott, Gary Anderson, and Marion Anderson. To Jack Pecover, whose book, *The Work of Justice, The Trials of Robert Raymond Cook*, became my well-thumbed reference, I am indebted for a wealth of information, the acuity of his analysis, and his understanding of my obsession with finding the family buried in this infamous case. I am grateful to Jack as well for reminding me of the pleasures of old-fashioned correspondence, of opening an envelope and holding a real letter in hand.

My thanks to UBC's Creative Writing program for the course of studies that helped me find my way through the story, and to Terry Glavin for his encouragement, and the wisdom of "truth matters" and "the inviolable trust that exists between the writer and the reader."

As always, love and thanks to Robert, Elisabeth, Eric, and Stefan, my ordinary family, extraordinary each of you in the best of ways.

Other Oolichan Titles By Betty Jane Hegerat

A Crack in the Wall (2008)

The stories in *A Crack in the Wall* take the reader on a voyeuristic walk down suburban streets, a glimpse into open windows at people yearning for what was, and making their reluctant peace with what is, and what will be.

Delivery (2009)

A "domestic" novel in the tradition of Carol Shields, Delivery is a story with a large theme painted on a small canvas. Betty Jane Hegerat delivers an elegantly written mother-daughter story most mothers and daughters will adore – and plenty of dads and sons too.

    - Dave Margoshes.

Betty Jane Hegerat is the author of two novels, a collection
of short stories, and a book of creative non-fiction. She lives
in Calgary, and teaches creative writing at the University
of Calgary and the Alexandra Writers Centre. *Delivery*
(Oolichan, 2009) was a finalist for the George Bugnet fiction
prize in the Alberta Book Awards. Juror's comment:
"Domestic dysfunction never had it so good. This novel
lactates with life."

Visit www.bettyjanehegerat.com.